Praise for Dana Marie Bell's *Bear Necessities*

"I had to let this piece sink in for a while before I decided to put it on the prestigious "Keeper Shelf" but I can now say that Ms. Bell has provided a lot a good paranormal content that sets her writing apart from the other authors in this genre."

~ *IReadRomance.com*

"I think Bears may be my new favorite shifters."

~ *Dark Diva Reviews*

"This story perfectly balanced the light hearted humor with the underlying serious issues. I giggled like a mad woman throughout the book. If you want a story to lift your spirits and make you smile, this is the book for you."

~ *Two Lips Reviews*

Look for these titles by *Dana Marie Bell*

Now Available:

Halle Pumas Series
The Wallflower
Sweet Dreams
Cat of a Different Color
Steel Beauty
Only in My Dreams

Halle Shifters Series
Bear Necessities

True Destiny Series
Very Much Alive
Eye of the Beholder

Gray Court Series
Dare to Believe
Noble Blood

Print Anthologies
Hunting Love
Mating Games
Animal Attraction

Bear Necessities

Dana Marie Bell

Samhain Publishing, Ltd.
577 Mulberry Street, Suite 1520
Macon, GA 31201
www.samhainpublishing.com

Bear Necessities

Print ISBN: 978-1-60928-122-9
Digital ISBN: 978-1-60928-117-5

Cover by Kanaxa

First Samhain Publishing, Ltd. electronic publication: July 2010
First Samhain Publishing, Ltd. print publication: June 2011

Dedication

To Mom, who was always there when I needed her, and sometimes when I didn't. We may not always agree, but it doesn't matter. We're family. That means you're stuck with me, no matter how many times you tell people you're my much younger adopted sister.

To Dad, who puts up with our crazy antics and sometimes eggs us on just to see the vein in Mom's temple throb. How many times do we have to remind you that she knows where you sleep AND she cooks your food?

To Dusty, my necessity. Despite the fact that my Alienware laptop rocks, you will always have more geek cred than me. You're the only man I know who's actively working toward surrounding himself with monitors...and succeeding. I'll know your master plan is complete when you finally hook up the automatic Mountain Dew/Snickers bar dispensers to your Uber Leet Gaming Chair with Built-In Massage.

Last but not least, to Molli, Jambrea, Sandie and the rest of the Samhain Café who begged me for a werebunny. This one's for you.

Chapter One

"Goddamn it, Bunny. That was the last piece of bacon."

This was starting out to be a really great day. Alexander "Bunny" Bunsun grinned and swallowed the crispy, greasy, salty bit of heaven. "Yes. Yes, it was." And it had been delicious. The extra-special flavor came from the amused frustration in his cousin's eyes.

Ryan sat back with a low growl. "And you ate all the cantaloupe."

"Yes I did." He sat back and rubbed his stomach. Damn, but the food here was *good.* He'd have to keep this place in mind the next time he traveled this way, especially if Chloe decided to make Pennsylvania her permanent home.

Ryan snagged the last grape with a warning glare, popping it into his mouth. "At least you left me *something.*"

"Quit your bitching. You got four eggs, all the sausage, six pancakes, all of the green melon thingies and an entire pot of coffee."

"Green melon thingies?" Ryan chuckled, wiping his hands on his napkin before dropping it onto his empty plate.

Bunny rolled his eyes and signaled the waitress. He never could remember what they were, but they were always put in salads with the cantaloupe and made it taste funny.

The hell with it. Let Ryan laugh. Bunny wanted to pay his check and get back on the road. It wouldn't take them more than a few more hours to get wherever the hell they were going, and he was determined to enjoy every moment of it, despite Ryan.

They paid the check and headed for their Harleys. He pulled on his jacket against the early fall weather. The cool had come early this year. It was late September, yet it felt like November.

He had to hope that whatever was wrong with Ryan's little sister could be fixed fairly quickly. He'd had to skip his yoga for two days now, and he was feeling the lack.

Chloe Williams had moved away from home to get her degree in veterinary medicine from the Halle branch of the University of Pennsylvania, and slowly but surely, the cheery little girl who'd gone off to find a home had lost some of her sparkle. She refused to discuss what was going on, only that she had some *personal troubles* that she didn't feel comfortable talking about with her brother or her male cousins. Bunny figured that maybe there was a problem with the sheriff she'd been dating for a while. If that was it, he'd see to it that the man fixed it before more than a day or two passed. Either that or he'd fix the man who had caused her grief.

He blew out a frustrated breath. A part of him hated that he'd left home. He had a life to get back to. Hell, he wasn't even sure why he'd come on this little trip at all. There was this sweet little she-Bear who'd been giving him the eye recently. He'd been tempted to have a taste, but something, some nagging sense that something wasn't right, had sent him on this trip with Ryan instead. It was weird. He'd never gotten the feeling that he needed to be out and moving quite like this before. It was almost a compulsion, and Bunny knew he'd regret it to his dying day if he didn't follow it.

Bunny shook his head and strapped on his helmet, shaking off the feeling that he needed to go *now*. Whatever the hell was wrong with him, he had every intention of returning home and finding himself a nice, sweet fuck. The dreams he'd been having since they left home had him so goddamn horny, he'd considered jacking off, despite Ryan being in the next bed over. Bears had good hearing and Bunny didn't feel like living with whatever humiliation Ryan would come up with if he heard *that*. So he'd held off, and now he was one cranky-ass Bear. It didn't help that each of the dreams featured a woman who alternated between looking like a dark-haired angel and a kick-ass heroine from one of his manga/anime fantasies. He was the only one in the family who had an obsession with the Japanese style of drawing and animation, but he couldn't help himself. He'd been in love with it since the first time he read *Sailor Moon* and *Tenchi Muyo!* He had the whole *Sailor Moon* series on DVD, in the original Japanese (with English subtitles, of course). His family just laughed and indulged him at Christmastime, and he ate it all up like a greedy child.

Unfortunately, no real woman could stand up to the fantasies he'd been having. He shook off the desire to have something a little out of the ordinary. With any luck, the she-Bear would be waiting for him, preferably naked under a trench coat and sitting on his doorstep. Bunny gunned the motor and eased into traffic, whatever it was that was driving him appeased now that his wheels were turning.

This was starting out to be a truly shitty day.

Tabby limped out of the woods, her right rear paw dripping blood. How she'd managed to slit her pad open she had no idea. She was usually careful not to run in places where campers or kids tended to go, since the litter on the ground could be dangerous to Wolves. One broken bottle could result in severe bleeding, causing shifters serious problems if they couldn't shift. She'd have to make sure she had a little chat with one of the local kitties. Maybe one of them could find out if some of the college kids had been running off into the woods for beer and sex. If so, she might have to request permission to move to different hunting grounds.

She was grateful the Pumas had granted her the right to run in their territory. Hell, she was grateful to the Pumas, period. If it hadn't been for Gabe Anderson, the Marshall's Second and sheriff of the small town of Halle, Tabby would have been forced to move on again. It wasn't every Pride that would allow a Wolf to live among them, even on the say-so of someone as high up in the Pride hierarchy as the Second, but Halle had turned out to be a lot more open to the idea than she'd ever thought possible. She was just grateful the rest of them had agreed to give her leave to stay on a trial basis.

Alpha, Beta, Marshall, Omega; those were the primary rulers of a Pride or Pack. The Marshall's Second fulfilled similar functions to the Beta did for the Alpha, but without the broad range of powers a Beta enjoyed. He was the right hand man of the Marshall, the one who enforced Pack or Pride law and helped see to the physical well being of its members. The Second, in many ways, had the ear of the Prides and Packs in ways the rest of the leaders didn't, as he straddled the line between ordinary member and leader. Some Prides and Packs lumped the Second in with the rest of the leaders; such was the case in Halle, were Gabe had as much say as the Beta, Marshall and Omega. She never wanted to leave Halle. The town was warm and inviting in a way her old Pack had never been. The Alpha of the Pumas, Dr. Max Cannon, was a hottie. His alpha female Emma, called a Curana by the Pumas, was a tough cookie with a heart of gold. She'd asked Gabe what Curana meant, and she'd been told it was an altered form of the word *çuçuarana,* the Portuguese word for cougar. The rest of the Pumas were, for the most part, really nice people. She felt at home here, something she hadn't felt in a long time. She'd made friends and built a life for herself. She never wanted to go back to the Pack that had shoved her out so long ago.

But no matter how nice the Pride members were, they weren't Wolves. They weren't Pack, something she was reminded of every full moon since she'd been granted leave to stay.

She was still Outcast.

She made it to her car and changed into the clothes she'd left on the hood. The shift caused the cut to bleed even more freely until it closed, leaving a sore spot on the bottom of her foot she felt after she put her sneakers on. She dug her keys out of her pocket, eager to get back to her apartment and the caffeine her roommates would have waiting for her.

"Well. Look who it is."

Tabby tensed at that hated voice, the one fly in the ointment of her happiness in Halle. He'd stayed downwind, or she would have noticed him approaching before now and moved a hell of a lot faster. "Gary." She turned to find her nemesis and his two best friends standing naked behind her. They must have shifted and run from somewhere else. There was no other car here, and none of their clothes littered the ground.

"Outcast."

She held back her Wolf's growl with difficulty. She was terrified. This wasn't the first time the other Wolves had confronted her, but this was the first time they'd managed to catch her alone. From the gleam in Gary's eye, if she didn't get away, she'd be in a world of hurt. "What do you want?"

Gary grinned, his fangs sharp, his eyes going from hazel to light brown. He rubbed his hand up and down his growing cock suggestively. The other two moved to flank her and she knew she was in deep shit.

As an Outcast, technically Tabby was fair game for any Wolf who wanted a bit of sport. So far, very few Wolves had made their way to Halle. Most of the shifters who attended the college were local themselves, and therefore part of the Halle Pride. She'd stayed out of the way of those who weren't part of the Pride, especially the Wolves. She'd been terrified of what would happen if she approached them. The Alpha of the nearest Pack wouldn't be any help. She'd seen him once from a distance, and he was large and scary looking. Rick Lowell had the coldest blue eyes she'd ever seen. Tabby was too afraid to approach him, to try to become a part of his Pack. He'd take one look at her and know she wasn't worthy of a home.

Now she wished she'd been able to find the courage to ask. Maybe she might have to earn her way into his Pack. Maybe she would be safe from the advances of Wolves like Gary, but it would have meant leaving Halle and placing every aspect of her existence in the hands of someone else again. And that was the last thing Tabby wanted to do. At least here in Halle the Pumas were fairly laidback. She didn't bother them, they didn't bother her. They were friendly, but distant, and she liked it that way.

Tabby shivered. Three against one were not good odds. She had her keys in her hand, but the car was locked. If she hit the button to unlock it, they'd be on her before she could get the door open.

But there was the other button...

Bravado was the only way she could see out of this. She knew some of the Pumas had been out running the night before. With luck, one of them would wander by and stop Gary before he did what he so obviously wanted to do. "Fuck off, Gary!"

He glared at her shout. "You think anyone is gonna come and save you, *Tabby*?" He sneered the nickname, his idiot Pack brothers laughing like a group of hyenas. "You're Outcast. Your ass is mine." He took a step forward, his eyes shifting to brown.

Wolf's eyes. Just what she'd been waiting for.

Tabby hit the panic button on her remote. The car horn began blaring, the lights flashing. The trio slapped their hands over their ears, their faces screwed up in pain, their sensitive ears assaulted by something that wouldn't bother their human senses.

Taking advantage of their surprise, Tabby hit the button that unlocked the car door and scrambled for the handle.

"Stop her!"

She got the door open and herself inside before any of them reached her. She slammed the door on the fingers of one of Gary's goons, his scream almost as loud as the alarm. He pulled his fingers free and she got the door shut, locking it before Gary could pull the driver's side door open.

He began punching the glass. She flinched, but kept moving, sliding behind the steering wheel. She started the car, screaming when Gary's third punch cracked the glass.

She took off, peeling out of the gravel-strewn parking lot, her tires kicking up stones. She fishtailed before getting the car under control, heading straight for the road back into Halle.

Back to safety.

Tabby was shaking like a leaf. This was the closest Gary had ever come to laying hands on her. He and his goons had been content before with taunting her or egging the storefront where she worked. She'd been careful to never be alone. How could she have been so thoughtless? Still, she hadn't thought they'd resort to... She shuddered again. She didn't even want to think about what she'd just escaped from.

Tabby needed help. She just hoped Gabe and the other Pumas would listen to her, because if they turned her away, she had every intention of running until her paws gave out.

"Wow. Your life's a mess, sweetheart." Julian Ducharme popped another kernel of popcorn into his mouth and grinned. "Good thing you have someone like me around to help."

Tabby snorted. She wasn't the only outsider who'd drifted into Halle recently. Julian had come into Living Art Tattoos a month ago and managed to endear himself to each and every one of the girls who worked there. Even tough Cyn, the owner, had taken a liking to the friendly Bear with the heart of gold. "And how do you think you can help me, hmm?"

He put the bowl down and wiped his greasy hands on a paper towel. The movie they'd been bickering over continued in the background, neither of them paying any attention to it. Although she did risk a peek when Aragorn was on screen. Viggo Mortensen was *hot* in *The Two Towers*. "First, I'm going to do something about that sore foot of yours."

She winced. She couldn't hide the slightest amount of pain from Julian. It freaked her out sometimes. The first time he'd said something, she'd gotten a splinter not seconds before. He'd frowned, turned her hand around and pulled the splinter out before she could even say "ow". "I think I stepped on a chunk of glass or something."

"Or something," he muttered darkly, pulling her bare foot onto his lap. "This will only take a sec." One finger smoothed down the ball of her foot and Tabby, who was outrageously ticklish, felt...nothing. "Wiggle your toes."

There was no pain. "Dude. You rock."

Julian grinned and stood, heading for her apartment's kitchen. "I know."

She shook her head.

"When are your partners in crime due home?" He turned on the faucet, the sound of the water muffling his voice, but she still heard an odd note in Julian's voice. She tried to bite back a snicker. She knew exactly how he felt about at least one of her roommates.

"Cyn said she was going to stay late, work on some paperwork." Cyn owned Living Art and was Tabby's boss, as well as one of her roommates. "Glory had a date, so I have no clue when she'll be back." Glory also worked at LA, doing piercings, and was her other roommate. The faucet stopped and Julian came back. He shook his hands at her, spraying her with water. "Hey!"

He flopped back down on the sofa and grabbed the popcorn bowl. He studied the screen, tilting his head. She waited to see what outrageous thing would pop out of his mouth this time. "Why is it that Orlando Bloom can look good as a girl *and* a boy?"

Tabby picked up a kernel and threw it at him. "Legolas isn't a girl."

He turned, raising one black brow, his full lips quirking in a smile. "Isn't she?" He tilted his chin toward the screen, his expression turning devilish. "You think Aragorn doesn't want a piece of that, Arwen or no?"

Tabby put her feet up on the coffee table and stretched out. "Yeah, and when Aragorn lifts Legolas's kilt, he's going to find the special surprise inside." Julian choked on the popcorn and started laughing. *Score one for me.* She stole the bowl out of his lap and settled in to watch the movie.

"This is it? This is what Chloe left Oregon for?" Bunny walked down the street, pausing to peer into the window of a store. It was very...pink inside. A group of women sat on an old sofa, drinking tea and laughing, while a short, dark-haired female rang up purchases on an old-fashioned cash register. He shuddered and looked up at the sign. *Wallflowers. Should be called Hen House.* He moved away before any more testosterone could be sucked out through his pores.

Ryan chuckled. "She loves it here and swears we will, too."

Bunny shrugged. "Whether or not I stay is still up in the air." He paused, looking in another store. Comic books. Much more his style. *I wonder if they have a good manga section?* He was always on the lookout for a good store, and if he was going to stay here—

"Oh, no, you don't." Ryan grabbed hold of his collar and pulled him away from the glass. "I swear, it's like those French pigs and truffles. If there are comic books around, you'll sniff them out."

Bunny rolled his eyes, but allowed his cousin to pull him away. He made a mental note to come back later without the two-hundred-and-twenty-pound wet blanket. "I swear, Ryan. You're getting old."

"I'm twenty-seven! And you, asshole, are twenty-eight!"

Bunny put his hand on his heart. "But I'm young *inside.* Where it counts."

Ryan shook his head and let him go. "And this is why you're not allowed out on your own."

Bunny just grinned and followed his cousin down Main

Street, Halle. They'd find Chloe, who hadn't been either at her apartment or the diner she usually worked at. Her problems would be over, whether she liked it or not.

Then he'd be going home.

Now if only he could figure out why his Bear growled every time he thought of home, he'd be golden.

Tabby stared out the window of Living Art at the sunny spring day and sighed. "Today is going to be another shitty day."

"You're just saying that because your roots are showing."

Tabby turned to her friend Cyn and growled, the sound deep and feral and in no way human.

Cyn laughed. "Hon, if I was afraid of you, I'd never have hired you."

Tabby rolled her eyes and turned her attention back to the front window. "We haven't had a customer all day."

"Mondays." The women looked at each other and echoed, "They suck the big fat hairy one." Very few people came in for a tattoo on a Monday afternoon.

Glory, the one who handled all the piercings at Living Art, twirled in her chair. Her long blue hair flared out around her. "Preaching to the choir."

Cyn shook her head, her dark hair startling with its new hot pink stripes. "And then there's Saturdays."

The three women exchanged a look and shuddered. Saturdays had become something of a pain in the ass for the three women. Gary and his friends had stepped up their harassment of Tabby since the incident in the woods, often enough that the police had been called out to the store twice now thanks to the catcalls, thrown eggs and worse. She was pretty sure Gary was responsible for the graffiti they'd found on the window one Saturday morning. The spray-painted "Cunts" had caused Cyn to break out in foul-sounding Hispanic curses. It was turning into a problem that not even the hunky Sheriff Anderson could deal with. While he might be a Puma, he was only *one* Puma, and since it wasn't affecting the Pride, she didn't feel comfortable discussing it with Dr. Cannon or his Curana. She wasn't Puma, she was Wolf, and her problems weren't theirs.

She'd traveled for years as a wolf, living off the land, before arriving in Halle six months ago, half-starved and ready to reenter the human race. She'd passed out in the backyard of a woman named Sheila Anderson, and that was the luckiest break she'd had in years. Her grandson, Sheriff Anderson, had quietly found her a place to stay, food to eat and a place to work. She now apprenticed under Cyn, had gotten her driver's license and a car, and almost had her GED. It was weird to think that she owed all that to a Puma lawman and his bossy grandmother who weren't even Wolves. She didn't want to cause him or his family any more trouble than she had, despite the fact that every time he found out about one of the little stunts Gary and his friends pulled, his jaw clenched tighter. Life had been good right up until the Asshole Pack had found her. She still didn't feel comfortable asking the Pride for help, and the Poconos Pack Alpha, Rick Lowell, was still a freakishly scary man. Rumor had it his new Luna, a Puma who'd lived in Halle, was even scarier. She'd never met the Puma Luna and had no intention of doing anything that might get her attention. She shook her head, catching sight of her lime green bob in the mirror behind the register. She grimaced as she noticed the dark roots starting to show again. "Gah. Cyn? Hair emergency."

Cyn laughed. "C'mon, honey, we have time. Have a seat."

Cyn grinned, pulling out the crème bleach. The tattoo parlor had once been a beauty parlor, and Cyn had opted to keep one of the sinks in place to do the girls' hair. "Glory, keep an eye out front."

"Will do." Glory flipped her hair over her shoulders and smirked. "Make sure to get all those roots or she'll look like she needs to be mowed."

"Lucky bitch." Tabby leaned back in the chair as Cyn began applying the lightener to her roots. "Wish I had naturally blonde hair *like some people*!"

Glory's giggles almost drowned out Cyn when she clucked her tongue. "Tabby, you are the only woman I've ever met who makes a lime green bob look sexy."

"That's because I'm the only woman you've ever met with a lime green bob." When she'd first met Cyn and Glory, her hair had been long, scraggly and depressingly brown. She'd taken one look at their hair and nearly cried in relief. Finally, some people she could relate to, who understood her! She wasn't some evil little troublemaker; she was just someone who was different. Cyn had offered to do her hair and the rest, as they say, was history. She'd sported the lime green ever since, and damn if she didn't rock it, even if she did say so herself.

Cyn ignored her. "So, who cares if it takes a little work?"

"Luscious alert!" Glory sounded positively giddy.

Tabby and Cyn peeked out from behind the curtain as a man walked past Living Art. He paused, looking in the window at the flash—the artwork depicting their most popular tattoos—they'd taped up. He was an absolute to-die-for hunk of a man. His light brown skin glistened over muscles that made Tabby's mouth water. He was bald, and from this distance she couldn't tell if it was a style choice or nature that made him that way. Some sort of tattoo circled the biceps closest to the window, but

Tabby was too far away to tell what it was. Something about the way he moved had every one of her senses sitting up and begging. "Dibs."

Cyn poked her. "Bitch. What if he likes the taste of Mexican instead of Hushpuppies, huh?"

Tabby giggled. "You are so bad."

"What?"

"You heard me." Tabby looked back to find the man peering in the window. One dark brow rose as he caught them looking at him, a smile flirting around his luscious-looking mouth. Oh, the things she would love to have that mouth do to her.

Tabby ducked back behind the curtain. "Shit. I think he caught us."

Glory darted behind the curtain. "Ohmigod!" She collapsed, laughing. "Oh shit."

"You think he'll come in?"

"I don't know." The sound of the bell brought on a quickly smothered giggle. "Oh hell. Glory?"

"On it, but now I'm calling dibs." Glory rushed out before either Tabby or Cyn could protest.

"Greedy bitch."

Cyn bopped her on the head with the brush. "Look who's talking." She picked up the bottle of bleach and a comb. "Now lie down and hold still. I have some roots to kill."

Tabby sat back in the chair and wished that she'd waited five more minutes to ask Cyn to fix her hair. It could have been *her* out there checking out the hottie instead of sitting in Cyn's chair getting bleached.

Bunny entered the tattoo parlor, pulled by the sight of bright, rainbow-colored hair and pretty, feminine smiles. He looked around and smiled. This place was pretty nice.

The tattoo parlor had that feminine touch to it without being the homage to estrogen that Wallflowers place had been. The walls were a bright aqua color, displaying the flash to advantage. The women had hung a nice, big art piece behind the counter that was rather more than flash. It looked like a giant, full-color pair of dragons, one red, one blue, circling together in a yin-yang, but was obviously a full-color tattoo inked onto someone's back. The counter was made completely of glass and housed more flash in one section, both black-and-white and color, and jewelry for piercing different body parts. He eyed the Prince Albert and shuddered, resisting the urge to cup himself protectively. The flash in the windows and on the walls was in silver frames, making it look even more like art. Two large books lay open on the counter, bound in brown leather and containing more tattoos. The floor was wood, a dark ebony stain that would hide spilled ink. Looking down the long length of the corridor, he could see four curtained-off cubicles, probably where the women worked. At the very end was a last curtained-off area marked "Employees Only".

The women, if they were the owners, had made the place look both welcoming and classy. He could see both men and women coming in here and being comfortable.

The tan-colored chairs near the window looked soft and inviting, but he had no interest in them. What he did want was down the aisle, behind the employees-only area. He could smell her, and she smelled *wonderful*. It was the same scent that had tickled him when he'd opened the door to Living Art Tattoos; a sassy, succulent scent that drew him like nothing else ever had. He'd almost barreled into the back room to find the owner of that scent when a blue-haired girl stepped out from behind the curtain and intercepted him. She brought with her the scent of the three women, but the citrusy scent that was hers alone was strongest, and not the one he was looking for. Curly, pale blue locks fell almost to the woman's waist. Bright blue eyes almost the same shade as her hair watched him with a mix of desire and sweetness that would have attracted Bunny on any other day. She was looking at him like he was a tall glass filled with chocolate mousse and she happened to have a very long spoon.

"Welcome to Living Art. I'm Glory. Can I help you with anything?" She batted her lashes at him, but Bunny wasn't interested. It was disappointing, too. She looked just like one of the heroines in the manga he liked to read, all big eyes and hair and sweet, innocent smiles. He could see himself spending a pleasant evening or two in her bed and finding out just how innocent she really was.

But that tantalizing scent tickled his nostrils again, sending a definite message to his cock to rise and shine. The gleam in the blue-haired girl's eyes said she'd noticed and approved. Bunny backed out of pinching reach. "Excuse me, but the other two ladies who were in here. Where are they?"

The woman made a face, disappointment lighting her features. The flirtatiousness disappeared. "Cyn and Tabby are in the back. Cyn owns the shop. Would you like to speak to her?"

He had to come up with something plausible. "Actually, I was thinking of getting a tattoo." He had a few already, so another one would be no big deal. A lot of women seemed to enjoy tracing the spiral triskelion design on his left biceps, the dark angel on his right shoulder. He had a black-inked, woodcut-style tailed bear with colored stars for the constellation Ursa Major on his lower back.

"What kind?"

A sudden image flashed before his eyes, so strong it startled him. "A bear and a wolf, I think." *Wolf? Is that what I'm smelling?* He didn't know there were any Wolves living in Halle. The only non-Puma he was aware of was his cousin Chloe, and she was Fox.

She blinked. "I think we can do that."

"The bear will need to be pretty specific too." He wasn't about to go into details, not until after he'd met the owner of that scent. He was pretty sure that was his mate behind that curtain and he didn't want to scare her off.

A Wolf? Really? He almost laughed. It seemed he was carrying on the family tradition of non-Bear mates. Ryan and Chloe's mother was a Fox, and his Uncle Ray had also married a Fox. Bunny's mother had been human, but despite that, his father had still caught flack in his mostly human community for marrying a black woman. His relatives had known better, and welcomed his mom with open arms. Fighting fate on your mate never worked out the way you expected it to, and you usually wound up in your mate's arms at the end anyway, so why give yourself the grief?

"Oh." She bit her lip. "Well, I do mostly piercings, but I could see if Cyn is available."

"Please."

She nodded and headed for the curtained-off area at the back. He could hear the murmur of voices, but neither one set off his senses.

"I wonder which one Cyn is," he muttered. "Green or pink?"

"Pink." He turned to find the woman with striking dark hair with broad pink streaks smirking at them. "I'm Cyn." She held out her hand. "So, you want a tattoo, big guy?"

Bunny hid his grimace. Damn it, he wanted to see his mate, and pink Cyn wasn't her. Cyn's scent was sharper, harder. More lemony. "Yes, actually I do. The other young lady, what does she do?"

Cyn eyed him with suspicion. "Tabby is an apprentice tattoo artist."

Bunny coughed. Nah. He could not have just heard that his Wolf mate was named after a kitty cat. No Wolf parent would be that cruel. Maybe it was Gabby or Darby or—

"Whose hair is about to fall out if you don't get the bleach out *now*!"

Bunny shivered as that deep southern drawl prowled over his skin. His dick had gone from zero to hero in two seconds flat.

Oh yeah. He'd found his mate. Now he just had to claim her.

Oh shit. Oh, fucking shit. Tabby waited as Glory rinsed her hair out. *My mate is out there. My* mate. *What's even weirder? Bear. My mate is a* Bear. *And I have orange roots.*

She was damn near hyperventilating. When she'd called dibs on the dude, little did she know she'd actually *get* him! And now she was going to wind up meeting him for the first time with *orange roots*. She was going to look like a half-melted Skittle. She grabbed Glory's arm. "Y'all tell him I'm dead. Please?"

Glory grinned. "What is wrong with you?"

"Remember the whole woof-woof thing?"

"Yeah."

"That guy out there?"

Glory's eyes widened. "He's a woof-woof too?"

"Er, no. More like grrr-grrr."

Glory blinked.

Tabby shook her head. "Never mind. That whole werewolf

mate thing in romance novels?"

Glory's mouth did that really wide "O" thing. "Really? He's your mate?"

"Yes! And I am having serious hair issues." She put on her best pleading look. "So, tell him I've been killed in a horrible vegetable-dye accident."

"Tabby!"

She held up her hands in mock-prayer. "Pleeeease?" She blinked, trying to look desperate. Hell, she probably *did* look desperate.

"Excuse me."

Tabby quivered. That deep, rich voice rolled over her, making her think of wicked things involving dark, melted chocolate and lit candles. "No customers allowed in the back room!"

Glory, bless her heart, threw a towel over her face, hiding her hair. "Sorry, you'll have to wait out front." Of course, now the towel was soaking up the still-running water. She was going to be drowned by a towel.

"Is everything all right in here?" The man's voice was pure sin, deep and slightly gravelly. "Why is her head covered in a towel?"

"Please. Tabby will...be a while." She could hear Glory clap her hands and tugged on her shirt, desperate to have the water turned off. She was spitting water back out onto the already-soaked towel. "Why don't you hit one of the diners in the area for lunch? Maybe do a little shopping? Um, oh! Frank's Diner has the best burgers in town!" Finally, someone turned the faucet off, saving her from a watery grave. She could just see the obituary. *Woman Drowns In Towel With Horrible Hair. Film at Eleven.*

There was a deep, happy sigh. "All right, if...Tabby, was it?...will be more comfortable."

He sounded like he was choking back a laugh when he said her name. Tabby snarled, knowing he'd hear it even if he couldn't see it.

Mr. Melted Chocolate coughed. "When can I return?"

"Uh..." Glory was obviously at a loss. Cyn was the one who usually took care of Tabby's hair.

"Try around seven." Cyn sounded amused, the bitch. "You can take her out to dinner. In fact, Tabby has the rest of the night off."

I do?

"But she has to be back at work by two tomorrow afternoon. Oh, and the lady *loves* steak." Tabby groaned behind her towel. *That's an understatement.* "Glory, see to it he has our address, okay?"

"But—"

"Trust me, just do it."

"Okay, boss." The curtain swished, but the scent of Bear remained. Glory must have stepped through the curtain.

"Ladies, it was a pleasure meeting you." The curtain swished again. The Bear was gone.

"Oh, honey. You are so screwed. Literally."

"*Cyn.*"

The towel was whisked off her head. Glory bunched it up, wringing the water out over Tabby's face. "You always were a greedy bitch. I should get Cyn to leave you with orange roots."

Tabby sputtered and wiped the water away from her eyes. "Don't worry, Glory. Some day your prince will come."

Glory blinked her big blue eyes, trying to look innocent.

Tabby had seen that look more than once just before something outrageous came out of Glory's mouth. "God, I hope so. What would be the point otherwise?"

"You are *so* bad."

Glory smiled her sweet, happy smile. "I know."

Bunny stood at the diner, wondering why he was here instead of back in the tattoo parlor waiting for his mate. He hadn't even gotten a good look at her face. How screwed up was that?

It had been pure impulse that made him wander the town. Ryan was off looking for his sister again, but Bunny had decided he needed some time on his own. He'd felt the urge to roam, discover the town his cousins were planning on living in, maybe visit the comic book store Ryan had pulled him away from the day before. Hell, if he liked it enough, maybe he would move his business here. The Alpha Puma appeared pretty open about other shifters living on his territory, and his father had been looking into the area anyway for Ryan and Chloe's family.

If the Alpha had been a Wolf, they wouldn't even be thinking about it. They'd have avoided Halle and looked for another place to live. Wolves hated having other shifters in their territory, even Bears who didn't give a rat's ass about that kind of thing.

He'd found the tattoo parlor almost by accident, the sound of feminine laughter faint through the picture window. He'd caught a glimpse of three women and gone in expecting to find three lovely ladies, perhaps even a date for the night.

Instead he'd found his future.

"Can I help you?"

Bunny turned around to find a tall, dark-haired man in a sheriff's uniform staring at him, a hard expression on his face. He nodded to the other man, taking a surreptitious sniff. *Puma.* "Sheriff Anderson?" Bunny held out his hand when the other man nodded warily. "Alexander Bunsun. You're dating my cousin, Chloe."

Sheriff Anderson winced, but visibly relaxed. "No, actually, I'm not. Never was. Chloe and I are just friends."

Bunny frowned. "That's not what it sounded like when we talked to her."

The sheriff sighed. "Common problem. Trust me, we've never dated." He shook his head. "Are you here to see Chloe?" He led the way into the diner and guided Bunny to a table. He settled in and laid his hat on the table next to them.

Looked like he was having lunch with the sheriff. Now to see if the man would try and run him off. "Yup. Her brother is heading to the university as we speak." He'd have to ask Ryan to find out what had happened between Chloe and the sheriff. Why had Chloe made it sound like they were together if they weren't?

"That sucks, because she's here right now." Anderson pointed toward a bright red ponytail bopping behind a counter. "She always works Monday afternoons."

"Oh." Bunny turned back to the sheriff, trying to keep his expression blank. "So what's this about you *not* dating my cousin?"

Anderson grimaced. "Long story short, Chloe and I are friends. *Just* friends."

"Really?" One of Bunny's brows rose questioningly.

Anderson winced again. "Let's just say my wife wasn't happy with the amount of attention I paid to Chloe and let me know about it. It took me a while to prove that Chloe doesn't mean nearly as much to me as Sarah does."

Ouch. He hoped the man's mate hadn't given him too hard a time. A jealous mate on the warpath was nothing to sneeze at. "I'll call Ryan and let him know Chloe's here." He pulled out his phone but hesitated. "Do you know anything about a woman named Tabby? She works over at the tattoo parlor." She'd carried the vague whiff of the sheriff's scent. Getting some information from the sheriff seemed like a good idea.

"Tabby?" Anderson eyed the triskelion tattoo on Bunny's arm. He sat back, the edges of his lips curving up in a knowing smile.

Bunny grinned. Just the thought of his mate made him feel like his heart was filled with sunshine. "Yup." He leaned in close, barely whispered the words. "She's my mate."

"Oh? *Oh.*" Bunny growled. The blank surprise in Anderson's voice was shadowed by a tinge of concern. Just because he'd be mating a Wolf instead of a she-Bear didn't give the sheriff the right to say anything. Anderson nodded, his expression turning grim. "Then there are a few things you'll need to know before things get too serious between you."

Bunny nodded. *Why do you think I asked, dumbass?* "Do you think the local boss will have any problems with us living here?"

Anderson's brows rose. "*Live* here? In Halle? I knew Chloe's family was coming, but I didn't know that included her cousins."

Bunny shrugged. "Tabby's here." Bears didn't mind moving to where their mates were happiest, and Wolves were, well, *territorial.* Odds were good Tabby would want to stay, so moving to Halle was Bunny's best option. The last thing he wanted was a grumpy Wolf chewing on his ass all the way back to Oregon.

Anderson opened his mouth, but before he could respond

there was an ear-splitting shriek.

"*BUNNY!*"

The sheriff nearly got bowled over by a pint-sized redhead hurtling toward Bunny at top speed. Bunny laughed, standing just as Chloe reached them. She hurled herself into his arms, giggling like a schoolgirl, her legs wrapping around his waist. Bunny took it, giving her a bear hug that had her gasping to be put back down.

"When did you get here? Where's Ryan? Did Mom and Dad come too? Where's Uncle Will and Aunt Barbra?" Chloe was practically bouncing in place, her ponytail waving gaily. Bunny watched his little cousin with an indulgent smile, his heart singing at the happiness in her face.

He'd missed the little squirt.

But there was something behind her eyes, a sadness that hadn't been there before. If it turned out that the sheriff *had* broken Chloe's heart, he'd have to have a few very private words with the man. "We're staying at the Holiday Inn, checking out the town. Ryan's on his way here to see you, Aunt Laura and Uncle Steve are still in Maryland with Mom and Dad, but they're thinking of visiting soon if we all decide to stay here. And we got here yesterday."

Chloe bounced again. "It will be so good to have family around again." Her smile turned wistful for a brief second before her innate sunshine came out once more. "So, what's new with you?" She nudged Bunny's arm.

He leaned in and whispered in her ear. The joy of finding the one woman who could complete him still rode him. "I found my mate."

Her jaw dropped. "No shit! Since when?"

Bunny was struggling with a smile. His cousin's bubbly personality was infectious. "Today. She works in the tattoo parlor."

"Living Art?" When Bunny nodded Chloe's eyes went wide. "Does she have blue hair?" Bunny shook his head. "Okay, not Glory then. Pink hair?" Bunny grinned and shook his head again. "Not Cyn, either. Oh! Tabby? Cool!"

Bunny started to laugh. He still couldn't get over his mate's name. He planned on having some fun finding out what in hell her parents had been thinking.

"Chloe! Order up!"

"Be right there, Frank!" She turned to Bunny, giving him a quick hug. "Get the fruit salad, you'll love it." She laughed and waved goodbye as she headed back for the kitchen.

"Bunny?" Anderson was hiding a smile behind his coffee cup. "Seriously?"

Bunny gave Anderson the one-finger salute. He still wasn't certain he shouldn't rip the good sheriff's arms off just to be on the safe side.

Something was bothering him, though. That look in Chloe's eyes was so wrong. His cousin had always known who she was and where she was going in life, and today she looked like she'd lost her way. "Is she having problems with something?"

Anderson shrugged. "I'm not certain what's going on. She's not talking, but I think the man she's...*interested* in is giving her fits."

Huh? Bunny stared at Anderson, startled. At Anderson's nod, he damn near reeled in his seat.

Chloe'd found her mate? Since when? Bunny took a deep breath, but couldn't detect anything other than Chloe's lingering scent. Ryan was gonna love that. His little sis, still in college, and already mated? The man would go ballistic. "Why? What's wrong with him? Chloe's cute as a button."

Anderson shrugged. "I'm not sure. But I wouldn't worry too much." He smiled tightly. "I'm sure she'll help him figure it out. And if she doesn't, I'll rip his head off and give it to her wrapped in a bow." And he sounded like he'd relish the opportunity. The kind of eager happiness on the sheriff's face was usually reserved for kids and Christmas presents.

Bunny snorted. The only way Anderson would lay his hands on Chloe's mate was if he beat Ryan to the man.

Pumas might be fast, but Bears, when motivated, were faster.

"Ohmigod, ohmigod." Tabby pulled her hair, staring into her closet. It was six forty-five and her mate would be here any minute, she didn't know his name and she had *nothing* to wear.

"Little black dress." Cyn stuck her head in Tabby's bedroom, grinning at the pile of clothing around Tabby's feet. "Can't go wrong with a little black dress."

"Guh." The panic was threatening to tear Tabby apart. She stared at the three black dresses hanging in her closet, her hand moving between them like a demented butterfly.

Glory's head peeked in from the other side of the doorway. "The sleeveless one."

"Uh?" She held up her sleeveless black dress, the one with the red belt and matching shoes.

Two heads bobbed in agreement.

Tabby stripped, more than used to being naked in front of her roommates. Hell, when she'd first moved in with them, they'd been shocked at how easy she felt being nude. Glory had actually asked her if she was gay and trying to tempt them to "the dark side". She'd giggled and said that she might be susceptible to temptation if the dark side had chocolate. Tabby had just shaken her head and put some clothes on. She'd spent so long as a Wolf, she'd forgotten some of the basic parts of being human, like pants. The first time she'd used a toilet after so many years had been an interesting experience, something Mrs. Anderson still chuckled about.

When Cyn and Glory had found out what she was, they'd freaked a little. They hadn't accepted her immediately. In fact, there'd been another girl, Brit, who'd worked at Living Art. Brit had left, refusing to believe what she'd seen the night Tabby, drunk off her ass for the first time in her life, let her Wolf loose in the middle of the apartment. She'd gone so far as to quit her job when Glory and Cyn refused to fire Tabby or kick her out of their apartment. But Glory and Cyn, after the initial shock had passed (and after, they claimed, they wiped up the dog drool), had accepted her without reservations. Hell, they'd mocked her once the hangover had passed. There was still a huge bag of Kibbles N' Bits in the pantry the bitches refused to throw away "just in case".

If she thought they'd take it, she'd make them Pack in a heartbeat. She missed having that connection, the knowledge that there were others for her to rely on without a shadow of a doubt. Part of her wondered if her dipshit ex had ever told his father the truth, or if he'd shrugged and let it go. Let her go.

Tabby shook her head and reached for her hairbrush, smoothing down her hair. That didn't matter now. Her mate would be here any minute. She slicked on some berry gloss and stared at herself in the mirror. Then she stuck out her tongue and made a face. She was so nervous, her Wolf was whining. She slipped her feet into the red high heels, grabbed her favorite purse and headed for the living room. "Well?"

Cyn circled her finger. "Twirl."

Tabby twirled.

Glory wolf-whistled. "See you at work tomorrow."

Cyn snickered and threw a bunch of condoms at her. "You'll need these."

Tabby swallowed. "I'm gonna throw up." Nausea roiled in her belly. She bent and picked up the condoms just as the doorbell rang.

Glory had the door open before Tabby could hide the packets. "C'mon in!"

In stepped the hottie from the store. He wore a green shirt that really emphasized his hazel eyes, dark wash jeans that looked painted onto his thighs and thick-soled black boots. Now that she was upright, she could see how tall he was. He towered over her, the top of her head barely reaching his upper lip, even in her four-inch heels. She'd hit his chin in her bare feet. His bald head gleamed, his jaw clean-shaven. She could see the tattoo that circled his biceps and her fingers itched to trace the design. In his hand, he held a daffodil.

My favorite flower. How did he know? Tabby smiled, knowing her mouth was trembling. She couldn't remember the last time someone had given her flowers. "For me?"

He held it out, a smile on his full lips. "Hello, Tabby."

"Thank you." She reached for the daffodil.

He coughed. "I'll take those." He reached over and removed the condoms from her hand, grinning at her embarrassed squawk. "It's okay, honey. I'm just glad one of us is, um, prepared." He eyed the condoms. "*Very* prepared." He unrolled them, one eyebrow rising in disbelief. "And optimistic."

Glory was practically doubled over with laughter. Tabby's face was beet red. She snatched the condoms back with her free hand, snarling as one got left behind in his big paw. She could hear Cyn snuffling and snorting behind her and just knew they were practically choking on their laughter.

She turned to her two roommates with a smile. “Don’t make me forget I’m housebroken.” They stopped, but from the way they were clinging together, Tabby figured it was only a matter of time before one of them broke again. She turned back to her new mate. “And you, whose name I don’t even know.” She smiled at Mr. Chocolate. “Thank you for the flower. My name’s Tabitha Garwood.”

Mr. Sin held out his paw, the condom miraculously gone. “Bunny.” She wondered if he’d dropped it or shoved it into his pocket for later.

Wait. “Bunny,” she repeated carefully.

“Alexander Bunsun, but everyone calls me Bunny.” He grinned.

She sniffed. *Nope, his scent is definitely Bear.*

“Are you laughing at my name?” Bunny’s hands went to his hips, but she could tell he wasn’t pissed by the way his lips quirked up.

She blinked. “Yes.”

He coughed, but she could tell he was trying not to laugh. “Dinner?” He held out his arm.

She gave him her sweetest smile and took it. “Yes.”

“Hold on.” Glory stopped them by placing her hand on Bunny’s arm, her expression worried. For all that Glory liked to flirt like mad, when it came down to actual dating she could be a real worrywart.

Bunny chucked her under the chin. “I’ll take care of her. My word on it.”

Glory studied him, and Bunny stood still, allowing her intense scrutiny. Glory relaxed and nodded, looking relieved. Tabby wasn't sure she felt the same.

Chapter Two

"Tabby? Seriously?" Bunny shook his head and helped her off his bike. "And you're making fun of *my* name?"

"At least I can blame my seriously screwed up parents. What's your excuse?" Tabby nodded at Bunny regally as he held open the door to Noah's. He'd asked Anderson to recommend a restaurant in the area and from his enthusiastic endorsement he had decided to give Noah's a try. He'd made the reservations and requested a nice, private table.

"It's taken from my last name. It's a nickname."

"It's a sucky nickname for a shifter to have," she muttered softly. "Bunny. Geez. Might as well call you Food." She shuddered delicately as they waited for the hostess to seat them. "Who came up with that anyway? And why didn't you tell me to wear pants?"

Bunny grinned, knowing it looked predatory. "*I* enjoyed it." She'd ridden on the back of his bike, those long sleek legs of hers bared almost to the point of indecency. The heat of her had been intoxicating.

Tabby rolled her eyes and followed behind the hostess. "Are you *sure* you aren't a Wolf?"

Bunny began singing "Little Red Riding Hood" under his breath, that deep, gravelly voice sending shivers down her spine. But when he reached the point about being everything a big, bad wolf could want, Tabby had to stop for a moment. She shook her head at him, amusement lighting her face. "Don't you mean big, bad Bear?"

Bunny held out her chair, a wolfish grin on his face. She allowed him to seat her, shaking her head. Lime green strands drifted across her face. And damn, what a face. She had the exotic good looks of a woman who had some Mediterranean blood somewhere in her gene pool. She was golden-skinned and full-lipped, with big brown eyes and lashes a mile long that perfectly framed a strong nose and determined chin. She wasn't classically beautiful, especially with her hair the way it was, but Bunny was already hooked. He could almost taste her. Like a ripe golden apple, she'd be tart and sweet on his tongue, a craving that would never go away.

This was going to be fun.

"Well? Out with it, *Bunny*. Who, what, where, why and how badly did you mangle them afterwards?"

He chuckled, trying to hide how uneasy the word mangled made him. She had no idea. "My cousins. I have five of the little shits. Ryan, Chloe, Keith, Heather and Tiffany are all my first cousins. They're the ones who gave me my nickname."

"Wow. Your aunt must have been churning them out."

"Don't make me order you a bowl of milk." Bunny didn't even flinch when Tabby punched him in the arm. She, however, got a very pained look on her face and surreptitiously tried to shake out her hand. "Ryan and Chloe are brother and sister and the children of my dad's first cousin, Uncle Steven. Keith, Heather, and Tiffany are my Aunt Stacey's kids. Aunt Stacey happens to be Uncle Steven's twin sister."

"Big family. Must be nice." She looked sad for a moment then shook her head. He wondered what that was all about. "You have any brothers or sisters?"

"Eric. He's my younger brother. He thinks, like you do, that Bunny is a stupid-ass nickname. He refuses to call me that. He mostly calls me Alex." And that meant something to him, that only those closest to him called him Alex. He'd never tell the cousins that, though. They loved the nickname they'd given him and, frankly, he was amused by it.

"Good for him."

"He also calls me SFB."

"SFB?"

"Shit For Brains."

She choked on her water. "Seriously?"

He nodded, and waited for her to stop laughing. It took longer than he'd thought it would.

"So? Why Bunny?"

He shrugged. "I hate fighting. They'd try to get me to fight and I'd do my best not to. After a while, they started calling me Bunny because, and I quote, I'm 'soft, fuzzy and completely harmless'."

It had taken him *years* to shrug off the fury that sometimes rode him with vicious spurs. Meditation, yoga, even avoiding certain foods helped him keep control of the anger that had been his bane as a teenager. Now he wore the nickname Bunny as a badge of honor, a way to remind himself of where he'd been and was now headed.

That direction now included the woman toying with her water glass across from him. He couldn't wait to get started.

"So, what do you do for a living?" Tabby took a bite of her twelve-ounce steak and moaned. Bunny damn near came in his jeans at the sound. She opened her eyes to find him staring at her mouth. "What?"

"Nothing." Bunny took a bite of his own seafood alfredo.

"This is good. Remind me to thank Gabe."

"So. What do you do for a living, Bunny?"

Bunny swallowed another bite of alfredo. "I'm a landscape architect."

She stared at him. He waited for the question most people asked him. "What's the difference between a landscaper and a landscape architect?"

"It means I have a Bachelor's degree in landscape architecture. I've worked in a corporate environment for years designing landscapes, both soft and hard. I understand the horticulture of the area I work in, and what laws need to be followed where. I design for people who have pools, need stonework, or want their landscape graded but have to deal with county restrictions on water drainage. I design structures to code, and help them deal with regulatory boards. In other words, I'm fully licensed and accredited in the state of Oregon, and I'm usually in a suit."

His mate stared at him like he'd grown a second head. Finally Tabby gulped. "Is that Bunsun with an 'e' or a 'u'?"

He smiled. He was surprised. She didn't look like someone who would have dealings with corporate landscaping. Maybe she had a relative working for him? They had branches all over the United States, and he'd pegged her accent as Deep South right from the beginning. "U. My parents are Will and Barbra Bunsun."

"Holy hell." Tabby sat back and stared at him. "I thought your name sounded familiar."

Bunny held up his hand. "Before we go too far, I live off my wages, not my dad." He put his hand down. He'd been thinking about this for a while. "And not even that right now. I've decided I don't want to do corporate anymore. I want to start working residential."

Tabby stared at Bunny in shock. "Bunsun Exteriors. Damn. Never thought I'd meet one of the Bunsuns this far north."

"I'm surprised you've heard of us." Most people not in the business didn't even know who Bunsun Exteriors were. From the sound of her accent, she *had* to know his name from someplace other than their Oregon branch. They had some southeastern branches, but they were small. His father was looking at expanding further up the east coast, but it was going to take time.

Tabby's face closed up tight. "I have an uncle who works for your company."

Bingo. From her southern accent, she had to be from Georgia, or one of the Carolinas. Maybe Tennessee? All of them had a smallish Bunsun branch, nothing like the corporate offices they had on the west coast. "Dad's company." Bunny leaned back, wondering why she'd suddenly gone cold. "Tabby?"

She blew her bangs out of her eyes. "Guess you should know. I'm Outcast."

Bunny paused. Being Outcast was a serious thing among those who lived in Pride or Pack families. Bears, not being pack-minded, didn't have nearly the same reaction to that sort of thing. Bears were more into small family groups and, unlike wild bears, the males stuck by their mates. "Mind if I ask why?"

She bit her lip, that small hint of vulnerability waking every protective instinct Bunny had. "I was seeing the son of the Alpha. Micah. He was...sweet, and kind, and liked being around me. The Alpha didn't approve, he thought I was trouble." She shrugged. "Maybe I was, maybe I wasn't. I liked to dye my hair different colors, I had some trouble in school, and I had a tattoo."

She had a tattoo? He couldn't find one on her arms, legs or

shoulders. He'd definitely have to explore that later.

"But I never broke anything that belonged to someone else," she continued, "I never hurt anybody who didn't throw a punch first, and I *never* stole anything."

The fierce way she said that last had Bunny growling. "You got Outcast for stealing?"

She winced. "Yes."

Bunny was already shaking his head. "You're not a thief."

Her eyes went wide. "You believe me?"

"Yes."

Her hands covered her mouth, those brown eyes of hers filling with tears. "Oh, God. How can you believe me? You don't even know me."

Bunny covered her hand with his. "I just do." Not that it would matter if she had. She was his *mate*. He'd tell her the sky was orange if it would make her smile. "Tell me what happened." Maybe he could find out what had happened and clear her name for her.

Tabby took a sip of her water. Her hand was visibly shaking. "Um, I was seeing Micah, like I said. Well, he asked me to come over to his house when his parents were out. I did, and we wound up in his room. His parents came home before we got too far, though, so I tried to sneak out of the house. Of course, the Alpha caught me trying to leave, but instead of asking me what I was doing there, he assumed I was there to rob the place."

"What?" Bunny was outraged. How could an Alpha make assumptions like that? Where had the Omega been during all of this?

She nodded. "He was fed up with me. So he gathered the Pack and asked if anyone would speak for me." She swallowed hard enough for Bunny to see, and she wouldn't look him in the eye. "Not even my parents would."

"What about your lover?" And didn't it just bite his ass to say that?

She laughed. "Are you kidding? Micah couldn't stand up to his father. The Alpha was *furious*, I mean scary angry, and if Micah had tried to defy him I don't know what would have happened to him." She rubbed at her wrist. Bunny wondered if she was remembering a bruise there, or some other damage.

"So he declared you a thief and threw you from the Pack." Bunny could feel the rage building under his skin. "How old were you?"

"Fifteen."

"*Fifteen?*" Bunny could feel his chest rumbling. He held back his roar of outrage with difficulty. Some Alpha bastard needed to die painfully. He controlled his Bear with difficulty. "How did you live?"

"I ran mostly in Wolf form, lived off the land, avoided everyone and everything, for fear they'd be able to tell what I was. I wound up in Mrs. Anderson's backyard about six months ago, and I've been here ever since."

"How old are you now?" Bunny knew he was about to lose it. That Alpha had thrown an innocent child out into the woods, no Pack or family to protect her.

"I'm twenty-three."

He felt his eyes turn brown. Bunny stood and walked away, knowing he was inches away from shifting. Eight years. Eight *years* she'd been without protection, alone and hungry and afraid. He could feel his Bear shifting beneath his skin and knew that if he listened to her story for one more minute, he'd be asking her the name of her Alpha. If he knew the name of her Alpha, there would be a Pack looking for a new one. He'd be on his bike and heading for Georgia to maul the son of a bitch.

He walked out into the cool spring air and took some deep breaths, hoping with everything in him that he'd be able to calm himself before he did something stupid. Because Bunny wanted to kill for her, and until he got that side of himself under control, he couldn't go back into the restaurant.

Tabby would have enough to deal with when she found out exactly what he was capable of.

Tabby watched Bunny stalk out of the restaurant, leaving her alone at the table. Totally humiliated, she waited for the waiter to come and give her the check. She hoped she had enough credit to cover the cost.

How could she expect anyone to understand what it was like to be unjustly Outcast? She was lucky the Pumas had taken her in. At least she hadn't made the mistake of going to the Poconos Alpha. If her own mate reacted like this, she could just imagine what the Pack Alpha would have been like.

A warm hand covered hers. "Tabby?"

She stared at Bunny, his image wavering before her, and only then realized that she was crying. "I'm sorry." And she should be. She was an Outcast. Someone no one wanted to be near.

Who had she been kidding? Bunny could go his merry way now. Outcasts had no place in their society. She hadn't even bothered trying to make her way back into a Pack. As far as he knew, she really was everything her old Alpha had accused her of being.

"Shit." Bunny crouched next to her, his expression full of sincere regret. "Don't cry. I'm sorry, Tabby. I didn't think about how you'd take me walking away." A soft kiss landed on the top of her head. "Do me one favor."

"What?" She sniffed.

"No matter how many times I ask, don't ever tell me the name of your ex-Alpha."

"Why not?" Her Wolf snapped to attention as his hazel eyes bled slowly to dark brown. A predator looked out at her through them. He looked lethal, ready to take out the world if she asked him to. It was strange to see that look in the eyes of a Bear. She'd thought Bears were more like her friend Julian, soft and sweet with a quirky humor, but Alex's eyes were those of a hunter. Maybe they were only that predatory where a mate was concerned? "Oh. That's why." She knew her mouth was trembling. Hell, all of her was trembling. No one had stood up for her in years, other than Cyn, Glory, Julian and Gabe.

She darted a glance at Bunny and caught him smiling at her. He was still stroking her fingers, sending tingles down her spine. His heat and scent surrounded her, his eyes still a deep chocolate brown. God, she actually felt *safe*. How the hell had that happened? She hadn't felt truly safe since the day her parents and her Pack turned their backs on her.

"Is everything all right?"

She looked up to find the waiter standing by their table, a concerned look on his face. "Everything's fine." She pulled a tissue from her purse and wiped her eyes.

"Can we have a moment? I think we're going to have dessert and coffee. The tiramisu looks really good." Bunny took a seat next to her, scooting his chair closer, angling his body in between hers and the waiter's.

Big goof. From the look on his face, he wasn't about to let anyone near her he didn't approve of personally. It was sweet, in a caveman sort of way, but could be a real pain in the ass if he chose to act that way at LA. She could feel her lips curving up in a smile at the protective gesture. She cleared the last of the tears from her throat. "I'm thinking of the French silk pie."

"Two coffees?" The waiter left to fetch their desserts after they nodded, leaving them alone.

He stroked her fingers, refusing to let go of her hand. His eyes turned back to the warm hazel they'd been before she began discussing her Outcasting. "Did you really live in the woods all those years?"

"Yes. If it wasn't for Gabe and his grandmother, I'd still be living out there." Or dead. But she wouldn't say that in front of the increasingly growly Bunny. His chest was actually rumbling.

"Where are you from originally?" The question was innocent, but Bunny's expression was anything but. In the dim lighting, she couldn't quite see the color of his eyes, but she thought they might have darkened just a hair.

She decided it couldn't hurt to answer in a roundabout way. "Georgia."

"Near Marietta?"

She shot him a look. No way was she confirming that he was right. Besides, she'd probably given it away when she mentioned her uncle worked for his father.

Bunny sighed. "Is there any way for you to join a local Pack?"

"The closest sanctioned Pack is in the Poconos, about two hours away."

Bunny smiled sweetly as the waiter set the deserts on the table and left. "Ah. So, whereabouts in Marietta is your Pack, anyway?"

Tabby decided to try a little soothing of her own. She reached up and patted Bunny's cheek. "Down, Baloo." Bunny looked startled. "For a Bear, you're awfully growly." Tabby shook her head before taking a bite of her pie. *Mmm, chocolate.* Screw that whole “chocolate isn’t good for canines” shit. After what she’d just gone through, she needed her fix.

“What’s that supposed to mean?”

“Nothing. I know a Bear or two, and I thought most of you were pretty laid back.”

Bunny scowled. “And you think I’m not laid back?”

Tabby tried to hide her growing grin behind her coffee mug, but knew she’d failed when Bunny just shook his head.

They left the restaurant in total accord. Bunny helped Tabby onto the bike and climbed on after her, careful not to jar her. “Want to head to my place?” He had every intention of claiming her tonight, but had no desire to do so in her tiny apartment with her roommates down the hall. He took a deep breath. He longed for the scent of his mate to fill all the empty places inside him.

Instead, he caught the scent of something else, something terrible. “Chloe?” And blood. Lots of blood.

“Chloe? What about Chloe?”

“Tabby?” The scent was stronger now, the breeze bringing him his cousin’s pain. He handed Tabby a helmet, the need to move, to protect his little cousin gripping him with steel hands.

“What?” She shoved the helmet on and wrapped her hands around his waist.

“I need you to hold on.” He started the bike, roaring out of Noah’s parking lot. He ignored Tabby’s squawk of surprise, concentrating only on getting to Chloe.

He turned the corner and found an ambulance, lights flashing in the darkness. They illuminated the body of his little cousin sprawled on the street, her red hair mingling with the blood under her, around her. The paramedics bent over her body worked frantically to save her.

"Sir!"

He was off the bike and charging for the scene before anyone could stop him. Chloe was hurt. Chloe needed him. Ryan was going to freak if anything happened to his baby sister. He needed to call Ryan...

Oh fuck. She looked dead. There was a stranger bent over her, obviously not a paramedic. The man had long, dark hair bound in a braid, but that was all Bunny allowed himself to see. "Chloe?" If he could just touch her, he might be able to help heal her.

One of the paramedics stared at him with sympathy in his eyes and shook his head ever so slightly.

Someone was tugging on the stranger's arm. "Sir, you need to step back and allow us to do our job."

"I'm a nurse," the man growled, deep, bass, primal. It went straight for Bunny's gut. The man was a Bear like him.

He trusted another Bear a hell of a lot more than he trusted a human paramedic. "How is she?"

The man pushed Chloe's light jacket aside, baring her shoulders. "She'll live."

The weary pain in the other Bear's voice was a dagger in his gut. "Live how?"

A car screeched to a halt next to them. A blond man stepped out, his eyes concerned. "Let me through."

Surprisingly, the men did. Bunny, however, wasn't moving. Not until he scented Puma.

"I'm Dr. Jamie Howard. I saw the lights." He knelt down next to Chloe, taking the bag a dark-haired woman, also Puma and smelling strongly of Dr. Howard, handed him. "What happened?"

"Julian Ducharme. I'm a nurse and acquainted with the patient. I don't know what happened, but her injuries are bad." Julian began a catalogue of Chloe's wounds in a cool, professional tone that left Bunny feeling left out in the cold.

"Bunny? Who is she to you?"

He turned to find Tabby standing in front of him, shivering in her light dress. He took off his leather jacket and wrapped it around her shoulders, pulling her against him. He needed comfort, the scent of Chloe's blood poisoning the air around him.

It was bad. He knew it was bad, just as he new his paltry gift was of no use here. "She's my baby cousin."

Tabby sighed. "Oh, sugar." She pulled his head into the crook of her neck, and held on tight. He took a deep breath but nothing could wash away the metallic tang of Chloe's blood.

Tabby could barely see what Julian and Dr. Howard were doing. Bunny took up a lot of space in her field of vision, but she could hear what they were saying and it wasn't good. Julian seemed to think he could help if he had time alone with her, but time was rapidly running out along with the other woman's blood. Bunny trembled in her arms, his hands fisted at the small of her back. She knew he wanted to help, but there was no way he could. Even Tabby could see Chloe was beyond saving.

So she held on as hard as she could, feeling the fine tremors racking her mate's body, while her friend knelt at the side of a dying woman.

"Make them go away, doctor. Get them away and I can save her." Julian's voice was intense.

"At what cost?"

Bunny stiffened in her arms at Dr. Howard's soft words.

"Let me do this. I can save her, they can't. Trust me."

She almost walked over to tell Dr. Howard that Julian could be trusted, but before she could the man sighed. "I'll see what I can do." Dr. Howard walked over to the paramedics who'd huddled off to the side. "These are her family. They want a moment alone with her."

"Sir, she's not going to make it."

Bunny keened softly, the sound full of anguish. His arms surrounded her, held her while he trembled.

"Let's grant their wish. It's not like it will hurt anything, or anyone."

Somehow Dr. Howard got them away, got the paramedics to give them a moment of privacy.

Bunny let her go, grabbed hold of Julian's hand and placed his other on Chloe's shoulder. Tabby watched Julian take a deep breath and...

That's when Tabby knew she was losing her mind.

Bunny relaxed and allowed Julian to direct the path of the healing. He might be a Bear, but Julian was trained as a nurse and had far more knowledge than Bunny could lay claim to. Modern medicine had made the healing the Bears did easier, allowing them to know the ways in which the body functioned, but it came at a price. A price Dr. Jamie Howard somehow knew about. The small amount of healing Bunny could do might keep his cousin alive long enough for them to get her to the hospital, but it would leave him exhausted. He knew he'd sleep around the clock after they were done.

He began to assess the damage. He could feel every cut,

every bruise, every single broken bone his cousin suffered from. There was no way, *no way* they could save her. Her body was too injured to sustain life. It was amazing she'd lingered as long as she had.

He owed Julian for giving him the opportunity to say goodbye.

Just as Bunny opened his mouth to thank the other Bear, the strangest thing happened. Julian took a deep breath, focused, and his hair turned pure white.

And then the *real* healing began.

Julian mended the broken bones, repaired the severed blood vessels, healed the damage to her skull. The fluid pouring into her cranial cavity was causing pressure her fragile brain wouldn't be able to tolerate. Julian drained it off efficiently and moved on to the next wound. Bunny could tell there was something wrong there, in the soft tissues of her brain, but he didn't possess the knowledge to figure out what it was. He was pulled along in Julian's wake, helpless to do anything but watch and marvel.

Bunny was stunned at the strength the other Bear possessed. Julian poured his energy into Chloe, revitalized flagging organs and sped the beat of her heart once all of the blood vessels had been properly repaired. He left enough outer damage that the paramedics would not be too suspicious of what had happened here this night.

He wouldn't have much time when he was done. Bunny could sense the fatigue that pulled at the other Bear, trying to make him sloppy in his healing, but Julian pushed through. His healing remained precise, catching even the tiniest details of the internal damage Chloe had suffered. Bunny offered his strength, letting Julian pull on him to complete what Bunny knew was impossible. It wouldn't be enough to keep the Bear on his feet more than five minutes, ten tops when they were done, but he would survive, thanks to the strength Bunny lent him. Bunny knew that Julian's selfless act would have ended his life. The man had to have known it before he even started.

Bunny owed him, big time.

Another source of energy poured into him. Alien, feminine, it wrapped around him, scented by wild forests and the feel of soft paws on leaves. The howl of a wolf, barely heard, the pull of the moon on a four-limbed body told him whose energy filled him. Savage strength held in check by a heart too big for its frame coursed through him, leaving him dizzy and so aroused he almost lost the spiraling tendrils of the healing path. Tabby lent them her strength, using the bare beginnings of their mate bond to channel her energy through Bunny to Julian and ultimately to Chloe.

That added strength allowed him to help Julian finish healing Chloe. Julian pulled back and released his hold on Bunny, his hair turning dark once more. Bunny watched the white fade from Julian's hair until not a pearly strand was left. Julian was visibly shaking, deep dark circles under his eyes, but when he lifted his face, his expression was serene. "I've done all I can, and it wasn't enough."

And then he collapsed like a broken puppet. Bunny barely stopped his head from cracking on the street.

"Shit." The blond doctor was suddenly there, concern in every line of his body. "I was afraid of this."

"What's this? He's exhausted, isn't he?" Both men turned and stared at Tabby. "I mean, I felt him...pulling on me, but it was weak. Like he was already tiring."

Dr. Howard nodded. "Exactly." He bent over Chloe, leaving Julian to Tabby and Bunny. Bunny checked Julian's vitals with his own healing power and smiled. He'd settled into a deep sleep and would probably be starving when he woke up, but he was going to be fine. He smiled at Tabby when she arranged Julian's legs more comfortably on her lap. "Damn, Bear. Not bad. She'll make it to the hospital." Bunny turned from Tabby to find Doc Howard smiling. "I need to have a long talk with him when he wakes up. We could use someone like him." Dr. Howard stood and motioned to the paramedics. Out of the corner of his eye, he saw the horror that flashed across Tabby's face and wondered at it. Could it have anything to do with the way Julian had collapsed after saving Chloe? How close was his mate to Julian anyway? "I want both Ms. Williams and Mr. Ducharme loaded into the ambulances. I'll want vitals on both of them when I arrive."

"But, Doc, the girl." The paramedic still had that horrible look on his face. It made Bunny want to smash something.

"She's going to make it. Just do what I say and load her up."

"Yes, sir." The paramedics didn't look convinced, but they put Chloe on the gurney anyway. She moaned as they moved her, startling the paramedics who quickly loaded her into the ambulance.

Bunny watched his cousin being maneuvered onto the gurney. Her face was white where it wasn't black and blue, her breathing shallow. She wasn't out of the woods yet. "We have to follow them."

"Of course." He shuddered and a small hand touched his arm. "I'm here, Bunny."

He turned and watched those amazing legs of hers stride toward his Harley. She straddled the seat, pulled on a helmet and waited for him.

The ambulance, lights flashing, started down the street. Bunny didn't watch it go. He had a horrifying thought to deal with.

God, if they crashed, nothing was between her sweet flesh and the harshness of the road. He studied her for a moment, mentally measuring her, knowing the next time she rode with him she'd need to be in denim or leathers.

Not even the amazing Julian could heal a case of dead.

He shuddered at the thought of the body on the ground being hers, of being forced to watch as her blood poured onto the road. She was his, quirky green hair and all. The fear he'd felt seeing Chloe broken on the road suddenly centered on Tabby. He couldn't watch that again.

He strode over to his bike and tugged the helmet off her head.

If anything happened to her on the way to the hospital, she would die his. It wasn't logical, he knew that, but right then, he didn't give a rat's ass. Someone he loved was on her way to the hospital. He needed something to reaffirm life, and marking his little Wolf would do nicely.

"Hey!"

He swallowed her protest, drinking deep of her sweetness. Her soft, full mouth opened in shock and he took complete advantage, thrusting between her lips hungrily. The urge to mate her, mark her as his, was overwhelming.

Thank God for sleeveless dresses. He pushed the leather jacket aside and, without a second thought, bit down into her shoulder. His mark formed under his tongue on her silky smooth skin. He felt her shudder, her head thrown back, her thighs clamping convulsively on the bike as she came. The mating enzyme raced through her system, the first hint of his scent mingled with hers. His Bear settled down, content now that she'd been marked.

She was his.

Tabby sat in the hospital chair and glowered at Bunny. Her hand reached up to touch her shoulder. The mark he'd placed on her burned against her skin. She kept the leather jacket on so no one would see the bite he'd left behind and ask if she'd gotten bitten by a fucking Bear. The only reason she wasn't more pissed off was because of Chloe. She'd seen how his cousin's accident had affected Bunny. She wasn't quite certain why he'd felt the need to mark her right then and there, but the way he'd gone from staring at the ambulance to the way he'd turned to stare at her gave her a clue.

It was touching, in a caveman sort of way. Still, she'd have liked a *little* more time before getting bit. There was so much he still didn't know about her, and even more she didn't know about him.

"Tell me the truth, Bunny. How bad is she?" The large man had come to the hospital in response to a phone call from Bunny. He'd introduced himself as Bunny's cousin, Ryan Williams, Chloe's older brother. He looked even more wild-eyed and pale than Bunny did. He hadn't stopped pacing since he arrived. His reddish-brown hair was mussed, his blue eyes rimmed with red.

"Mr. Bunsun? Mr. Williams?"

Ryan practically jumped the doctor. "Yes, Doc?" Poor guy. He really was worried sick. Bunny rose more slowly, but with just as much urgency.

Dr. Howard stood there and ran his hands through his blond hair. "Follow me." Bunny took hold of Tabby's hand and followed Dr. Howard. He led them to a private room and shut the door. "All right. Who do you want to hear about first?"

Bunny didn't even hesitate. "Chloe."

No surprise there. She was the only one of the trio who knew Julian. From the sick way Ryan swallowed, Bunny had made the right choice.

"She's going to have some scars from this. Chloe is incredibly lucky. To put it bluntly, if Julian hadn't arrived when he did, she'd be dead." Ryan moaned. Bunny shuddered. Tabby hugged his arm, offering comfort. Julian would never have allowed Chloe to die. She knew that like she knew the color of her own eyes. "Her recovery will take time. There will be some brain damage. We won't know until she wakes up exactly what we'll be dealing with."

"Fuck." Bunny began to pace. "She's working on her doctorate in veterinary medicine. I'll have to call her boss, let him know what's going on."

"I'll do it." She'd call the diner and the veterinary office where Chloe volunteered. She already had the diner's phone number, since she and the girls ordered lunch from there regularly, and it wouldn't be difficult to get the veterinary office's phone number. Bunny and Ryan needed to concentrate on Chloe.

"Our family is on the way." Ryan sounded like he was in shock. "Mom and Dad should be here by morning."

"Is she awake?" Tabby looked to Dr. Howard in time to catch his wince.

"No, and that's one of the reasons we're worried. I couldn't talk to Mr. Ducharme before he collapsed." Dr. Howard stared at the closed door for a moment before turning to Bunny. "Your friend is a Kermode Bear, isn't he?"

A what?

"He is?" Bunny frowned. "That explains a lot. How did you know?"

Dr. Howard smiled. "I dated one briefly before I met my

mate. I lived in Canada for about two years before coming back to Halle. She taught me a lot about Bears." He shook his head. "Only a Spirit Bear could have done what Julian did."

Ryan took a deep, audible breath and blew it out. "I owe him."

Jamie shot him a look. "You owe him more than you think. The paramedics tell me her injuries were extensive and Julian confirmed it. Quite frankly, I'm surprised he lived through the healing."

Tabby froze. Julian could have *died*? Her best friend, the man who'd laughingly declared that she could be the sister he'd never had, could be...gone? Now it was her turn to swallow. He was one of the few people who gave her the sense of family she'd lost eight years ago. She couldn't bear it if she lost him.

"My girlfriend told me there were limits to how far a Bear could heal someone, even a Kermode. So unless Julian is Super Bear, something had to have helped him."

Bunny nodded, but didn't elaborate. Tabby knew who'd helped Julian, and he was exhausted because of it. "He's still out?" Bunny's jaw looked to be clenched shut. She could see some serious dental bills in their future.

"We're not sure when he'll wake up, but knowing the healing capabilities of your kind, it shouldn't take too much longer, despite whatever it was he did to save your cousin."

"Was it an accident?" Tabby looked over at Ryan. The man was practically vibrating in place. "What happened to my sister? Did someone do this deliberately or was it an accident?"

"I haven't spoken to Sheriff Anderson yet, so I don't know. I do know he's been informed. Last I heard, he was at the scene, trying to figure it out."

Tabby frowned. "That doesn't make any sense. Why wasn't he there with the ambulance? Or hell, any one of the cops around here?" The men all turned to stare at her. "Seriously. Why was the ambulance there without a cop present? Someone had to have called it in, right? Was it Julian?"

Dr. Howard blinked. "I...don't know. Tell you what, let me find out who called 9-1-1 and reported her. Maybe the dispatcher just didn't think to alert the sheriff's office."

"Here's my cell phone number so you can contact me once you know anything." Ryan rattled off his number while Dr. Howard programmed it into his phone. "Can I see my sister?"

Dr. Howard nodded. "And I've left instructions that all three of you be allowed to see Mr. Ducharme as well as Ms. Williams."

"Thank you, Doctor." Ryan shook the man's hand.

"Thank you." Bunny followed his cousin, shaking Dr. Howard's hand.

"Take care, all of you." Doctor Howard opened the door and left the room, leaving behind three very tired, upset shifters.

"C'mon. We're not doing any good here." Tabby tugged on the two men. "You two go see Chloe. I'll be in Julian's room." She poked and prodded until they both got moving, knowing neither would rest until they knew Chloe was on the mend.

She got Chloe's room number from the nurse and pushed the men toward it, then headed to Julian's room. When he woke up, she had every intention of being there and finding out what *Super Bear* had done to save Bunny's cousin.

What the hell was a Spirit Bear anyway?

Bunny stared down at his sleeping mate. Tabby had curled up on a chair next to Julian's bed, her lime green hair glowing against the blue vinyl upholstery. He wished he could join her, but the need to stand guard, to protect the ones he cared about, was too strong. He'd almost lost Chloe tonight. Nothing was going to happen to Tabby. Ryan, just as sleepless, was guarding his sister.

Tabby snuffled in her sleep and he smiled. How had she come to mean so much to him so quickly? His gaze drifted across her. The pride he felt in her was startling. Of the three of them, she'd kept her head, dealing with each blow with a practicality that allowed him to lean on her when he'd needed her most. She didn't even know Chloe, but she'd called Frank at the diner and told him what had happened. She'd called the veterinary office and left a message about the accident, complete with Chloe's condition and her room number. After she was done, she'd kept watch over Julian, running back and forth between his room and Chloe's to check in with Bunny and Ryan to see if they needed anything. She'd done everything she could to take care of all of them, and the only one she truly knew was still unconscious.

He sighed and rubbed his hand across the top of his head, the soft stubble there rasping against his palm. Tabby growled and twitched in her sleep, her fingers tightening around the arms of the chair. He wondered what she was dreaming about.

His mate was an incredible person. He just hoped he was worthy of her.

"Alex?"

Bunny turned toward the door, shocked to find his father standing there. He should have known his parents would rush to their niece's side. "Dad?"

Will Bunsun walked into the room, his wife following behind him. "What the hell happened?"

Barbra Bunsun smacked her husband's arm. "Will! Keep it down." She rolled her hazel eyes, but grabbed her only son, pulling him down for a hug. "Ryan's parents called us. Sweetie, *you* should have called."

Bunny sank into the comfort that was his mother. She always smelled of cinnamon and home. "Hey, Mom. I wasn't sure you were still up. I planned on calling in the morning."

"You could have called to tell us about Chloe. And you should have called us the minute you found your mate." Only a mother could look at someone the way Barbra Bunsun was looking at him. Her eyes narrowed and he flushed, wondering why he felt guilty. He hadn't done anything wrong.

"We caught the first flight out." Will hugged his son. "There's no way we'd let you go through this alone, Alex."

"Thank you." Bunny blinked back tears. Of all his cousins, he was closest to Ryan and Chloe, and seeing her battered body had hit him hard. God, he loved his parents. William Bunsun might run an extremely busy company, but he always put his family first. "Where's Eric?" He was surprised that his brother wasn't right behind his parents.

"Aunt Laura and Uncle Steven are with Chloe and Ryan. Uncle Ray and Aunt Stacey stayed behind with Eric to help run the business." His mom pulled his face around. "Ryan told us we owe Chloe's life to Mr. Ducharme, and that we could find you here with your mate." She looked over at the man on the bed, her gaze snagging on his sleeping mate. "*Green* hair?"

Will chuckled. "You were expecting something else?"

Barbra Bunsun gave her husband an astonished look. "I'm surprised he didn't go for a Japanese blonde with two pigtails on her head and an insane love of fried rice."

Bunny rolled his eyes. He did *not* have a Sailor Moon fetish, no matter what that therapist had said. "Mom." He winced. He hadn't sounded that whiny in years. Leave it to his mother to have him feeling ten years old again.

His mother patted his cheek. "That's all right, dear. I'm

sure she'll fit right in."

God he hoped so. And he hoped the rest of the family was as welcoming as he knew his parents would be. Because so far Tabby was anything but ordinary.

Chapter Three

Tabby sipped the sucky hospital coffee and waited for Alex to step out of his cousin's room. Julian had insisted that she go check on her, but she didn't feel comfortable in there with everyone else. Chloe's parents were hovering over her and, despite how shitty Tabby felt about it, she found herself jealous. Tabby's parents had never cared that much for her. If they had cared at all, they'd never have abandoned her to the streets when she was fifteen.

"Here, this might make it a little better."

Tabby glanced at Alex's mother, wondering again at the sight of the smaller woman. The beautiful woman next to her looked nothing like a mom. She looked like a model, her eyes a startling light hazel, her skin a creamy bronze. The only imperfections were the laugh lines around her eyes and mouth and the light smattering of freckles across her nose. It was those laugh lines that showed her the resemblance between Bunny and his mother. "Thanks, Mrs. Bunsun."

"Barb, sweetie. And don't thank me until you've tasted that."

Tabby looked down at the cherry danish in her hand. "Hospital cafeteria?"

"Yup." Barbra sighed and leaned against the wall. "So. You're mated to my son."

Tabby winced. “Almost.”

Thin dark brows rose, questioning her without saying a word.

“He bit me before we followed the ambulance. Just pushed the jacket aside and bared fang, right in public too.” She took a bite of the cherry danish. She then took a nice, long sip of the coffee so she wouldn’t choke on the dry pastry. She tried desperately not to make a face. It had been a nice gesture, but dear God. “Um. Is there a convenience store around here?”

Barb’s lips twitched. “Bared fang, huh?”

“Mm-hmm. That’s as far as we’ve gotten, though.” Tabby froze, her gaze sliding away. “You’re...all right with that?” Hadn’t Alex told her that Tabby was Outcast?

“Are *you* all right with it?”

Tabby thought of her hotter-than-hell mate and nodded. “Oh, yeah. I’m fine with it.”

Barb smiled, looking relieved. “I was worried. My parents freaked when they found out my mate was white. They didn’t speak to me for weeks.”

Tabby snorted. “My parents are the least of my worries.”

Barb’s expression turned sharp. “Is there a problem I need to know about?”

Tabby threw away the inedible danish. She’d eaten better food out of garbage bins. Someone needed to smack the hospital nutritionist upside the head. “I’m Outcast.”

Barb blinked. “Hmm. What for?”

She studied her mother-in-law, relieved to see no condemnation in the other woman’s face. “For being a thief.”

Barb waved her hand. “And? Details, hon.”

“Long story short? I was dating the Alpha’s son. I snuck into his room to fool around, got caught sneaking out. The

Alpha assumed I was there to rob him and wouldn't listen to what I was saying. His son didn't even try to explain things to his father." Her lips twisted in a smile. "The Alpha never heard anything he didn't want to anyway. No one bothered to speak up for me and the Alpha Outcast me. I roamed for about eight years as a wolf and finally landed in Halle. I've been here ever since."

Barb studied her for a moment, her whole body relaxing. "Then we'll have to fix it."

Tabby blinked. How did you fix the unfixable? "How's Chloe?"

Barb sighed, the tension returning to her shoulders. "Not good."

She took hold of Barb's hand and squeezed. "I'm so sorry. Is there anything I can do to help?"

"Yeah." Barb's smile was weary. "Take good care of my son."

Tabby nodded, her eyes following Barb all the way back to the hospital room door.

"Tabby?"

Tabby grinned as her friend's sweet voice flowed over her. Glory was standing there in one of her colorful peasant skirts and glittery tops, her pale blue hair done up in a sweet-looking ponytail. She looked like a pixie gypsy. "Hey, girl. What are you doing here?"

Glory held up Tabby's gym bag. The bangles on her wrist jangled and her grin was wide and sparkling. "Not quite the way we'd envisioned you spending last night." She giggled. "Okay, bringing you work clothes after your night of debauchery, yes. Bringing you work clothes after a night in the hospital, no. And hey, no walk of shame, right?"

"Thanks a lot." Tabby rolled her eyes, but just the presence of her bubbly friend soothed her. It was hard to be upset when Glory was around. "Is Cyn all alone?" The store had opened over an hour ago.

"She posted that we were closed for a family emergency and moved the appointments we had to later in the week." She handed Tabby the bag. "I'm sorry to hear about your boyfriend's cousin."

"Thanks." Tabby headed toward Julian's room. She'd rather change in his bathroom than in the public restroom. And there was no way she was going into Chloe's room, not with all those people in there. Julian would guard the door for her while she changed. He was one of the few people she truly trusted to keep her safe.

"Where *is* your new man, anyway?"

Tabby shrugged. "Alex is getting some sleep finally." And hadn't that been a battle and a half? He'd argued with everyone but his mother until the woman had pinched his ear and literally dragged him off for some rest. He was due back any minute now. "Oh, I almost forgot. Julian's here."

"What for?"

She thought about trying to explain, but decided she wanted a nice tall pitcher of margaritas next to her when she did. She still hadn't figured out how he'd saved Chloe, or what was up with the funky white hair. "I'll tell you later, but he's fine now. He's waiting on his discharge paperwork in his room, so I'll change there."

"Well, Cyn says to take your—*oomph*!" Tabby spun around. Glory was sprawled on the floor. Ryan stood over her, the strangest look on his face.

Glory blew her pale blue bangs out of her face. "And hello to you too."

Tabby had to stifle her own giggles at the disgruntled look on her face.

Ryan blinked. His expression was stunned. Tabby had seen Glory have that effect on more than one man. “Hello.” Tabby shivered. Ryan had practically purred the salutation. “Who are you?”

Glory smiled up at Ryan. “Glory.” She held up her hand, every inch a dainty princess. “Help me up, please?”

Ryan jumped. “Oh! Right.” He took Glory’s hand and easily pulled her to her feet. “I’m Ryan, Ryan Williams.”

Glory’s expression turned much more genuine. “Chloe’s brother?”

Ryan smiled. “Yeah. She was admitted last night. You know her?”

Glory’s mouth dropped open. “You mean...?” She turned to Tabby. “You didn’t tell me it was *Chloe* in the hospital.” She tugged on her hand, frowning absently when Ryan didn’t let go. “Chloe’s a friend. I need to go get her some flowers or something.”

“She’d like that once she’s out of ICU.” Ryan took Glory’s hand and tucked it into the crook of his arm. “Maybe I can help you find some?”

Glory tapped her foot. “Your sister is in the hospital and you’re flirting with me?”

Ryan’s answer was a heated grin.

Tabby coughed. From the look on Ryan’s face, things were about to get interesting for her friend. “I need to borrow Glory for a little bit.” Ryan frowned at her. “Seriously. She’s my coworker, my roommate and one of my best friends.”

The frown left his face. “And?”

Tabby sighed. “Glory?”

"Yeah?"

"Grr-grr."

Glory tilted her head toward Ryan, her mouth hanging open. "Him?"

"Yup."

"Oh!" Glory yanked her hand free. "Shouldn't you be, I dunno, with your mate?" She hissed. Glory had a real hate-on for cheaters. Tabby still didn't know why, though she could guess. Glory's parents were divorced, and she knew Glory would have nothing to do with her mother.

"He doesn't have one, Glory."

Ryan threw his head back and laughed. "Not yet, anyway." He loomed over Glory, his expression intense. He towered over her petite friend. The move screamed possession.

Uh-oh. "Um. Ryan? Why don't you go check on Chloe?"

He looked over at her, and for a moment the predator he was peeked out of his suddenly deep brown eyes. She could tell he was debating whether or not to do what she'd asked. "Where are you two headed?"

Tabby held up her bag. "She brought me clothes. We're headed to Julian's room so I can get changed in peace."

Ryan studied her, his fingers absently toying with a lock of Glory's hair. "Keep her safe."

She gulped, the quiet warning in the Bear's voice clear. If Ryan had decided not to let Glory out of his sight, there wasn't much Tabby could have done to stop him. A lone Bear could whip the ass of a lone Wolf. "Yup. Will do."

Ryan took Glory's hand to his lips. "I will see *you* later." He tipped Glory's chin up and smiled down at her, his expression filled with wonder and a touch of satisfaction. "Glory."

Glory didn't take a breath until Ryan's form disappeared

around the corner. "What the hell was that all about?"

Tabby took Glory's arm and steered her back to Julian's room. "I'll explain it on the way." She pushed the button for the elevator. "How do you feel about bears?"

Glory looked stunned. She stumbled along, pulled by Tabby, her expression one of horrified fascination. She'd never dealt well with aggressive men, and a man on the hunt for his mate was about as aggressive as they came. "Please tell me we're discussing the teddy kind."

Tabby shook her head and escorted her friend into Julian's room.

Bunny pushed on the door to Julian's room. Ryan had told him that his mate could be found there. He'd also told Bunny that she was getting naked. He needed to find out if Julian was a dead man or not. Clenched in one hand was the stupid stuffed bear he'd had made for Julian at Tabby's insistence.

If Julian had gotten one glimpse of his mate's creamy flesh, Bunny was going to feed the toy to him one fuzzy piece at a time.

"I was wondering when you'd show up."

Bunny blinked. Julian sat on the edge of his bed, a smirk on his face. His Native American heritage was obvious in his dusky skin color, deep black eyes and high cheekbones. His long, dark hair was loose, falling to pool in his lap. Now that he got a good look at him, Bunny nearly growled. Julian was one of the handsomest men he'd ever seen. And Tabby was naked in this man's bathroom?

Hell to the no.

"Where's Tabby?" Bunny smiled, his fangs peeking out. *Mine.*

Julian rolled his eyes and snorted. “She’s getting dressed.” He pointed toward the bathroom. “She even waited until she shut the door to start with the nakedness.”

Bunny’s hands clenched. He owed the man, but still. That was *his* mate getting naked in another man’s room. “Tabby?”

“Yeah?” Her muffled reply sounded amused.

He ground his teeth. “Are you done yet?”

Julian covered his mouth, no doubt hiding his laughter from the way his shoulders were shaking. “Your mate thinks I’m going to sneak in there and ravish your lily-white ass.”

Bunny relaxed a bit. The other man had just acknowledged Bunny’s right to Tabby. He bowed his head in thanks, smiling back when Julian winked at him. The last thing he wanted to do was rip into the man who not only was one of his mate’s closest friends, but his cousin’s savior. Besides, Bunny hated fighting, but he’d do it for Tabby. It was nice to know there wasn’t a need where Julian was concerned.

The sounds behind the door had stopped. “He thinks what again?”

“Face it, hon.” Julian struck a dramatic pose. “You want me even more than you want Legolas.”

The door opened. Tabby stepped out and Bunny’s tongue nearly hit the floor. Those jeans looked painted on. “Of course. Legolas can’t do that thing you do with your tongue and a cherry stem.”

Bunny sighed. He’d explore those jeans later. He turned his attention back to Julian. “You need to die now.”

Julian laughed. “Nice to meet you, by the way.”

Bunny stepped forward and shook the hand Julian was holding out. He tried not to frown. The man looked like hammered shit despite the front he was putting on. “Alexander

Bunsun. Call me Bunny."

The Bear blinked, but didn't say a word. "Julian Ducharme. Tabby and I are good friends."

"I owe you for what you did for my cousin."

Julian grimaced. "I couldn't leave her like that." He shrugged. "Her pain pulled me from three blocks away."

Tabby's hand rested on his shoulder, calming him even further. "Are you the one who called it in to 9-1-1?" *Good question.* One that hadn't been answered yet, at least as far as Bunny knew.

Julian frowned and sat up straight. "No. They arrived just as I got there."

Tabby and Julian exchanged a worried look. These two obviously had some history, and his mate trusted the other Bear. He decided that was good enough for him. He relaxed, settling into a chair next to Julian's bed. "So who did call them?"

"That's a good question."

Tabby frowned. "I know just the man to answer that." She pulled out her cell phone and touched a number, then put the phone to her ear. "Hi, it's Tabby. Can you put me through to Gabe?"

"Good girl. I should have thought of that."

Bunny frowned when Julian settled back against the head of the bed. "Thought of what?"

Tabby moved to the door and opened it, stepping out into the hallway. "Hey, Gabe. Any news on Chloe's case?"

Julian folded his hands behind his head and crossed his ankles. "She's friends with the sheriff. She'll get an answer out of him faster than anyone but his mate, especially where Chloe's concerned." Julian gave him a speculative look. "She may have lost her family in Georgia, but she found a new one here. You understand?"

Bunny studied Julian and slowly nodded. Yeah, he understood. "Thank you again."

Julian shrugged. "I'm not the only one. There are a number of people who would go to bat for that girl without thinking twice about it. In fact, I think she'd be surprised at how many would."

"Including the Alpha?"

"Not sure, but I think so. From what I've seen, Max is pretty confident and he trusts his hierarchy."

"And if Gabe says she's family, he'll what? Accept that?"

Julian looked mysterious. A streak of palest white flashed through his hair, gone almost as quickly as it appeared. "I think when all is said and done, Tabby's going to find that she's got a lot more family than she ever dreamed of."

Julian and I need to sit down and have a nice, long talk. Soon. "She doesn't know about the Kermode." He grinned. "Can I be there for that discussion?"

Julian snorted. "Sure. Can you have it for me?"

Bunny rolled his eyes. "Remind me to introduce you to Ryan. You two should get along really well." He held out the bear. "Here. From Tabby and me."

Julian took the white bear and snorted. "Cute. But why the Superman costume?"

Tabby stepped back into the room before he could answer. She looked shaken, wild. Bunny stood, ready to comfort his shaken mate. "I just talked to Gabe."

Julian sat up slowly, all of his attention suddenly focused on Tabby. Bunny tensed all over. The look on her face was horrible. "What, baby?"

"Chloe." She gulped. "She wasn't hit by a car. They've confirmed that the marks on her body are consistent with a beating." She stepped forward and clasped her arms around Bunny, laying her head against his chest with a sigh. "Someone tried to kill your cousin."

Bunny blinked in the late afternoon light filtering in through the hospital window. He'd made sure Julian got home safely, following the cab to the small house on the outskirts of town Julian called home. He'd dropped Tabby off at work immediately afterwards and headed right back to the hospital. He'd been sitting there ever since.

"Go home."

Bunny blinked up at his father. He couldn't leave Chloe. What if something happened to her? He needed to be there to protect her. It was bad enough he hadn't been there before.

His father's hand landed on his shoulder. "I know what you're thinking. We're more alike than you know." Will pulled Bunny out of the chair. "I promise nothing is going to happen to Chloe while I'm here."

Bunny looked into his father's shifted eyes and nodded. He and his father were a great deal alike. Will would protect Chloe against anything and everything that came at her. The only difference was William didn't have the anger issues Bunny faced on a daily basis. The rage in him was much more focused and directed. He'd taken that anger and turned it on the land itself, creating his business with his own two hands. Just as Bunny used yoga, his father used physical labor, and it worked. "Okay. I'll go rest. Call me if she wakes up." He winced. He'd meant to say *when.*

"Sleep, son. You're exhausted. You helped heal Chloe. Now

it's time to heal yourself."

Bunny nodded again and shuffled to the door.

"And leave the bike here. Take a cab."

He froze. He *never* left the bike. That Harley was his baby.

"Maybe you could call your mate and get a ride?"

Now there was a thought. Maybe he'd convince her to come back to the hotel room with him. "Good idea." Maybe he'd do more than nap, too. He pulled out his cell phone and called Living Art.

"Living Art, Glory speaking."

"Hey, Glory. Can you put Tabby on?"

"Sure thing." She sounded so sweet and demure, right up until she screeched at the top of her lungs, "TA-BBY! PHO-ONE!" He pulled the phone away from his ear with a wince. Damn, that girl had a healthy set of lungs.

His father chuckled. "Isn't that the girl Ryan showed some interest in?"

Bunny gaped. Ryan had shown interest in one of the girls?

"Tabby speaking. How can I help y'all?"

He shivered. That deep drawl washed over him again, his cock perking up with insistent interest. Damn, he'd left her only six hours ago and already he was jonesing for the sight of her. "Can you do me a favor, baby?"

"Sure, sugar. What do you need?"

"Can you come pick me up? I'm exhausted and I've been ordered to leave the bike here."

There was a pause. "I can't. I'm expecting a customer in about ten minutes."

He hated to ask, but damn it he was starting to see double he was so exhausted. He hadn't slept a wink in that damn hotel room, pacing and worrying about Tabby and Chloe. His mother had taken one look at him and shaken her head, exasperated. "Can one of the other girls give me a lift?"

"I'll do one better. Wait there, someone will pick you up shortly. And don't even *think* about sneaking off on the bike. If you're tired enough to call me, you're too tired to ride."

He could feel himself blushing. "I wasn't."

"Good." She paused. A bell jingled in the background. It sounded a lot like the one attached to Living Art's front door. "I have to go."

Bunny frowned. Her voice had sounded tight. "Are you all right?"

"Yeah, I—" Something crashed. "Shit. I will be. Gotta go." She hung up, leaving him standing there, a red haze of anger rising inside him.

"Something's happening at Living Art." Bunny headed to the door. "Where's Ryan?"

"Trouble?" Will followed him.

"Yeah. Dad, you need to stay here or get Ryan to stay here. I need to head to the tattoo parlor and check up on Tabby."

"Not in your condition."

Bunny turned and growled at his father. He'd never challenged the older man, but he'd never had a mate before, either.

Will threw his hands up in the air. "I'll call Ryan, have him meet you there."

Bunny nodded and stalked toward the elevator, the possible threat to his mate thrumming through his veins. Suddenly he wasn't so tired anymore.

God help anyone who laid their hands on what was his.

Tabby called 9-1-1, but the damage was done. Someone had thrown something through the window and she had let Bunny know something was wrong. Fuck. Ten to one he was already on his way over here.

"What the fuck?"

She turned to look at the patron who'd entered the store just before the thing came through the window. What the hell was that anyway? It looked like some kind of metal tube. A pipe, maybe? "Ryan?"

He looked over at her, his pale blue eyes turning brown as she watched. "Where's Glory?"

"Here." Glory stepped out from behind the curtain, followed closely by Cyn.

He went right to Glory's side, his gaze roaming over her, his hands twitching at his sides. "What happened?"

"That came through the window." Tabby pointed toward the metal object. It lay less than a foot from her.

"Oh no! Are you all right?" Cyn was suddenly right there, checking Tabby over for damage.

"I'm fine. I called 9-1-1."

Ryan's gaze was glued to Glory. He sniffed and his nose wrinkled in disgust. "What's that smell?"

Tabby looked down at the tube, only then noticing the stench beginning to drift up from it. "Oh, hell. Grab your stuff. Everyone out."

They hurried out of the store, careful of the broken glass. Ryan scooped Glory up and carried her out, his eyes hard. He barely seemed to notice her weight, but as a Bear, he was much stronger than most men. She probably *did* feel like a feather in his arms.

Glory, on the other hand, was freaked. She was stiff as a board in his arms. Ryan set her down on her feet, his expression a mix of confusion and concern. "Did you get hurt?"

She backed away rapidly. "I'm fine."

He looked puzzled, the brown fading away, leaving behind the blue. "Glory?"

Tabby shook her head and moved away. It seemed Glory wasn't going to take to mating as easily as she'd thought she would. She saw Cyn snarl and pull out her cell phone, gesturing for people to get back, move away from the store.

Then the back of Tabby's head exploded and the world went black.

Bunny roared to a stop outside Living Art. He turned off the bike and ran toward the huddle of people. "What happened?"

The deputy speaking to Cyn and Glory pointed to the store. "Someone threw a pipe through the window with some kind of stink bomb attached to it. Oh, and that lady over there got attacked. Sheriff's dealing with her."

Bunny caught sight of Tabby's green hair on the concrete and lunged toward the sheriff. His heart pounded with fear. Visions of Chloe lying in a pool of blood haunted him.

Ryan grabbed hold of his arm, trying to stop him. "Tabby's hurt, but she's okay."

He ripped free of his cousin's grasp and lunged to the center of the crowd. He didn't care who he shoved out of his way. He had to get to his injured mate. "Tabby?"

She pulled her hand away from the back of her head with a wince. "Ow. I got hit." That Georgia drawl was slurred by pain.

The sheriff and a deputy stood aside and let Bunny get close to his mate. He knelt down, probing the back of her head with his fingers. Sure enough, there was a small, bloody wound forming into a lump. He reached for his Bear, grateful for the strength he gave him. He healed the wound, the exhausting drain worth it when she sighed in relief and sagged against him. He stroked her hair, grateful beyond belief when she smiled up at him. He muttered a silent thanks to Bear for healing his mate and looked up at the sheriff. "She'll be all right."

"Did you see who hit you?"

Bunny turned and glared up at the deputy standing next to the sheriff. The man had spoken in a bored tone, rasping across Bunny's protective instincts. How dare this man take the attack on his mate so lightly? Hell, even Gabe looked briefly disgusted before he once more controlled his expression. Bunny wondered if the deputy was the type of cop who figured anything that happened to a tattoo artist had to be linked to something illegal and was therefore deserved.

Tabby shook her head, wincing a little. "Nope. It was pretty much *bam*, then lights out." Bunny stroked her forehead, brushing away the last vestiges of the headache her attacker had caused.

"And no one else was injured." Anderson was staring down at her, his expression completely closed off. But there was a glint of gold in the man's eyes that Bunny recognized.

Bunny knew what Anderson was thinking. He closed his eyes, lest someone see the possessive rage boiling in their depths. Someone had deliberately targeted his mate. "Tabby's coming home with me."

He knew she was going to protest, but before she could, Cyn's voice cut through the crowd. "Of course she isn't. She needs x-rays and stuff, and no argument, you got it?" Tabby bit her lip. Cyn stood there with her hands on her hips, her eyes blazing. "Some son of a bitch thinks he's going to shut my shop down, take you out without a fight? I don't think so." Cyn pointed at Tabby. "You. Go to the hospital." She pointed to Gabe. "You. Find out who did this and stick their asses in jail, where I sincerely hope they will get reamed multiple times." The people around Cyn chuckled, but Bunny noticed Cyn wasn't joking. "Glory and I will clean up."

"I'll help."

Cyn eyed Ryan up and down. "Good. We could use some muscle around here."

Glory looked terrified. Bunny briefly wondered why, but got distracted when Tabby's hand landed on his shoulder.

She used his shoulder for leverage and stood up. "Yes, master." She bowed dramatically to Cyn, wobbling a little bit. Bunny reached up and steadied her with one hand on her thigh.

She still looked a little pale. He stood and pulled her gently into his arms, running his hands over her, healing her scrapes, doing his best to soothe her. She settled in against him but continued to pout. "Are you up to riding?"

She snorted. "I'm up to driving."

That might not be a bad idea. Bunny was beginning to shake, a reaction to his exhaustion and the adrenaline rush. "Good idea. Hospital?"

She glared at him. He'd healed almost all of her injuries. He knew she didn't need any x-rays, and apparently so did she.

"Right." He pulled his key out of his pocket and handed it to her. "The Marriott near the college."

"Got it." She twirled the keys around her finger and swung onto the bike. "Ready?"

He narrowed his eyes. She looked incredible straddling his bike. Her black tank top made her skin glow, emphasizing her green hair. Those damn painted-on jeans strained against her thighs. Her high-heeled black boots rested comfortably against the blacktop, bringing forth every dirty image Bunny had ever had about women and motorcycles.

Fuck. He could see her sitting like that in nothing but those boots and a smile. He pictured it, her body hunched over the handlebars, her breasts swaying free, that saucy grin on her face and her ass in the air, ready for him to take her.

He growled. "You have no idea."

She pulled her helmet on and patted the seat behind her, enticingly close to her ass. "Come on, sugar. Climb aboard."

Bunny, his control almost shredded, did, fastening his helmet. She was in for more than one type of ride today.

"Hospital." He looked over at Cyn. "I mean it. She's got a lump on her head. Are you sure she should be driving?"

Bunny fought the urge to roll his eyes. There was no way Cyn could know he'd already healed Tabby's injury, and no way he could explain it in such a mixed crowd. "She's fine."

Cyn glared at him. "Lump. Head. Hell, even Tabby's thick skull isn't crack-proof."

"Hey!" Tabby yanked off the helmet. "I feel fine now, thank you."

"I don't." Cyn grabbed Tabby's helmet and held out her hand. "Hospital. Pinky-swear."

Tabby rolled her eyes and held out her little pinky. "I swear I'll get my head checked out." Of course, they both knew Bunny had already taken care of it, so her oath wasn't necessary. And she'd phrased it in such a way that she could honestly say she hadn't lied.

Cyn grabbed it with her own pinky. "Good." She stepped back, obviously satisfied. "Take care of her for me."

"I will." He wrapped his arms around Tabby. This might even be better than when he drove. He thrust his hips forward, cradling his cock against Tabby's luscious ass. "Believe me, I will," he muttered for her ears only.

She shuddered and started the bike. She pulled out into the street, careful until they were out of sight of the store. "You know I don't need a hospital."

He did. He'd never have let her drive if he thought for one minute she was impaired in any way. The healing was complete. "I know." He rubbed his hand briefly across her breast. "But I know what you *do* need." And, dear God, what he needed more than anything.

They pulled up to his hotel and found a parking spot close to the front door. "Really? You think so?"

He reached around her for the keys and turned off the bike. "I know so." He helped her up, tucking their helmets away. "Shall we?"

She looked...disappointed. He knew he had to hold it together until they were in his room. Once he had her in his temporary den, all bets were off.

They rode the elevator in silence, Bunny's hand wrapped around hers. It felt so small in his big paw. His chest rumbled with a low growl. The thought that anyone would try to harm his mate was inconceivable. She deserved so much more than she'd gotten out of life so far. And he was just the man to see that she got it. But first, she was going to mark him.

The elevator dinged and she sighed, her shoulders slumping wearily. So far it had been a hell of a week and they were both exhausted. That sigh quickly turned into a gasp when he dragged her out of the elevator and almost threw her into his hotel room. God, he needed her. If he didn't feel her around him soon, he was going to fucking explode. He had to erase the scent of her attacker from her skin, the feel of him from her mind. He closed the door, pushing her up against it. "Mine."

"Yours." She was breathless, trying desperately to soothe him.

He wasn't in any mood to be soothed. He bit her right through her shirt, marking her again, forcing her into orgasm. The scent of her pleasure teased him, drove him insane. She had to be naked. He wanted the feel of her soft flesh in his palms. He pulled at her shirt, ripping it half off her body, exposing her lacy bra. He pulled one cup of the bra down, exposing one full breast to his hungry gaze.

Oh, fuck, she's pierced. A little gold ring dangled from her brown nipple, a green bead glowing against her golden skin.

He bent down and sucked her nipple into his mouth. He pulled on it relentlessly, tongued the gold ring, and reveled in her soft cries. Her body began to undulate against him, her hips pushing up against his erection.

He grabbed her around the waist and picked her up, holding her against the door so that he stood upright, her breast right where he wanted it. She wrapped her legs around his waist and grabbed hold of his head, pushing his mouth right where they both wanted it.

He ripped his mouth away only to suck her other breast into his mouth. Her head slammed back into the door. "Fuck, Alex."

He snarled. She'd called him Alex. No one called him Alex except his immediate family.

Possessiveness roared through him. She was family. She was *his.*

He looked up to find her staring down at him through Wolf eyes. Her fangs were bared. "Put me down."

He let his fangs scrape her breast. The moan she let loose was music to his ears. “Why?”

She grinned. “I want to mark you.”

He shuddered. “My way.”

“What?”

He turned and threw her onto the bed, ignoring her startled screech. “My way.” The boots had to come off before he could peel those jeans off her legs. He yanked them off and quickly pulled off her jeans. He eyed the boots lying on the floor. He wasn’t sure he’d allow her to wear those to work again. They screamed *fuck me* to him.

He was the only one who got that pleasure.

Next went the underwear. She lay there, watching him pull her clothing off, the delicate lace ripping under his hands. He was using too much strength, leaving bruises behind, but he couldn’t seem to stop himself. He needed to feel her coming around him.

Once she was naked , he stood up. “Play with yourself.”

Her eyes widened for a moment before her lids dropped, her hands reaching up to pluck at her nipples. Her thighs spread, allowing him to see the juicy lips of her pussy.

He nearly dropped to his knees, eager to worship the woman writhing on his bed. He dragged his clothes from his body, not caring where they fell. He only knew he had to climb up there and bury his face between the thighs of the woman he’d claimed.

Tabby watched Alex crawl up the bed. There was no way in hell he looked like a *Bunny* to her, not with that look in his eye. The expression on his face was one of wicked intent, his gaze glued to her pussy. He licked his lips and everything in Tabby quivered in anticipation.

Oh, hell. He was going to eat her out.

At the first swipe of his tongue, she gasped. Rough and wet and warm, it was almost too much to bear. He licked and sucked and nibbled at her clit like a starving man at a five-course meal.

It almost made her forget about what *she* could do with *her* tongue. "Turn around."

He paused. "Hmm?"

She shuddered. She'd felt that hum through her entire body. She looked down at him. "I want your cock in my mouth."

If possible, his eyes turned even darker. He knelt and tapped her hip. "Switch places with me."

She grinned. If he knew what she had planned, he might not be so accommodating. "Sure thing." She let him settle down on his back before swinging her body over his. She lowered her face to his cock, licking the drop of pre-come off. The salty sweetness flowed over her tongue. "Mmm. You taste delicious."

He grabbed hold of her hips and tugged her down to him, sucking her clit right into his mouth. She gasped, thrusting her hips back at him. Oh, yeah. The man knew what he was doing.

Then again, so did she. She wrapped her hand around the base of his cock and took him in, sucking on the flared head. She felt him pause before he attacked her pussy with a vengeance. Her thighs trembled.

Hell if he was going to get her off first. She had every intention of milking an orgasm out of him before she marked him. She laved his slit with her tongue, wringing more drops from him. He groaned, the sound vibrating through her pussy.

Oh, fuck. He'd moved his tongue to her hole, fucking her ruthlessly with it. His thumb danced across her clit while he drank her juices. She bucked back into him, fucking his mouth. *Shit.* She didn't know how much longer she'd be able to hold off that orgasm.

She reached over and bent his knees for him, tugging on his hips to get him to start fucking her mouth. It took him a few moments to get the idea, but once he did, he fucked her in earnest, his tongue matching the movement of his cock in her mouth.

She suckled him in earnest now, dying for a full taste of her mate. The heavy weight of him on her tongue was incredible, his scent driving her to the brink of ecstasy.

Then he did something, twisted his tongue or his thumb somehow and she was coming, screaming around him, desperately licking at his cock to drag him along with her.

His mouth pulled away from her on a gasp. "So good." His hands landed on her hair, pushing her head down onto him. "Fuck, take it baby." He damn near choked her, but she didn't care. She wanted him to come. She knew what would happen when she marked him and wanted him primed and ready.

"Fuck!" He poured down her throat, his body bowed. He came so hard, she did choke, unable to catch all of it. She swallowed what she could, damn near purring at the taste.

Then she pushed his spent cock aside and marked him right where his balls met his thigh.

"Oh *fuck*!" She was sucking on the mark she'd given him, her pretty little ass swaying in front of his face like she was wagging her damn tail.

His cock was rock-hard in an instant. He waited until her fangs pulled free of his flesh before grabbing her by the hips and lifting her up off the bed. She squeaked in surprise. "Fuck me. *Now.*"

He dropped her onto his cock. He didn't even bother turning her around. She'd marked him and now he was going to fuck her until the animals in both of them were satisfied. He grabbed hold of her waist and pulled until he was sitting upright, her thighs draped across his, her pussy dripping on him. He reached around and began to strum her clit. "Ride me, baby."

The want he'd felt before was nothing compared to now. If she didn't come on his cock, he'd go insane. At least he thought so until she began to move, gliding up and down his length with languid strokes designed to drive him crazy.

When she rolled her hips, he felt his eyes cross from the exquisite torture. Fuck, she was incredible. "Play with your breasts."

She moaned, throwing her head back against his shoulder. Her hands reached up and began tugging on her nipples. He could feel the ripples moving through her pussy with each stroke of her eager fingers. "You want more, baby?"

"Uh-huh."

He pinched her clit then soothed the minor hurt. "You want to come?"

She cast him a sultry look over her shoulder. "Do you?"

He grinned and thrust, letting her know without words how much he wanted. "Play with your clit."

He moved his hands to her hips. He was going to give his woman a little help.

One of her hands moved down to her pussy. He looked over her shoulder to watch, wanting to see the rhythm her fingers moved in. He'd memorize it if he had to.

She rolled her hips again, riding his cock while she stroked herself.

"It's so good." She moaned, pressing into her own hand. Just the sight of her riding him and touching herself damn near sent him over the edge.

He lifted her up slightly, ignoring her mewl of protest. He wanted a little room to maneuver and he could easily hold her weight while he fucked them both to orgasm.

She gasped at his first hard thrust, sighed over his second, and tried to take back control on the third. She turned wild on him, leaning forward and thrusting back into him. One hand sank into his thigh while the other remained busy at her pussy. He could feel her fingers stroking him every time he exited, the butterfly touches sending his need skyrocketing.

She had to come. He needed her to come now.

He got to his knees behind her and bent her over the rest of the way. He positioned her so that her head and shoulders were on the covers and her ass was up in the air. All the while, he never left her body and her fingers continued to work frantically.

He leaned down so that his chin rested on her shoulder. "Now we *really* fuck."

Her eyes went wide. "What was that before, pretend fucking?"

He licked her neck and took her like the animal he was.

Oh my God. Tabby desperately tried to ride the storm called Alex. He pounded into her, his body locked to hers, his arms tight around her. She couldn't move, couldn't fuck him back. She was impaled, imprisoned on his cock, in his arms.

And she loved every minute of it.

She couldn't even reach her clit. One of his big paws was holding her arms hostage. The other held her head down, keeping her teeth away from him. Smart man. If anyone else dared treat her like this, she'd bite his face off.

But this was her mate laying claim to her at last. She settled down, her body relaxing into his, her head tilting even further to the side. She submitted to her mate, the one man who could bring her to her knees with a look and a smile.

She could hear the slap of his thighs against her ass, felt the trembling start deep inside her. She'd only come once or twice without touching her clit, and boy did it feel like the third time was going to be the charm. Her entire body strained for release. "More."

With a savage growl, he gave her what she asked for. She'd unleashed the beast in him with her demand, and she was going to pay the price for it with a very sore, very happy pussy. *Then again, he's got those wonderful healing powers...*

If she thought he'd been pounding into her before, she was sadly mistaken. He began in earnest, ignoring her howls of pleasure. The big paw holding her arms in place let go, only to take hold of her breasts. He squeezed her nipples to just this side of pain. She whimpered, her breath stolen, unable to beg for more. The hand holding down her head clenched in her hair, holding her steady while he took what he wanted and gave her what she needed.

Her orgasm began, rolling through her, the pleasure so intense she could barely draw the breath to scream. Every muscle in her body clenched, the pleasure damn near tearing her apart.

He quivered around her, in her. How he held back his own orgasm she'd never know. "Oh, fuck yes. Do that again."

She tried to shake her head no, she wouldn't survive another one like that, but he was moving again and she couldn't stop it. The first orgasm rolled right into the second, her body pulsing, her breath lost to her. Her body obeyed his command, heedless of the impossibility of it. He owned her, body and soul, and let her know it in no uncertain terms.

She clenched around him, determined to take him with her this time. She snarled up at him, whimpering when his hand tightened, reminding her of who she belonged to. God, it was incredible, and nothing like what she thought being with a Bear would be like. She'd expected something like this with a Wolf and had felt a small pang that she'd never know the kind of mating that she'd always dreamed of.

Alex was taking those dreams and shattering them with reality.

It was happening again, her entire body shoved into orgasm. This time she had enough breath to scream his name. "Alex!" His fangs pierced her shoulder, intensifying the orgasm until she damn near blacked out, spots dancing in front of her eyes as her body shook.

Alex roared, the sound more feral than any other she'd ever heard. His cock twitched inside her once, twice, and liquid heat poured into her. He'd come, finally, his fangs still buried in her neck, her body quivering at the intensity of her own pleasure.

If he kept fucking her like this, she might never leave his bed. She now understood the meaning of the phrase *dying from pleasure*. She was wrung out, limp, damp and sated to her toenails.

He pulled out of her and dropped to the mattress beside her. His big chest heaved, glistening with sweat. He rolled his head and looked at her, her head still on the comforter, her ass still in the air. "You okay?"

Her muscles were too weak to move even enough to lower her ass to the mattress. Maybe she could sleep just like this? She smiled, knowing exactly what it looked like. "Best. Fuck.

Evah."

Alex chuckled. She almost growled at the smug male satisfaction on his face, but really? He'd earned that look. He pulled and pushed until she was practically on top of him, their feet propped up on the pillows. Neither one appeared to have the strength to move right way around on the bed. They lay there for a few minutes, dropping sweet kisses wherever they could reach without actually moving.

Eventually Alex stirred. "Do me a favor? Next time bite my neck." He grumbled, but his lips were twitching. "What am I supposed to tell my father when he asks to see my mate mark? Should I drop trou and proudly point?"

She hid her face in his chest and giggled. Her mate had just given her the best orgasm of her life *and* he was fun in bed? She'd died and gone to Tabby heaven.

Chapter Four

Bunny frowned and tried to figure out what it was that had woken him up. He couldn't remember the last time he'd slept so damn well. He woke up wrapped around the warmth of his mate, his erection nestled between the cheeks of her ass. She was snoring lightly, her green hair plastered to her cheek. Their feet were still propped up on the pillows; they'd never bothered turning right way round. The low hum of the air conditioner reminded him that he'd need to start looking for a place if he was going to stay in Halle. He had no intention of living with the three women in their tiny apartment. He'd have to ask Tabby if there was any particular neighborhood that appealed to her.

There. He heard it again. Beethoven's "Für Elise". He carefully climbed out of bed and dug through his mate's pants. Her cell phone vibrated in his hand, Beethoven blaring out until he got it open. "Hello."

Silence.

"Hello?"

"Who is this?"

Bunny pulled the phone away from his ear and glared at it. "This is Bunny. Who is this?"

"This is Tabby's boyfriend." A long-suffering sigh sounded through the speaker. "Fuck. Is she cheating on me again?"

Tabby's boyfriend? He stared at the woman sleeping in his

bed. "I guess so."

"Damn. Dude, I'm sorry, but I need you to do me a favor. Would you tell her Gary called? I heard she got hurt yesterday and I want to make sure she's all right." The concern in Gary's voice grated on his nerves. "Despite everything, she's...she's everything to me, you know?"

Something about this just didn't feel right. All of his instincts were screaming at him that Gary was a lying sack of shit, but how much of that was due to his mate bond with Tabby? "Yeah. I know the feeling." He took a deep breath and tried to calm the rage inside him. "I'll make sure she knows you called."

"Thanks, man. And don't blame yourself. We've been having problems recently and, well, Tabby doesn't handle stress well."

Bunny shut the phone and cut him off, unable to listen to another word. He studied the woman on the bed. How well did he really know his mate? Could she have a boyfriend? A fucker named Gary?

Tabby yawned. "Hey, was that my phone?"

Her voice was husky with sleep and affection. He crushed the phone in his hand. The flimsy plastic shattered easily. "It was."

"Alex?" She sat up with a frown. "What's wrong?"

He took a deep breath. He'd give her a chance to explain, to make this right. "Do you have a boyfriend?"

"Other than you? No."

Damn. Right now, he wished he was a goddamn Coyote. They could smell a lie at fifty paces. "You sure?"

"Yes," she drawled. She pulled the sheet up around herself, hiding her beautiful breasts from him. "Who told you otherwise?"

"Gary did."

She blinked, fury blanketing her features. "*Gary.*"

Something inside him eased. That was not the response of a guilty woman. "Ex-boyfriend?"

Tabby stared at him for a moment before carefully blanking her features. "Nothing you need to worry about."

Oh, hell. Now that wouldn't do at all. "Bullshit."

"Alex," she sighed, rubbing the bridge of her nose.

"He called because he heard you'd gotten hurt, but as soon as he heard my voice, he asked if you'd cheated on him again. He told me he was your boyfriend." The possessive fury rose in him again. He battled it back down, knowing he'd failed when her expression turned wary. "So if he's a pain in your ass that makes him a pain in *my* ass." A pain he'd be more than happy to rub out if it came down to it.

"Let Gabe deal with him. Please?"

"This is something the sheriff knows about?" He settled on the edge of the bed.

"Yeah. It's an ongoing pain. I'm just having trouble finding the right medicine to get rid of it." She smiled weakly. "Can we go out for breakfast now?"

He stared at her, deliberately letting his eyes bleed to brown. "I'm more than willing to take care of Gary for you."

She shook her head, panic drifting across her face. "No. Alex, no. You have more than enough to worry about. Let Gabe handle it. Please?"

Tabby was rubbing his arm, her expression pleading. He didn't understand the hint of worry in her eyes, but she was obviously upset. He closed his eyes and let go of the anger. The last thing he wanted to do was get into a fight in his new hometown. He couldn't risk losing this place when it meant so much to Tabby. "Are you sure?"

"Yes."

"Could he have been the one who hit you?"

She blinked, looked shocked. "I don't know. Maybe? Whoever it was stayed downwind, and no one saw anything."

He nodded. He'd definitely be paying the sheriff a visit. "If he did, he'd better pray the sheriff gets to him first. Understand?" She nodded, her shoulders relaxing in what looked suspiciously like relief. He cupped her cheek, his chest rumbling happily when she nuzzled into his hand. "I have to do my yoga before we go, and I'm thinking we could both use a shower. What would you like to eat?"

She tilted her head. "Yoga?" Her lips twitched. She looked both amused and intrigued.

This wouldn't be the first time someone teased him over the yoga he did every day. "Don't. Please. It helps more than you know." If it wasn't for the peaceful meditations he did each day, he probably would have killed someone by now.

"Does it hurt? I've seen some of the positions people get into and it looks massively uncomfy."

He smiled, relieved. She wasn't going to give him shit. "Not once you're used to it, no. It's a nice, slow stretch that helps to center me."

She nodded. "Yoga, huh? That explains your truly epic ass." She tilted her head and tried to sneak a peek.

He felt himself blushing. No one had ever called his ass epic before.

"Can I watch?"

He'd have felt more comfortable about it before the comment about his ass. "Sure. Just do me a favor and keep quiet, especially after I put my music on, okay?"

She looked intrigued. "Sure. But afterwards I want bacon."

He'd talk to Anderson once he got to the hospital. She might not want to give him the details on Gary, but he bet the Puma would be more than happy to fill him in. "Not sausage?" He pointed to his groin and waggled his eyebrows.

She giggled. "Alex!"

"Fine." He stood up and tugged her out of the bed. "Yoga, shower, then food."

"Then work."

He grinned. "You going to do some ink on me?"

She stumbled. One finger traced the Ursa Major stars on his lower back. "What kind?"

The heat in her voice had him nearly growling with need. "You'll see."

"I should hope so if I'm going to be tattooing you." She settled back, ready to watch him stretch.

He unpacked his iPod and plugged it in, selecting the music he'd learned put him in the best frame of mind for his meditation. He settled into the routine, ignoring her start of surprise at his choice of music. Granted, not many of his friends were familiar with Loreena McKennitt, but the Celtic music soothed him, the woman's voice and style calming the beast in him.

"Damn. Just...damn. I'm going to like mornings with you. Naked yoga doesn't sound nearly so skuzzy now."

He felt his cheeks flush again and glared at her. The lust on her face was making this difficult. Triangle pose was a real bitch with a hard-on. "Tabby," he growled, moving to Proud Warrior, arms outstretched, legs wide, his weight evenly balanced between his straight back leg and his bent front one.

His erection bobbed between his legs, shooting the calm he was aiming for all to hell.

"Sorry." She headed into the bathroom to presumably take care of business. Once she was out of sight, he was able to concentrate on the movements of his body, allowing his muscles and mind to ease into his day. He slipped into the final pose, legs crossed, hands resting on knees, his eyes closed. A fine sheen of sweat covered his body. His slow breath cleansed his mind. He felt invigorated and completely at peace.

"You finally done, Gandhi? I have bacon to hunt down."

He opened one eye. "You're going to be a serious pain in my ass about this, aren't you?"

She leaned against the doorjamb and smirked at him, showing fang. "What part of hungry carnivore did you not get?"

He shook his head and stood up. "Fine. You're hungry and I smell bad. Shower first, remember?"

She waltzed into the bathroom and grabbed his toothbrush. She started to brush her teeth.

His stomach rumbled. Suddenly he was ravenous. "You know what? Hurry up, I want my strawberry pancakes."

She made a face. "Ew."

"What's wrong with strawberries?"

"Real strawberries? Nothing. That syrupy crap they put on pancakes? Blech." She shuddered delicately and handed him his toothbrush. "Here. You can join me in the shower when you're done."

"I can? Really? May I borrow my shampoo while I'm at it?"

She chuckled and stepped under the spray. "Maybe. We'll see."

He grinned and brushed his teeth. He stepped into the shower a few minutes later and thanked God he'd decided to stay in a nice hotel. No tiny little shower stall in this place. It had a full-size tub.

And that meant he could have some fun with his wet, naked mate.

Tabby squeaked when a large set of paws landed on her ass. "Behave, Alex."

"Since when am I Alex?"

She was wondering when he'd ask that. She was the only one who called him that other than his brother. "Since I decided there was no way I could moan "Bunny" while you're fucking me. *Especially* when you're fucking me." She glanced behind her at his lengthening cock. "You may be furry, but you sure ain't cute."

His lips quivered. "Why, thank you, ma'am." He leered down at her, his soapy palm skating across her nipple. "I aim to please."

She tilted her head and decided to keep playing. She cupped his balls, rolling them in her palm before letting them go. "And these are *not* rabbit ears. They don't vibrate or anything." She then tapped the head of his cock with her fingernail. "Although, come to think of it, it does kind of look like his little nose is quivering."

His hand stopped. His chin dropped down onto her shoulder. The leer had turned into a wide grin. "That's because he smells something delicious." He grabbed hold of her hand and dragged it back to his hard flesh. "Have I mentioned he loves to be petted?"

She curled her hand around his shaft, but refused to be coaxed closer to the head of his cock. "Are you sure it's safe? He's drooling an awful lot. Has he had his shots?"

She giggled madly when he picked her up and pinned her against the wall. "Drooling?" He palmed her thighs, spreading her wide. She didn't fight him. She wanted this just as much as he did. She wrapped her legs around his waist, let her heels rest on the top of his truly amazing ass. "I'll show you drooling, you little witch."

She wasn't afraid of him. How could she be? He was smiling down at her, his hazel eyes gleaming with laughter and something else, something it was too soon to put a name to. At the most, she was willing to call it affection. It was a good start, one they could build on.

An even better start was when he began to kiss her, the minty taste of his toothpaste mingling with his own heady flavor. His palm slid down her body. His fingers paused at her nipple ring, twisted it until she was gasping into his mouth. Tabby tightened her legs and tilted her hips, an invitation he accepted. His hand wandered south again, curled around her pussy until his fingers were stroking her clit in easy circles. He slid his cock between the wet folds of her pussy, teased her until she was damn near ready to beg. "Alex?"

"Tell me you want me."

She gulped. His eyes were bleeding to brown, his fangs descending. The mark on her neck throbbed in time with her clit. "I want you, Alex."

The head of his cock slid home, stretching her wide. His lips brushed against hers, kept them in an almost-there kiss. He ignored her attempts to deepen it, to bring him into her mouth the way he'd entered her body. He rocked them together with lazy motions, their gazes locked together. It was a coupling completely unlike what they'd done the night before. Last night had been about staking a primal claim on each other.

This was...something else. Something she hadn't known

was possible. The hurried fucking she'd done with her teenage sweetheart, the one-night stand she'd had since rejoining the human race, hadn't prepared her for making love with Alex.

She clenched around him. She understood what this sweet, lazy fucking was. This was just as much a claim on her as the other, but where last night had been about her body, this morning was about her heart.

His lips pursed and he took the kiss his mouth had promised. The hot water beat down on his back. His buttocks flexed beneath her heels as he thrust over and over, the sweet slide dragging her closer and closer to orgasm. His hand left her pussy to curl around her hip, the strength of his hold almost bruising. "Tabby," he breathed into her. His eyes closed and she knew he was close.

She wanted, needed to come with him. Her hand reached down and took off where his had left off, stroking herself. She was so damn close. "Alex. Bite me. Please."

His eyes flew open. His chin brushed against hers, his mouth nipping its way down to her shoulder. She felt her own fangs descend and knew she'd mark him when they came.

His teeth pierced her, throwing her into her orgasm. He groaned as she bit into him, marking him once more. She rode his cock and the never-ending orgasm that flowed through them both.

They were both quivering at the end. Less intense than last night, it was nonetheless just as profound. She'd never had an orgasm last that long before, the sweet flood of pleasure going on and on that way.

She wanted that again, that feeling of belonging.

She licked his wound closed. Her head dropped back against the tiles. The only thing she wanted to do was crawl right back into the bed in the other room, wrapped up in her mate.

He lifted his head from her shoulder, a thin line of blood trickling down her chest. The wound was already closing. He rested his forehead against hers, his lips taking hers in a gentle kiss. “Good morning.”

She smiled. “Yes indeed.”

His answering smile matched hers.

Bunny walked into the hospital, still torn about leaving Tabby with the other girls at Living Art. She’d insisted on it, saying that she had to work and he had to check on Chloe. She was right, damn it. He almost called his father to ask him to go protect his mate, but with Chloe still unconscious and her attacker still on the loose, there was no way he could divide his family’s attention that way. He frowned. Maybe he could enlist Julian or some of the Pumas to keep a surreptitious eye on the place for him. But first he needed to know how his little cousin was doing before he went to see Sheriff Anderson.

That part of his day he hadn’t discussed with his mate. He had every intention of finding out just who the fuck Gary was and what kind of a threat he represented to Tabby. If he found out the fucker was the one who’d hurt his mate, Halle would be short one asshole. There would be nothing that could stop him from ripping Gary apart.

He entered Chloe’s hospital room to find Ryan, his father, Aunt Laura and Uncle Steve already there. “How is she?”

Aunt Laura looked like she hadn’t slept in weeks, her eyes red-rimmed and weary. “No change. She won’t wake up, damn it, and I’m at my wits’ end.”

Uncle Steve placed his hand on his mate’s shoulder, his

own expression full of fear and grief. "She could wake up at any minute, sweetheart."

"Then she needs to." The determination in Aunt Laura's voice came as no surprise. The tiny Fox female had to be strong, surrounded as she was by Bears. "Dr. Howard suggested we find something to stimulate her with. Can you think of *anything* that might trigger a response?"

He sighed. "No, I..." He blinked. "Wait." The sheriff had said something the first time they met, when Bunny was still shocked over finding his mate.

Mate.

"She has a mate."

The uproar that followed was loud. "What?" Uncle Steve's voice was full of hope.

"Since when?" Ryan bellowed.

"Is it Sheriff Anderson?" Aunt Laura asked. She stood, somehow towering over the men in the room, though she barely topped five foot three.

"She knows who it is, but from her scent I'd say she hasn't claimed him yet. And no, it's not Anderson. The man already has a mate." Bunny pulled out his cell phone. Right after the attack on Chloe, he'd programmed Dr. Howard's number into it. He knew Dr. Howard had Anderson's phone number, and Bunny needed it. "Let me make some calls, see what I can find out. Maybe if we get her mate in here it will be just what she needs."

And maybe he could get some of his own questions answered while he had the sheriff here.

"Speaking of mates, how's yours?"

Bunny grimaced. "She got attacked yesterday."

"What?"

"By who?"

The family chorus of outrage was strangely soothing. "I have no idea." He breathed deep, afraid he would accidentally shatter the phone in his hands. "By the time I got to the shop, she was on the ground, a lump on the back of her fucking head."

Ryan's hand landed on his shoulder. "Do you need help?"

He stared at his cousin, knowing what Ryan was offering and what it would do to them both if Bunny took him up on it. One of the ways they sometimes blew off steam was by fighting each other. The way Bunny was feeling, if he took Ryan up on that offer, one or both of them would be lying in the bed next to Chloe's. He shook his head. "Nah. I'll make sure to do an extra twenty minutes of yoga."

Ryan rolled his eyes. "You have to get over that some day."

Bunny shrugged, uncomfortable with the direction the conversation was going. "I need to call the sheriff."

"You need to remember you were sixteen when it happened. Let it go, Alex."

The soothing sound of his father's voice did nothing to help. "I have. I make sure it's never going to happen again." Nearly killing someone because you'd lost your temper was a sure-fire way to teach you how to control yourself. He'd done everything in his power to see to it he'd never hurt another living soul.

Still, there were times when he longed to roughhouse with his cousins without the fear that he'd hurt them. He was large and strong in his human form, larger than all of his relatives, except for his father. He was even more so in his Bear form. And even his father didn't have the depth of rage Bunny had learned to conquer. His father was one of the most even-tempered men he knew.

Bunny dialed the phone. If he had his way, he'd never fight

again. He couldn't live with the consequences if he did.

"Are you sure you're all right?"

Tabby shoved Cyn's hands away from her head. "I'm fine, okay?"

"No headache?"

"Other than the one you're giving me? No." She snapped on the rubber gloves and smiled weakly at her nervous client. If Cyn didn't knock it off, Tabby was going to lose her customer.

Cyn glared at her. "Fine. I'll let it go for now." She smiled down at the nervous college boy. "So, what are we having done today?"

The boy gulped. If he didn't calm down, he was going to shake apart from nerves. "Um, I want a wolf, a timber wolf." He held out a picture. "Just like this."

Tabby frowned down at the wolf. It looked familiar. "Where did you get this?"

"Gary gave it to me."

Tabby put the picture down on the counter and leaned back with a sigh. "Why did Gary tell you to get a wolf tattoo?"

The boy shook some more. "He said it was cool."

This kid is what, eighteen? What the fuck is Gary up to? She took a sniff. *Nope, he's human.* "Do you like wolves?"

The boy nodded eagerly. "Oh yeah. I contribute to a bunch of charities trying to save endangered species and their habitats."

Her brows rose. He didn't look like he had the money for an Egg McMuffin, let alone donations to charity. "Where are you from?"

"Ph-Philadelphia."

She stroked a finger down his arm, trying to calm him down. "Okay," she glanced at the form he'd filled out, "Tim." *How do I explain to you that Gary wants his own ugly face tattooed onto your body?* Talk about claiming someone! "If you had a choice, what tattoo would you get?" She held up a hand when he opened his mouth to speak. "Remember, whatever I ink in will be on your body *forever.* I mean old and wrinkly forever. They've found intact tattoos on mummies. So make sure it's what *you* want before I do this, okay?"

"What about Gary? He said I couldn't join his fraternity without it."

She nearly growled. *Son of a bitch.* "Did he give you the money for the tattoo?" She'd already explained that she charged by the hour, and how much. The complex tattoo she'd have to make from the picture would wind up costing him almost three hundred dollars.

"No."

"Are you paying for it?"

"Yes."

She sighed and decided to fill this poor kid in before he became a Wolf snack. "Gary isn't the nicest person in the world, Tim."

Tim scowled. "He's been very nice to me."

"Yeah, well, he's been less than nice to me." She fingered the picture again, wondering how to get through to this poor guy. "Gary's threatened me more than once. He's egged the shop. We've had to call the cops on him a few times." She frowned. "Did Gary tell you to come *here* for the tattoo?"

Tim shook his head. "No, he told me to go to the place on Fifth." Tabby exchanged a glance with Cyn. That place was a dive. “But I asked around. A lot of people told me you guys were the best, and that your prices were fair.”

That explained a lot. No way was she letting this kid out of here with Gary’s mug a permanent fixture on his body. “If I pick up that phone there and call Sheriff Anderson, will you listen to him about Gary?”

He gulped nervously. “The cops? Why would you call the cops?”

“We’ve had to call them out because Gary won’t leave us alone.”

He bit his lip and frowned, obviously thinking.

She picked up the phone and handed it to him, rattling off the number for the police station. *C’mon, Tim, make the right decision.*

His expression cleared. He was familiar with the phone number, which raised a whole host of other questions she didn’t have the right to ask. “Can I take another look around the shop, please?”

She smiled and nodded, getting up off the swivel stool she sat on when she worked. “Sure thing, Tim.”

She watched him walk with a bit more confidence into the front of the shop.

“Good job.”

“Thanks.”

“What made you question him?”

She picked up the picture of the wolf and showed it to Cyn. She could hear the murmur of voices and knew that Glory was talking to Tim. She would ease his fears better than anyone else. “That’s Gary as a wolf.”

Cyn whistled. “Damn. Is the little bastard building a club or something?”

Tabby jerked. *Could* he be trying to build a Pack? She took another look at Tim.

Damn if the boy didn't have Omega written all over him, and not in a good way. "Fuck." There was no law against changing a human against their will. If there was, more than one mate would be in big trouble, including the current Halle Pride Alpha. But a prick like Gary with a Pack of handpicked assholes? "That would be bad."

"I've decided." They turned to find Tim standing there, a smile on his face. Glory stood next to him. She winked at Tabby. "I want this one." He held up a piece of flash.

Tabby looked down at the stylized dragon and grinned. "Good choice."

She set up the inks, pleased that Tim had relaxed. She began the tattoo and did her best to hold back the smirk.

Gary was going to shit a brick when he saw it. She just hoped Tim would be protected. She made a mental note to let Gabe know all about Tim. If anyone could protect the boy, it would be a Hunter like Gabe. Gary didn't know what train was about to hit his pompous ass, but he was definitely pissing on the tracks.

She hoped it hurt. A lot.

Bunny stood as the sheriff entered Chloe's room. The man's eyes went immediately to Chloe. He didn't even try to hide his wince. "Still no change?"

Bunny shook his head, watching closely. The sheriff approached Chloe's bed. He took one of her pale hands into his and bent down, his hat nearly falling off. He grabbed it before it could land on Chloe's face. "Hey, little vixen. You need to wake up now. Sarah's threatening to bake cookies, and you know how she is in the kitchen."

There was no response, not that Bunny had expected to see one.

"Do you know who my daughter's mate is?"

Anderson lifted his head and stared at Aunt Laura. He nodded. "Yeah. I know who he is."

"And?"

He straightened up and let go of Chloe's hand. "He's not in town right now. Sarah called him and let him know what's going on. He told her he'd be back as soon as he could." Anderson shifted, looking uncomfortable. "There are a few things you should know. First, he doesn't know about us. He's human."

They all nodded. Bunny's mother had been human, and the stories about how his father had cornered and claimed his mate still had the power to reduce grown men to giggles. The fact that Barbra Bunsun had every intention of being caught only added to the joy of the story.

Still, everyone knew you had to be careful when claiming a human mate. Not everyone would respond well to finding themselves furry. In the past, there had been those who had attacked their shifter mates, thinking them possessed by the devil.

"Second, he had the mistaken impression that Chloe and I were dating."

Bunny folded his arms across his chest and snarled. Next to him, Ryan growled. They, too, had thought the sheriff and Chloe were dating. The way Chloe spoken about him, the bracelet he'd given her for Christmas with the little cats and foxes on it, had all said *girlfriend* as far as the Bunsun-Williamses were concerned. Hell, as far as he knew Ryan still thought it, despite being told Chloe had a mate somewhere out there.

Anderson's hands went up. "We *weren't*. Damn it. My mate still gives me fits about that." He rolled his eyes. "But Jim blames both of us. The third problem is he thinks Chloe's too young for him. He even told her as much."

"Will he come for her?"

Aunt Laura was still staring at Anderson, her gaze boring into him.

Anderson nodded. "I think he will. Sarah says he loves Chloe, he just needs to deal with his issues. I wouldn't be surprised if he's here before morning."

"How would Sarah know this?"

Anderson's whole face softened. "My mate is the Omega of the Hallc Pride."

Bunny was confused. As the Omega, Anderson's mate should have known exactly how the man felt, both about her and about Chloe. The way he understood it, Omegas were the emotional lynchpin of whatever Pride or Pack they belonged to. How could there have been any confusion over which one he wanted? There was no way, once he met his mate, that he could confuse it for anything but the mate bond. Had he met his Sarah after he'd begun dating Chloe, or had it been some sort of cosmic misunderstanding? Unfortunately Bunny didn't feel he had the right to ask the sheriff that question. He barely knew the man, after all, and only trusted him because he'd helped Tabby.

"Any idea who did this to my daughter?" Uncle Steve's voice was low and threatening. His hand reached out and stroked Chloe's hair.

"I have some theories, but until I'm sure, I'm not going to say anything. Don't ask me, I won't tell you."

And that was when Bunny realized exactly what sort of man stood in front of them. Anderson radiated an aura of power he'd only felt once before. "You're a Hunter."

Anderson's smile was grim. "Yup. How'd you know?"

"I had a friend once, James. He's a Hunter." It had been a long time since he'd seen James. He was the Bear Senator as well as a Hunter. He was a charming rogue with a core of steel. The aura of power faded, leaving Bunny feeling a little off balance.

"James Barnwell?"

Bunny's brows shot up. "You know him?"

Anderson grimaced. "The son of a bitch trained me."

Bunny snorted. He'd heard more than one person use that tone of voice when describing James. Hell, he'd heard him called much worse than that.

"He's also the reason we're in this fix with Chloe and Jim, in a roundabout sort of way. He convinced me not to claim Sarah before I left, Sarah and I almost imploded and we each turned to other people to get over it. Chloe and I were friends and we talked a lot. I asked her to keep an eye on Sarah. Sarah started hanging out a lot with Jim Woods, Chloe's destined mate, and Chloe got jealous. I don't think she even realized what she was doing, but Chloe was the one who had everyone thinking we were dating." He shook his head. "If I hadn't come back when I did, both Chloe and I could have lost our mates."

Bunny winced in sympathy. He couldn't begin to imagine spending eternity without Tabby now that he'd had her. But to lose her before he got to claim her would have been torture.

"It doesn't surprise me that James told you to hold off on your mating. He doesn't believe Hunters should be mated at all." Bunny shared a glance with Anderson. Someday James Barnwell would find his own mate, and when he did, he knew *exactly* how the Hunter would react.

Poor girl. I hope I get to watch the mighty Hunter fall. The sheriff was watching him, a questioning look on his face. "When he finds her, call me. I'll bring the popcorn."

Anderson shook his hand. "Done."

"I hope this Jim person gets here soon," Uncle Steve said, his hands curling into fists at his sides.

"I just hope she responds to him." Ryan stalked out of the room, his tension obvious. Watching his baby sister lying motionless in that hospital bed was hitting the other man hard.

Bunny held out his hand, pointing to the door Ryan had just walked out. "Could I ask you a few questions outside?" He led the way after Anderson nodded his agreement. He made sure the door was shut before asking the question burning in his gut. "Tabby got a phone call this morning, and I need to know if this person is a threat to her or not. And before you ask, she's refusing to talk to me about it."

"I'll answer if I can."

"Who the hell is Gary?"

When Anderson's midnight blue eyes turned to gold, Bunny knew the answer.

Gary was trouble.

"So?"

Tabby winced. Cyn was behind her, guarding the end of the counter, trapping her behind glass and artwork. Glory was leaning over the counter, her face full of mischief. The shop was empty, and the moment she'd been dreading all day was finally here. Her nosy-ass friends had her cornered. "So what?"

The two women exchanged a glance. "How was it?"

Tabby's cheeks heated up. "It?"

Glory's head tipped back, exposing the long line of her neck. "Oh, *Bunny*," she moaned. "Bunny, Bunny," she chanted, each one becoming more breathless, until, "*Bunny!*"

Cyn was laughing her ass off as Glory faked an orgasm. What neither woman saw was Ryan right outside the door, his eyes narrowed as he glared at Glory. When Glory threw her head back and shuddered, his fists clenched, his eyes turning deep, dark brown.

If Glory didn't stop, Ryan was going to do something seriously drastic. She just hoped drastic didn't involve Ryan's claws and Alex's face.

"Knock it off, guys."

Glory giggled and waved her hands like a hula dancer. "Well? How was the motion of his ocean?"

"Screw that." Cyn propped one hip against the counter. "I want to know about the size of his boat." She held her hands at least seven inches apart and waggled her eyebrows.

The bell over the door jingled and Ryan sauntered in, his gaze glued to Glory. "Don't you dare answer that."

Cyn pushed herself back up. "Don't sweat it, Glory. It's not like we won't get it out of her once we get home."

Glory nodded, looking angelic. "Yup. We know her weakness."

Uh-oh. Tabby stiffened. "Oh, no, you don't."

"All we have to do..." Cyn smirked.

"...is break out the box..." Glory was smiling that innocent pixie smile that fooled only the very young, the very old, and the terminally stupid.

"...and hide all her shoes." The triumph in Cyn's voice demanded retribution. Too bad Cyn didn't seem to *have* a weakness.

Tabby glared at her so-called friends. “I hate you bitches.” They would, too. The only hope her poor shoes had was if she got home before they did and managed to hide them all.

“Is this a private party or can anyone join?”

She would have lost it if she hadn’t heard the bell again. “Hey, Julian!”

“Julian Ducharme?” Ryan held out his hand when Julian nodded. “Ryan Williams, Chloe’s brother.”

Julian took Ryan’s hand and shook it. “How’s she doing?”

“She hasn’t woken up.” The anger and grief in Ryan’s voice was unmistakable. “I owe you.”

Julian shrugged uncomfortably. “It was nothing.”

“My sister would have died on that street if you hadn’t risked your life like that. My family is in your debt.”

Tabby saw Julian’s jaw clench for a moment and wondered at it. “Any one of us would have done the same.”

“You almost lost your own life in the process.” Out of the corner of her eye, she saw Cyn start. “That’s not something we’re likely to forget.”

“I couldn’t let her die.” For a brief second, white flashed through Julian’s hair, there and gone so quickly that if she hadn’t seen it before she would have declared it a trick of the light. “Her journey isn’t over yet.”

From the way Ryan’s eyes widened, he’d seen the flash of Julian’s hair as well. Whether the Bear knew more of what that meant, she didn’t know. All she knew was she needed to corner her friend, tie him down, and get some goddamn answers. “Feeling better, Julian?”

He nodded, his gaze darting to Cyn before he answered Tabby. “Yeah, I’m good. I’m going to stop in the hospital, see if there's anything more I can do for Chloe."

"No!" Ryan and Tabby's voices rang out, startling Cyn and Glory. Tabby coughed. "All things considered, I don't think a hospital is a shiny, happy place for you to be, Jules."

Glory inched away from Ryan, who'd been trying to put his arm around her waist. "Why not? He spent the night there just fine."

She shared a look with Julian, raising her brows. Did he want to reveal to the other two women what he was capable of?

He sighed, his shoulders slumping a bit. "No, it's not. It's fucking horrendous, but I'll do what I have to do." His knuckles rapped on the glass. "I'll head there now. Maybe I can wake her up, maybe not, but I have to try."

Cyn glared at him, eyes narrowed dangerously. "One of these days you're going to tell me what the fuck is up with you, *aren't you.*"

Tabby could tell that was a statement, not a question. Cyn was on the warpath and apparently felt one of her own was threatened. Tabby hid her grin.

Julian wasn't going to know what hit him when Cyn decided to let him claim her.

They shared a long look before Julian nodded slowly. "When everything is in place, you'll know everything."

Cyn just rolled her eyes and headed into the back room. Julian's expression was completely closed off, but the tick in his jaw was back. She'd never seen the easygoing man look like that. He was staring at that curtain like he wanted to storm through it and lay siege to the woman hiding behind it.

"I'll head back with you." Ryan tugged one of Glory's curls. "Be good."

"Excuse me?" Glory glared up at him.

He tugged a little harder before letting Glory's hair go. "And stop thinking about my cousin's junk. I'd hate to have to rip it off."

Tabby growled.

Ryan rolled his eyes. "Fine. I'll just beat the shit out of him."

She kept the growl going.

Ryan smiled weakly. "You can nurse him back to health."

Now it was her turn to roll her eyes. "Get out of here." The two men turned to leave. "Do me a favor? Tell Alex he owes me a new cell phone." The two men left the store, shaking their heads. "Glory?"

"Hmm?"

"Could you give the poor guy a break? His sister's in the hospital."

Glory didn't try to pretend she didn't know what Tabby was talking about. "He's just too much, you know? Big and overpowering and doesn't know the term personal space."

Tabby decided to tell a little white lie. "He likes you." He more than liked her, he was a man trying to land his mate.

"Maybe too much." Glory blew her bangs out of her eyes. "What would I do with him, anyway? Feed him, water him, build him a tree house? Can bears climb trees? Should I buy a house and put in a big fishpond? I could put in a fireplace and let him flop in front of it."

Tabby stared at her friend. She crooked her finger at Glory. "C'mere."

Glory leaned over the counter. "What?"

Tabby sniffed. "Nope, no drugs or alcohol. That means you're insane. Ow." She rubbed the top of her head. Glory could have bopped her with a little less enthusiasm. "Glory and Ryan sitting in a tree, k-i-s-s-i-n-g," she sang.

Glory stomped her foot and marched into the back room, her back ramrod straight.

Tabby sighed and grabbed a piece of paper. She was going to wake the two of them up if it was the last thing she did.

Chapter Five

"What the fuck is his problem?" Bunny rubbed the back of his head. Ryan stomped away from him again, a low growl in his throat. If he didn't know better, he'd think Ryan was warning him away from his sister. It was starting to piss him off. He'd have to do a full hour of meditation or wind up *accidentally* breaking Ryan in half the next time he tried to smack Bunny.

"I have no idea." Julian pulled his long hair back out of his face. "I'm sorry, there's nothing more I can do. She *will* wake up, I can guarantee that much. How she'll be when she does, I have no idea."

Uncle Steve's hand landed on Julian's shoulder. "You've done more than anyone had the right to ask. Thank you."

"You're welcome." He stood and stretched wearily. There were deep circles under Julian's eyes, a testament to how much the healing took out of the Spirit Bear. "I'm going to head out. Being here is difficult for me."

"Understood." Bunny turned to Uncle Steve and Aunt Laura. "I'm leaving too. I'm going to pick up Tabby at work." He bent to give Aunt Laura a kiss. "Call me if you need me."

"We will." Uncle Steve pulled him into his arms and gave him a hug. "Call your parents, let them know you're heading back to the hotel."

"Have you decided yet?"

He stared at Aunt Laura. "Decided what?"

"If you'll be staying here?"

He nodded. "This is Tabby's home." He'd already discussed it with his father. This area was a great place to expand into and would bring them closer to being a coast-to-coast company. They might even be able to get Eric down here to take a look around, if they could get his little brother to leave Oregon.

His aunt smiled. "I thought so."

"Does she know that?"

Bunny shook his head at Julian. "She will when I take her house hunting."

Julian chuckled. "Good luck with that. She's got a definite idea of where she wants to live. Hope you've got a *lot* of money."

Bunny just smiled. He didn't feel the need to enlighten Julian.

The two Bears left Chloe's hospital room. The scent of antiseptics and sickness was strong in Bunny's nostrils. The urge to go into each room and do what he could to ease the suffering of the patients was almost more than he could bear. He couldn't begin to imagine how Julian was feeling. "How are you holding up?"

Julian took a deep breath and let it out slowly. "I hate hospitals." The weary desolation in his voice told Bunny more than anything else the other man could have said.

He nodded and left it at that. They exited the hospital together and headed for the parking lot. "I'll tell Tabby to call you. She'll want to know you're all right."

Julian held out his hand. Bunny took it. "Take care of her. She needs you more than she realizes."

"Thanks." He paused. "What do you know about Gary?"

Julian's shoulders tensed. "Has that little bastard been bothering her again?"

"He called Tabby's cell this morning and asked me if she was cheating on him. Tried to pass himself off as her boyfriend."

Julian's lips twitched. "What did you do?"

"After I broke her phone? Listened to what Tabby had to tell me."

Julian laughed. "That's what she meant when she asked us to tell you that you owe her a new one. She loved that phone."

"I'll buy her one with a different number." One Gary wouldn't have. He'd get one that was unlisted.

"Say hi to the girls for me." Julian climbed into his truck, moving like he'd been beaten.

"Are you all right?" Tabby would kill him if he let anything happen to her friend.

"Nothing a little sleep won't cure." Julian shut his car door and waved goodbye before pulling out of the parking lot.

"Right. Sleep." Bunny shook his head and climbed onto his bike. "And you have a lovely bridge to sell me, right?" Julian needed to stay away from hospitals. They made him look like the walking dead.

Bunny took off into the night, eager to be with his mate. Rain was coming soon, the damp scent heavy in the air. He breathed it in and smiled. He loved the way the air smelled in the fall just before it rained.

He pulled into the lot behind Living Art and parked next to Tabby's Jeep. He covered the Harley with the tarp he kept in his saddlebags. No way was he letting his baby get soaked. He headed for the front of the store, smiling at the sight of all the flash in the windows. He'd have to see about getting that tattoo done before too much longer. The thought of wearing Tabby's ink on his body had him drooling.

He grinned, remembering Tabby's shower comments on drooling—and the lovemaking they'd indulged in afterwards—and pulled open the door. The bell over the door jingled. It had been a long day, both in the hospital and out. He waved hello to Glory, who was helping some little blonde pick a navel ring. The urge to just take hold of his mate, breathe in her scent, was overpowering. Bunny stared around the shop, a tattoo gun the only thing he heard. He frowned up at the sign over the curtained-off area of the store. *De Nile* had been drawn in flowing script and tacked up crookedly. "Tabby?"

The sound of the gun stopped. "At my station, sugar."

Just the sound of her voice was enough to soothe him. They were going to have a nice, long talk about Gary tonight, after he fed her and fucked her senseless. She wouldn't be able to hold anything back from him by the time he was done with her.

He went into the back of the shop and found his woman. She was finishing up a tattoo of an elaborate cross on a woman old enough to be his grandmother. "Hey, baby."

Tabby grinned up at him. "Hey, Alex."

Cyn popped her head into the cubicle. "Hi, Bunny."

The woman in the chair looked him up and down and snorted. "Bunny?"

Tabby shook her head. "Long story, Mrs. H."

"You a biker?"

"Yeah, but not in a gang. The nickname's from my last name." He held out his hand to the woman. "Alexander Bunsun."

The woman shook his hand. "Evelyn Hagen. Nice ta meet'cha, Bunny."

"You almost done, Tabby?" Cyn crossed her arms over her chest

"Yup. Just have to finish up the last initial." She started the gun back up, waiting for her client to settle back down. "Here we go."

He watched her draw the long line of an *H* in the center of the cross. It looked like a tribute tattoo, the initials *MH* inked in the center of the cross. "All right, done." She took the needles off the gun and disposed of them in the hazardous waste bin under the counter. "You know the drill. Don't get it wet, use the creams we give you, yadda, yadda, blah, blah."

Mrs. H watched as Tabby carefully slathered something over the tattoo and taped it up. "Good job." She grinned over at Cyn. "This one's a keeper."

"I think so, even if she is a smart-ass." Cyn stuck her tongue out at Tabby. "As soon as I find the ladder, that sign's coming down."

Mrs. H. cackled. "You're going to have to explain that one to me." As Cyn blushed, the cackle turned into a full-belly laugh. "Oh, with that look on your face you're *really* gonna have to tell me."

Tabby snapped off the rubber gloves and disposed of them. "Are you done with me for the night, your majesty?"

Cyn waved her away. "Get out of here, you pain in the ass."

Tabby laughed and got out.

Bunny followed her to the front of the store. Behind him, he heard Mrs. H. begin to grill Cyn, but found himself too distracted to listen. Tabby was wearing another pair of those painted-on jeans and a black lacy top that exposed an inch of creamy skin just above the waistband of her pants. It had sleeves halfway down her arms ending in more black lace, and gleaming buttons he wanted to bite off. Oh yeah, and those fucking boots. She looked like a kick-ass heroine out of one of his favorite comic books.

If he didn't get her out of here, he was going to get arrested for indecent exposure. He wanted to rip the lace off her body, strip those jeans up and fuck her up against the wall while she wore nothing but those boots, her nipple ring and a smile. Bunny's cock twitched at the thought. If he could just hold on until he got her back to the hotel room, he'd see to it his fantasy came true.

Glory was trying to hide her smile behind her hand. "Hey, Bunny."

"Hi, Glory." He wondered what the half guilty, half amused look on her face was all about. "Hey, what happened here today? Julian told me he and Ryan were here this morning and for some reason when Ryan came back he smacked me."

Tabby choked.

Glory's face took on an innocent expression that didn't fool him for a moment. "I have no idea. We were talking about the ocean and boats when he showed up. Does he get seasick?"

Tabby snickered.

Okay, something's going on here. Ryan had practically bitten his head off more than once today. "Please tell me you didn't do something that's going to make my cousin try to kick my ass."

Glory shrugged. "I have no idea what has him upset. Did you say something to him, Tabby?"

Tabby shook her finger at Glory. "Keep me out of this, your pixieness."

He growled down at Glory, careful to keep the sound human. "What happened? If I'm going to die, I deserve to know why."

"Glory decided to, um... And Ryan walked in while she was...heh." Was Tabby blushing? "You know what? You're better off not knowing."

Now he was intrigued. "Glory?"

She sighed. "Fine." She tossed her head back. "Oh, *Bunny,*" she moaned. Tabby leapt toward the counter, but Glory evaded her easily. "Bunny, Bunny," she chanted, each one becoming more breathless, until "*Bunny!*"

Now it was Bunny's turn to blush. "Yeah, that will do it." He pinched the bridge of his nose and tried to figure out how to explain to the little pixie that moaning another man's name was a surefire way to get her mate to lose his damn mind. "Do yourself a favor and don't do that again, okay? Not unless you want to find out exactly what Ryan's capable of where you're concerned." Knowing his cousin, Glory would find herself marked and claimed before she could blink. "You ready to go, baby?"

"Yup. Let me grab my purse and we're out of here." She glared at Glory. "Behave, your pixieness."

Glory laughed. "Enjoy your boat ride, Tabs."

Tabby's blush deepened.

"Again, do I want to know?"

Tabby clamped her lips shut and practically ran out the front door. By this time, even the tips of her ears were red.

Bunny's lips twitched. Hell, with these three around, at least his life would never be boring.

"Tabby," a voice drawled out of the darkness. "Where are you off to, Outcast?"

She stepped back before she could stop herself. "Gary." She let her eyes bleed into her Wolf's, checking around the darkened street for Gary and his goons.

"I asked you a question, bitch."

She turned so rapidly she almost lost her balance. There, just stepping out of the alleyway next to the store, were Gary and his buddies. "Leave me alone, asshole." She had to get away before these guys went after Alex or worse, Glory and Cyn. Hell, Mrs. H. was still inside. She didn't know if they'd go after a harmless old woman, but Mrs. H. wouldn't stand by and let someone she liked get hurt. She'd try to save Tabby and wind up getting savaged.

An arm slipped around her waist, her mate's scent filling her senses. "Is there a problem here?"

Oh fuck. Alex. She felt herself tense, ready to defend her mate. "No, no problem." *Please go back inside.* A Bear could hold off one Wolf, but a Wolf Pack? He'd be mangled. She wouldn't allow Gary to lay a hand on Alex. She'd never forgive herself if anything happened to her mate.

"No, no problem," Gary echoed. He smiled slowly. "Your voice sounds familiar."

"So does yours." Alex's arm tightened around her waist. "You're Gary, right?" Alex's voice sounded soft and menacing. Shit. He sounded just like he had at Noah's that night. The muscles in his arm were tight with tension.

"That's right. And you are?"

"Tabby's mate." She could feel his claws against her waist, but didn't dare look down. She'd seen Julian's nails turn black, the tips become deadly sharp. She didn't need to see them to know Alex's were the same way.

Gary did look. His eyes widened briefly. "Oh."

One of Alex's claws began rhythmically tapping against her stomach. She held perfectly still, knowing he would never intentionally hurt her. "That's right. We're not going to have any trouble, are we, boys?"

Gary's eyes gleamed in the light of the streetlamp. "You're not Wolf, so allow me to explain a few things to you." Those tapping claws stopped, scraped across her skin. She twitched when one scratched her belly. "You're right. I'm not Wolf. I'm Bear."

Gary laughed. "Wait. You mated a *Bear*?" His three goons laughed along with him. "A fucking Bear? You're kidding me, right?"

Tabby clamped her lips shut. Whatever the hell Alex was up to, there was no way she could stop it now.

"Listen, *Bear*. Tabby is Outcast. That makes her fair game to any Wolf who wants a piece, got it?"

For some strange reason, Alex relaxed behind her. "Is that so? Well, let me tell you something, *Wolf*. Tabby is no longer a Wolf problem. She's mine."

Gary laughed again. He wiped away an imaginary tear. "Oh, that's good. A Bear." He shook his hand at Tabby and Alex. "Run along. I'll deal with you both later."

Gary turned his back on them and motioned for his Pack. They grinned at Tabby and Bunny before turning and following Gary down the street, the small Pack still laughing.

"What. The. Fuck?" Tabby turned in Alex's arms, heedless of the claws scraping along her flesh. The scratches would heal quickly enough. "What the hell was that all about?" And why hadn't Gary attacked them?

Alex shrugged, but his narrowed eyes were glued to Gary's retreating form. "I have no idea." His hands absently stroked her flesh, healing the scratches he'd made.

"I would guess that he didn't want his ass in jail."

They both turned to find Gabe standing behind them. "I thought maybe I should update you on the prints we found on the stink bomb." He gestured toward the door of Living Art. "Mind if we go in, get it all over with at once?"

"Sure, no problem." Alex steered her back inside. She was still a little dazed at how easily Gary had backed down. Then again a Puma, a Wolf and a Bear could easily defeat his small Pack. And when one of those shifters was not only a Marshall's Second but a Hunter?

Yeah. One order of Gary's ass on toast, coming up.

They went back into the store. "Cyn! Glory! I found a sheriff on the front step. Can I keep him?" She winked at Glory, who giggled behind her hand. She ignored Alex's low growl and Gabe's chuckle.

Cyn stepped out of the back room. "Hey, Sheriff. Any news on the vandalism?"

"That's why I'm here." He took off his hat and ran his hands through his black hair. "The prints we lifted aren't on file, either with us or with the national database."

"Damn it." Cyn collapsed into one of the chairs lining the walls. "That means we'll never get him."

"Not unless he gets arrested, no." Gabe looked around. "Is anyone else in the store with you?"

"Nope. Mrs. H. left the back way. Said she'd left her Harley back there."

"Fine." Gabe eyed the two humans thoughtfully. "Know that the only reason I'm telling you this is because you know about and accepted Tabby." Cyn frowned, Glory looked puzzled. "I'm running the prints through...other channels as well, just to make sure we're not dealing with a shifter problem."

"Shit." Cyn tugged her hair. "Like Gary isn't enough of a

problem. Any way we can fingerprint him?" When Gabe shook his head, she took a deep breath and blew it out, straightened in her seat and did her best to stare a hole through Gabe. "You tell us what we need to do and we'll do it."

Gabe smiled. "Let us deal with it if it turns out to be shifters. I'll let you know if anything shows up. At that point, it's out of your hands and I'll have to call in some backup." He knelt down in front of Cyn. "I'm obligated to make this offer."

She eyed him warily.

"I or one of my other Pride members could change you." He turned his head to share a look with Glory. "Either of you, or both of you. You know about us already, so it wouldn't be too much of a hardship for either of you."

Tabby blinked, then bit back a possessive growl. If anyone was changing her girls, it was going to be *her*.

"What would I be if you did?"

"A Puma."

"Really?" Glory stepped forward. "I'd be a shape-shifting kitty?"

Gabe dropped his head. "Ah. Not exactly."

"That would be a really bad idea, Anderson." Alex pointed with his chin. "At least for Glory."

She put her hands on her hips. "And why is that?"

Tabby nodded. Alex was right. "Because Ryan would pitch a fit."

"Who cares what Ryan thinks? I like kitties. What if I want to be a kitty?"

"Ryan Williams, as in Chloe's brother?" Gabe stood up and studied Glory. "Right. I'll talk to him." He turned back to Cyn, ignoring Glory's gasp of outrage. "What about you?"

Tabby doubted she was the only one who heard Gabe's

unspoken question. *Do you have a mate too?*

Cyn smiled, her expression wicked. “I think I’d make a fine-looking cat.”

No. Bad idea. Very bad. “Uh, Gabe?” Tabby grinned weakly. “Not a good idea.”

His brows rose. “*Both* of them?”

She nodded.

He crossed his arms over his chest. “Why the fuck are they unclaimed?”

“Uh, ex*cuse* me? Unclaimed? Like my ass is in some ratty lost-and-found bin?”

“Glory,” Tabby groaned.

“I have a *mate*?” Cyn stood, her entire body quivering. “He’s going to fucking *claim* me?”

Oh hell. “Cyn, calm down.”

“Fuck no! Who is it?”

Tabby pinched her lips together. No way was she getting in the middle of this.

Cyn’s eyes narrowed. “I know where you hide your shoes.”

Tabby’s shoulders shrugged. “So not fair, Cyn.”

“Including your favorite fuck-me pumps. They’re history.”

“Oh, hell, not my black patent leather pumps. You bitch!”

“Hello, Wolfgirl, that’s kind of the pot calling the kettle black. Like those pumps—”

“Okay, okay, it’s Julian.”

Glory growled. “No need to ask who thinks he owns my ass.” She began pacing, her skirts swirling in a crazy Technicolor display.

That was way better than the controlled ice Cyn was showing. “Julian thinks he can just claim me whether I like it or not?"

"No! Why do you think he's waited, Cyn? He knows you're not ready yet!"

Cyn's glare turned deadly. "Does he, now?" She smiled at Gabe. "Turn me."

"Uh... Yeah. Maybe not." Gabe backed off, holding his hands up.

"If Julian thinks he's going to wait to claim me until *he* decides I'm ready, I'll be fucking old and gray. Put me on equal footing. Let *me* decide."

Gabe's jaw clenched. "You know this is irreversible, right? If I do this, you'll be answerable to Max Cannon, our Alpha, and his Curana, Emma. You'll bow before them whether you want to or not. Can you handle that?"

Cyn frowned. Some of the ice surrounding her thawed. "Emma's cool. I've met her once or twice at the coffee shop. I don't know Max."

"There's more than one type of shifter, Cyn." Tabby took hold of her arm. "If you really want to do this, I could make you Wolf. Hell, I'd *love* to make you Wolf." She'd have the Pack she'd always wanted, one that loved her.

"Or I could make you Bear." Alex shrugged when Tabby turned and growled at him. "It's an option, but I think she needs to know *exactly* who and what Julian is before she makes that decision. Being the mate of a Kermode is considered an honor among my people."

Cyn blinked. "The mate of a what?"

Alex sighed. "The Kermode Bears are also known as Spirit Bears. They live exclusively in Canada, somewhere near British Columbia. They have powers beyond what a normal Bear has, but there are so few of them, it's rare to meet one. It's unheard of to find one outside of Canada.

"I don't know much about them other than they're so reclusive my grandfather thought they were a myth until Jamie Howard came home from Canada. He told us some stories about the ones he'd met." Gabe sighed. "If your mate is Kermode, he's the closest thing we shifters have to a mystical priest."

"So you're telling me he has magic powers?" Cyn's expression turned cynical.

"Not quite. Hell, I'd try to explain it, but I don't understand it myself. Bunny?"

Alex shook his head. "Sorry, we know a little more, but not much. The Kermode are..." He got a far-away look in his eyes. "They're treasured. Respected. They have powers other Bears only dream of. It's said Bear Himself walks with them and guides their dreams."

"Then why is he here?" They all turned to Glory, who shrugged. "Seriously? Why is he here if they never leave Canada?"

Gabe looked thoughtfully at Cyn. "Good question. Has anyone ever asked him?"

"We're getting off topic." Tabby sat in Cyn's abandoned seat. Her feet were killing her. "I'd really suggest letting your mates claim you. If they scent another man on you, they'll freak the fuck out."

"Maybe that would be a good thing." Cyn began to pace around the room. "Besides, I'd like the ability to protect myself from Gary and the Gutless Wonders."

Glory giggled. "I agree. And don't try to tell me I need some big strapping man to do it, either."

Alex closed his mouth. "I wasn't going to say anything."

The three women stared at him until his cheeks began to turn red.

"So now it's a matter of deciding what we'd like to be." Cyn locked eyes with Glory. The mischief in them was daunting.

"It's like picking out a new dress that will never go out of style."

"Oh lord." Tabby put her head in her hands. It was going to be a long night.

Alex took the keys to Tabby's Jeep out of her hands. "Your friends are insane."

"Yup. Total Queens of Denial."

Alex shook his head. At least the sign over the curtained-off area now made sense. He opened the passenger door and waited for Tabby to climb in. "What do you think they'll decide?"

"Knowing them both?" She scooted in without protest and waited until he was settled behind the wheel before continuing. "Glory will jump the first shifter she sees and beg for a bite. Cyn will think about it and eventually go with her first instinct. I expect she'll call Gabe before the end of the week."

"I'm not sure that's fair to either Ryan or Julian." He started the Jeep and took off, leaving the Harley behind. It had begun to rain while they were in the shop and he had no desire to get soaked on the way back to the hotel. "They should be the ones to change their mates."

Tabby shrugged. "Here." She reached into his pocket and pulled out his cell phone. "Call Ryan. Tell him what Glory's pondering and see what happens."

He stared at her. She grinned back. "That's evil."

She nodded once. "Yup."

"You have Julian's number?"

Her grin turned into a snarl. "I did until *someone* crunched my phone."

He began dialing his cousin's number. "Right. First stop, the Sprint store."

"Damn skippy."

"Hey, Ryan. There's something you need to know."

"Shoot." His cousin sounded like absolute shit.

"Is Chloe okay?" He could be at the hospital in fifteen minutes if he needed to.

"No change. Mom's...yeah."

Bunny sighed. "Shit."

"Yeah." Ryan sighed. "So what's up?"

"Anderson came by Living Art and filled the girls in on some stuff he's checking out. He offered to change both Cyn and Glory so they can protect themselves if Tabby's attacker turns out to be a shifter."

"Son of a *bitch*." Ryan's inhuman growl filled his ear. "Where is Glory?"

"We just left her at Living Art."

The phone clicked when Ryan hung up on him.

Tabby took the phone he handed over and dialed, then put it back in his hands. He frowned but put it back up to his ear.

"'Lo?"

Julian didn't sound any better than he had an hour ago. "Julian, you sound like shit."

He could hear the rustling of cloth, possibly sheets. "Yeah, well I feel like shit. What's up?"

"Anderson came by Living Art. He offered to change both Cyn and Glory so they can take care of themselves if Tabby's attacker turns out to be a shifter and goes after either of them."

There was silence on the other end of the line for a moment. "And this concerns me how?"

Bunny pulled the phone away from his ear. "Cyn. Not a Bear." Still nothing. "Someone else's mark on her body."

That got a reaction. "Shit." The man sounded more awake now. "What did Tabby tell her?"

Bunny frowned. Wasn't Cyn's reaction more important? "She said it was a bad idea, but she gave Cyn the impression that the reason you hadn't changed her was because you were waiting for something. Cyn didn't handle that too well."

"Goddamn mother fucking son of a bitch." Julian sighed. "Let me see which way the woman's planning on jumping and if I need to stop her."

"Aren't you going to claim her?"

"*It's not time yet!*"

Bunny winced and pulled the phone away from his ear. Damn, Julian could *yell*. He checked the driver's side window to see if his brains were currently sliding down the glass. "Dude, I hate to say it, but your time might be up."

"Shit. Fuck!" He could hear more rustling cloth. "Who the hell told Tabby she could say anything?"

"I think *my mate* was trying to prevent *your mate* from making a mistake."

There was the sound of a huge crash. "Any idea who she was thinking of asking to change her?"

"I think she was leaning toward a Puma."

"That won't do. Tell Tabby that if she can't talk Cyn out of it, she has to get your Aunt Laura to change her into a Fox. That's the only other option."

"Oookay. Do I want to know, or should I flail around

blindly?"

Julian snorted. "Welcome to my world."

Huh?

"Trust me, Bunny. If I could have, I would have already taken Cyn. *Nothing* would have stopped me."

Bunny sat up straighter. Something in the other man's voice called to everything in him that was Bear.

"But the time isn't right. And until it is, I'll do everything I can to see that she remains *safe*. And that means she can't become either Wolf or Puma, understand?"

"What about Bear?"

"No. Not unless it's by my hand."

"Julian—"

"I forbid it."

"Understood." Bunny's foot hit the brake. He blinked. Since when did he take orders from anyone other than his father? "Julian?"

"Just…trust me. Please."

Bunny looked over at Tabby. The clueless, worried frown on her face told him she had no idea what was going on. But she trusted Julian with her life.

And Julian had almost given his saving Chloe.

"I do." He hoped the conviction he felt was obvious in his voice. If it wasn't, he'd reassure the man next time he saw him.

"Thank you." He barely heard the whispered words before Julian cut the connection.

"I'm going to say it again," Bunny muttered. He pulled back into traffic. "You have some freaky-ass friends."

Tabby shook her head. "What the hell was that all about?"

"Not a clue." *And something tells me Julian isn't much better off*. If the Kermode didn't know the answers, who the fuck did?

They couldn't reach Cyn before they hit the Sprint store, and by the time they were done, it was late. They stopped for some fast food and ate in the car before heading back to Alex's hotel room.

"Are you planning on living here?" She winced. She hadn't meant to ask that question yet. They were newly mated, still learning each other. She had no idea whether or not he'd meant what he'd said in Noah's that night, about possibly starting up a small business here in Halle.

He frowned. "You're here." They got out of the Jeep and headed for the front door of the hotel. "By the way, seen any houses you like?"

She stumbled. Real estate? That sounded permanent. "Um. Not recently."

Okay. That was a total lie. There was this adorable little red brick house not far from Simon and Becky Holt's that she'd totally fallen in love with, *and* it was for sale. The cottage-style house had both whimsy and dignity, with a black front door and shutters, but a garden with stone fairies in it. She was sure that the garden would be full of flowers come spring, hiding the fairies behind colorful blooms.

He nodded. "We'll need to make an appointment, see what we can find." He led her inside, his hand drifting down to her ass. "In the meantime, have I mentioned I love those fucking boots?"

Tabby grinned up at him. "Do you?" She put a little extra sway into her hips, his low growl music to her ears. After the night they'd had, they both deserved a little something special. After only two times with Alex, she already knew he'd make tonight memorable.

They entered his hotel room. She stepped inside, a wicked smile crossing her face at the sight of the bed.

She heard the door shut. "Tabby?"

"Hmm?" His voice had deepened, sending a quiver of anticipation down her spine.

"Strip."

She shivered at the note of command in his voice. She looked back over her shoulder. Her man stood there, his arms crossed over his chest, his legs spread wide. The bulge of his erection pulsed behind the zipper of his jeans. He looked dangerous.

She had two choices. Defy him and see what happened. Or strip and see what he had in mind.

Her hands went to the hem of her shirt and pulled it over her head. She was stubborn, not stupid.

The gleam of approval on his face told her she'd made the right decision. She wasn't in the mood to fight tonight. She was in the mood to fuck.

She sent him a wicked grin and turned around. She kept her back to him and undid the clasp of her bra, letting it fall from her shoulders to the floor. She reached up and played with her nipples, feeling the sting of arousal all the way to her clit. The ring slipped between her fingers, heightening her arousal. She loved having her nipple ring played with. She could hear his breathing speed up, but refused to turn to see what he was doing.

"Now the jeans."

His voice was a deep, husky rasp. She toed off the boots. There was no way she'd get her jeans off over them. She undid the snap to her jeans, pulled the zipper down and hooked her thumbs into the waistband. She pushed them down her legs, letting him see the thong she'd worn just for him.

"Stop."

She was bent down all the way, her pants almost to her ankles, but she stopped.

"Put the boots back on when you're done."

She smirked. Oh yeah. From the husky rasp of his voice, he *really* liked the boots. She tugged her jeans the rest of the way off and put the boots back on before straightening up. She stood there, her back to him, in nothing but her thong and her boots. The knowledge that he was thoroughly enjoying the view sent tingles down her spine. She'd never felt sexier in her fucking life.

She heard a noise behind her and risked a glance. He'd undone his jeans, pulled his cock out, and was slowly stroking himself, his gaze glued to her ass.

She let one brow rise. "See something you want?"

His eyes locked onto her mouth. "Hell, yes. Get over here."

She turned around and rubbed her lips with the tip of her finger. She wasn't certain he'd wanted her to see the shudder that passed through him, but damn if the knowledge didn't make her feel even bolder. From the way he was eyeing her finger, she had a pretty good idea of where his thoughts had wandered. "If you get my mouth, what do I get?"

He stalked toward her, his hand still wrapped around his cock. "Good point. How about an even exchange?"

God, just the thought of his mouth on her pussy nearly dropped her to her knees. "I do prefer sixty-nine to sixty-eight."

Those gorgeous lips of his curved. "I don't mind owing you one, but I'm not going to complain, either." He walked past her to the end table and pulled out a bottle with a black lid. He placed it next to the pillow and lay down on the bed. He was still fully dressed, only his cock standing free. “C’mere, baby.”

It was her turn to shiver. The thought of fucking him while he was still fully dressed and she was almost naked was an incredible turn-on. She wanted to feel the stiff cloth of his jeans under her fingers, the soft T-shirt between her thighs. And then she couldn’t wait to turn around and feel the denim scratching her inner thighs while she rode him. The only thing sexier was the feel of his whiskers scratching her thighs.

She pulled off her thong and crawled onto the bed, her Wolf close to the surface. She was going to take her mate, show him how incredible being mated to a she-Wolf could be. She knew the look on her face bordered on evil just before she bent down, lapping at the head of his cock.

Salty-sweetness exploded onto her tongue. *Yum.* The scent of her mate was strong here, mingling with the smell of his need. It was a heady combination. She buried her face in his balls and licked, sucking one into her mouth. The zipper dug into her chin, making her moan around the sac.

“Oh, fuck.” His hands buried themselves in her hair. “Get your ass up here.” She lifted her head from his lap and licked her lips. He glared down at her. “Don’t make me say it again.”

Fuck that. If he reacted that way to a little suck and lick, she wanted to see exactly what he would do while his cock was buried balls-deep in her mouth. She slowly sucked him, her lips sliding bit by bit down to the root.

He reared up, his hands pressing against the back of her head, holding her in place. “Oh *shit.* That’s it, suck it, baby.” He bent over her body, one of his hands going to her ass. He slapped it, hard enough to make her grunt.

She sucked, laving the sensitive opening of his cock with her tongue, drawing out the spicy-sweet taste of his come.

He groaned below her, his cock twitching inside her. His hands moved from her head to her hips, tugging on them. "Gonna let me have a taste, baby?"

"Mm-hmm." She nodded her head, but refused to release his cock. She'd figure out a way to keep him right where she wanted him while she gave him what he'd asked for.

He moaned, petting her hair one last time before he lay back down. She maneuvered herself until she was straddling his face, eager to feel that hot tongue on her clit.

He pulled on her hips until he had her right where he wanted her. His hands stroked the globes of her ass. "So beautiful."

That's when she felt it. The most wonderful thing she'd ever felt in her whole life. Alex pulled her pussy to his face and sucked her clit into that amazing mouth. She bucked her hips, riding him, unashamed. He was fucking *amazing*.

A slap to her ass reminded her of what she was supposed to be doing. She bobbed her head, taking him back down her throat, swallowing around the head of his cock. His rumble of approval was matched by the thrust of his hips as he began to fuck her face. She pulled back a little, wrapping her hand around the base of his cock, letting him control the blowjob while she held on and sucked for all she was worth.

Meanwhile, Alex was driving her insane with that tongue of his. He was eating her like a starving man at an all-you-can-eat buffet, leaving no part of her pussy untouched. His hands dug into her ass, pulling the cheeks apart, exposing that part of her that was still virgin.

He lifted his mouth away from her, much to her disappointment, but was soon back, his lips wrapping once more around her clit. She whined around his cock, so close to coming she was ready to scream from frustration. She tightened her legs, the feel of the cotton of his shirt ratcheting up her desire. She let go of the base of his cock and palmed his balls in one hand, rolling them back and forth to his obvious enjoyment. He planted both feet on the mattress and began to seriously fuck her face at the same moment he gently inserted a wet finger into her ass.

Apparently the bottle with the black lid was lube.

The slight sting, the dark invasion, pushed her over the edge. She came, screaming around his cock, riding that finger and mouth until he'd almost drained her.

He kept fucking her in the ass with that finger, stretching her out. She felt the slight burn subside, the pleasure slowly building again.

"More," he muttered, lapping at her pussy lips. She heard a click and wondered at it. One of his arms wrapped around her waist, holding her in place while he inserted something wider into her ass. Oh, that stung, stung so good. He must have gone up to two fingers. Warmth spread from where he was inside her. She had no idea what that warmth was, but it felt *damn* good.

She lifted her head from his cock, ignoring the wet slap of it against her cheek. Her hands dug into his thighs, the denim harsh against her fingertips. She rode his hand, his lips, felt the orgasm racing down her spine again. "Gonna come again."

He moaned and nibbled her clit with his teeth and that was it, she was coming around his fingers, whimpering and still wanting.

He pulled himself out from under her. "Down." He held up the bottle and shook it at her with a dark grin.

She went down, her legs so rubbery they couldn't hold her up anymore anyway. His hand stroked one of her ass cheeks, kneading the soft flesh. "I am going to enjoy this."

She heard the snick of a cap, felt the cold gel glide between her ass cheeks. It began to warm almost immediately. “Alex?”

He bent down and nibbled at her ass. “Mine.”

She felt she’d better warn him. If his cock felt as good as his fingers, she knew she’d enjoy it, but even she knew this wasn’t something you did without some preparation. “Never done this.”

“Good.” The dark satisfaction in his voice had her burying her face in her hands, her hips writhing in the bed. “Gonna fuck this tight hole of yours. You’ll think of me every time you sit tomorrow.”

“Hell.” Like she didn’t think of him too much already!

She jumped when she felt his fingers stroke between the cheeks of her ass, rubbing the lube against the tight pucker. “Gonna feel so good, baby.”

She felt the stretch when he inserted his fingers and wondered if someone could die of pleasure.

Bunny watched Tabby squirming beneath him. He’d never had a lover take to anal play the way Tabby had. She was practically humping the sheets, sucking his fingers into her tight body. And she’d never done this before?

Holy. Fuck.

No way was he going to hurt his virgin mate. Hell, if he’d known she’d never done this before, he would have used even more of the cinnamon-scented, self-warming lube. Not that she’d complained; she’d come as sweet as you please. His she-Wolf seemed to enjoy a little sting of pain with her pleasure.

Despite that, he wouldn’t give her true pain. She might be begging for it, but Bunny knew just how much she could take right now. He reached beneath her and began to strum her clit with his free hand, her sighs music to his ears. He inserted two fingers into her ass, scissoring them, stretching her wide for his cock. He wouldn't enter her until she was begging for it, her hole wide and inviting, ready for him.

He let her ride his two fingers, taking his time, noticing the way she moaned and squirmed when his jeans brushed her thighs. *My baby has a fetish, huh?* He'd have to take her more often while still fully clothed if she reacted like this.

"C-close."

He stirred, letting her feel the denim against her skin and inserted a third finger into her ass.

She stilled, her breath hiccupping. "Okay, baby?"

She snarled, the sound inhuman. One dark brown eye peered up at him through a fall of damp green hair. He could see her fangs descending.

He smirked, the satisfaction that he could reduce his mate to nothing but a mass of wanton need coursing through him. It was better than anything he'd ever experienced.

He fucked her with his fingers, gentle at first. He wanted her used to the stretch and burn of three fingers. He was wider around than that, especially at the head of his cock. When she relaxed back into him, he took his fingers out and added more lube.

She snapped at him, those sharp teeth flashing. Thank God. He was *very* happy his cock was currently nowhere near her very talented mouth.

He reinserted his fingers and she smiled. She pushed back as much as he would allow, rode his hand with a smile. His other hand remained busy at her clit, keeping her on the edge of orgasm.

When those sweet little whimpers began pouring from her mouth, he pulled his fingers free. "Gonna fuck you so good, baby."

Her hips lifted in invitation, one he had no intention of turning down. He put a thick coating of lube on his cock and stroked it, knowing she could hear the sounds of it squelching through his palm. "Ready for me?"

She nodded. "So ready."

He put the head of his cock against her asshole. "Push out, baby."

He entered her slowly, pausing every time a wince crossed that incredible face. He moaned when the head passed through the tight ring of her muscles. He stilled, letting her get used to the sensation. When she shivered and relaxed, he inched forward. He paused with each stroke to let her get used to his invasion. When his balls finally rested against her pussy, he sighed. "You okay?"

Her lip curled, a fang peeking through. "Peachy."

He almost laughed. Damn, she was extraordinary. Her ass pulsed around him. "Need a minute?"

She nodded, wiggling a little bit. Her eyes widened and she shuddered. "Oh fuck."

"Like this?"

She reached back and stroked his thigh, her nails scratching the material of his jeans. "Need."

And he would provide. He began with small movements, swiveling his hips every now and then so she'd feel the rasp of his zipper against her flesh, know he was fucking her still fully clothed. Hell, he hadn't even taken his boots off.

She began to respond. Tabby rocked against him, their movements becoming surer, sharper, the sensation indescribable. He could feel the tingling at the base of his spine, the pleasure already more than he could bear. He needed her to go over with him, needed to feel the clench of her muscles while she came. She was so tight, she might snap his dick off when she came, but fuck if it wouldn't be worth it.

There, that was the sound he'd been waiting for, that delicious little whimper that signaled she was close. She was pushing back against him, riding him, barely letting him guide her. He lowered himself over her, forcing her down, his hands on her hips keeping her ass in the air. He pulled her hair roughly to the side. He was almost there, his cock throbbing inside her.

Her face was red, her eyes scrunched up, and it was the most beautiful sight he'd ever seen. "Come on my cock."

He thrust one arm toward her face, hoping she understood what he wanted. He didn't wait though, he took what he needed. He bit his mate, forcing the mating enzyme into her system, throwing her over the edge into orgasm.

Oh. Oh fuck. So good. So tight. Her scream was muffled against his arm, her teeth clenched, her face screwed up. He could barely move inside her body, she was coming so hard.

It was too much, too tight, too hot and he was coming, pouring himself into her, coming so hard his world turned gray.

She collapsed beneath him and he followed her down, reluctant to leave the tight clasp of her body. He licked the wound on her shoulder, lapping at the blood, her taste exploding inside him.

"I think you broke me."

He smiled. Her ass was still quivering around his softening cock.

"Seriously. I think I'm blind. You fucked me blind."

He kissed her damp cheek. It was going to be so easy to fall in love with his mate. He said a silent prayer of thanks for the awesome gift fate had given him in the form of one small she-Wolf. “Your eyes are closed.”

“Oh.” He waited. He knew she wasn’t done yet. “Are you sure?”

He laughed silently. “Yes, I’m sure, baby.”

“Hmm.” She elbowed him until he rolled off of her, then snuggled into him, her ass resting against his hip. She wriggled and sighed happily, purring like her namesake. He got up long enough to clean himself and her off, then put his cock back into his pants and maneuvered until he was spooned up against her body. If his baby got off on the feel of denim, he’d buy fucking denim pajamas. They would be uncomfortable as hell, but Tabby was worth it.

He drifted off to sleep, a satisfied smile on his face.

Chapter Six

"So."

Tabby raised her brow, wondering what the hell Alex was up to. He'd let her shower by herself this morning, his demeanor quiet and thoughtful. He'd finished his yoga before she got out, and damn if she wasn't sorry to miss that. Watching him stretch that amazing body, his muscles quivering with strain, had been an incredible turn-on. After he was done, he'd led her to IHOP for breakfast, his expression still peaceful after his morning workout.

"Tell me about Gary."

She thudded her head down on the Formica table hard enough she'd probably have a red mark. "Bacon. Need bacon."

"Tabby."

She huffed out a breath, leaving her face on the table. "Fine. Gary is a student at the college who thinks it's fun to try to fuck with me." She couldn't go into too much detail; it was Saturday morning and the IHOP was packed to the rafters with humans and Pumas. One mention of shifters right now could lead to either a long life in a hug-me jacket or being forced to leave the only real home she'd ever known. Neither one was an option she wanted to contemplate.

"How long has this been going on?"

The quiet tone of voice had her stiffening. She was coming

to recognize that tone as a dangerous sign. She stiffened, wondering if Alex would lose it. He couldn't go after Gary. Gary, thanks to his *friends*, was too well protected. Besides, Gabe wouldn't be able to keep Alex out of trouble if he went after Gary unprovoked. Despite everything that had happened, they had no solid proof that Gary had ever threatened to lay a hand on her. It would be her word against his and his goon squad's. That would work against Alex in both human *and* shifter law. "Why?"

He gave her an innocent look, totally incongruous on his face. "No reason."

She glared up at him through the fall of her bangs. "Alex."

"You are so not allowed near my mother anymore," he grumbled.

"Why not?"

"You sound just like her."

She could feel a smile trying to break free. He sounded like a grumpy little boy. "After having met your mother, I'd say that's a good thing."

His eyes sparkled with approval even while he glowered at her. "Flattery will not get you out of telling me what I want to know."

"What about a BJ? Will that get me out of it?"

He blinked, his eyes blanking before the frown returned.

She lifted her head and grinned at him. "You had to think about it, didn't you?"

A slight flush crossed his cheeks. "Brat." He sat back as the waitress piled pancakes in front of him. Tabby sat back too, the scent of her own breakfast driving her crazy. "If he's a threat to you, I need to know. How can I protect you otherwise?"

The look on his face was hard, uncompromising. She

sighed, just knowing he was going to try to be her fuzzy knight in matte black leathers. "Gary arrived in Halle in August. He's a junior and a transfer from New Mexico, I think. I'm not sure what group he's affiliated with, and it's not like I can walk up to him and say, 'Hey prick, who's your boss? I'd like to complain about your customer service'." Tabby laughed at the look on Alex's face. Her old Alpha had hammered into his Pack how to talk around humans without giving them away. The Pack was treated as a company. The analogy wasn't that far off the mark. Most Packs came with bosses, employees, and yes, even customer service. Hell, the Senate actually *did* have a legal corporation headed by the Leo, the ruler of the American shifters, a charitable organization that was mostly concerned with the conservation of endangered species. They only accepted donations from shifters, so they didn't fall under public scrutiny. The Wildlife Conservation Foundation did a lot of good, helping to repopulate the wolves in Yellowstone National Park and giving the big cats born in the U.S. a safe environment to live in. She'd heard that there were more tigers living in the U.S. than any other place in the world, and the WCF helped to take care of them. Chloe would probably do very well working as one of their vets once she recovered from her injuries and graduated. "Anyway, he found out pretty quickly that I was an ex-employee and decided that harassment was A-okay."

"Tell me what he's done, Tabby."

Fuck. His voice had dropped, deepened until it rumbled through her. "He's egged Living Art, given me grief, harassed me on the phone, threatened the girls. You know, the usual." She wasn't sure if she should tell him about that time in the woods, when Gary had scared the shit out of her. She was afraid of what he'd do if she did. "You were there the other night. He's done stuff like that off and on the entire time I've been here."

"Have you tried petitioning the closest human resources office for help?"

She shook her head. "I've heard of the Poconos boss. He's a scary guy, and his COO is said to be a little insane." She heard someone in the booth behind her choke, but ignored it. "I heard she's from around here, but she left before I arrived." Tabby shrugged. "Besides, Gabe is aware of what's going on and he's doing his best to look out for me." Although she hadn't yet told Gabe about how Gary and his Pack had cornered her in the woods. Damn, with everything that had been going on, she'd forgotten she'd wanted to speak to the sheriff about that. It seemed like her life was both spinning out of control and finally finding its center.

Gary hadn't found out her new cell number yet, but that didn't mean he wasn't still stalking her.

"What's that frown for?"

She looked up from her plate. Seeing the look on Alex's face, she grimaced. "I need to talk to Gabe about something." One of those dark brows rose and she winced. "I just want to tell him that some of Gary's issues are beginning to spill over onto Cyn and Glory."

He looked unconvinced. "And then you're going to tell him about the butterflies that flew out of your butt."

Okay, the person behind them really needed to stop listening in on their conversation. Throaty feminine laughter floated over them and Tabby frowned, not sure if she was more pissed at the eavesdropper or Alex. "Look, he's begun harassing them too. He knows that if he hurts them, it hurts me, and it would be my fault." It would damn near kill her if something happened to Cyn or Glory because of her.

"Bullshit. It would be Gary's fault." Alex's expression turned thoughtful. "Maybe its time we called in some reinforcements then."

"I agree."

Tabby blinked and turned. There, standing next to her, was a short, curvy woman with long dark hair and laughing brown eyes. Behind her stood one of the handsomest men Tabby had ever seen, his sky blue eyes serious. His blond hair just brushed the collar of his blue shirt. The only flaw on that perfect face she could see was a small scar just along one side of his nose, so faint it was barely noticeable. Dr. Max Cannon, Alpha of the Halle Pride, slipped his arm around the waist of his wife and Curana, Emma Cannon. "I understand you're having some problems."

Emma rolled her eyes. "Thank you, Captain Understatement." She smiled at Tabby, her expression mischievous. "Lion-O and I heard everything." She rattled off an address Tabby knew was in one of the more affluent sections of town. Not quite in the same area as the truly rich, like the Howards, but still pretty respectable. "Come over to our place, both of you. We need to talk."

Tabby blinked. That hadn't been a request. "Okay," she drawled. She'd heard about the Little General who ran the Halle Pride alongside her mate. You did *not* want to be on her bad side.

Emma nodded. "Good. We'll see you there in half an hour." She pulled out her cell phone and began to dial. "Sarah? Listen, I need you and Gabe at our place in half an hour." She frowned. "Sleeping in? There's no time to sleep in." She began to march out of the restaurant with an absent wave at the stunned couple at the table. "We have an *issue*! Oh, and I need to grab a hold of Becks and Simon. You can call Adrian and Sheri. Yes, I *know* what time it is, Sarah. Why do you think I'm giving you half an hour?" Emma pulled the phone away from her ear and frowned down at it. “Do you kiss your husband with that mouth?”

Tabby bit back a giggle. She now understood the *other* nickname she’d heard in conjunction with the Halle Curana. *Hurricane Emma.*

Max shook his head, his lips twitching as he watched his mate walk away, still chattering on the phone. “I don’t know where the hell she thinks she’s going. I’ve got the car keys.” He turned back to Tabby, a small swirl of power surrounding him briefly, sending a shiver down her spine. She had the oddest urge to bow down to the Puma, his Alpha powers caressing her with a different flavor than that of the Wolf Alpha she’d once served. “I’ll see you both in half an hour. Whatever the problem is we can fix it. One way or another.” He nodded goodbye to Alex and followed his mate out the door.

Tabby gulped at Max’s ominous words. “Uh-oh.”

Alex frowned. “What? I’d think this would be a good thing. You have the local guys on your side, right?”

She bit her lip. “I don’t know if Gabe ever told them I...was fired, and what for. And they have strong ties to the Poconos boss.”

Alex shrugged, his eyes glued to the man leaving the restaurant. “It’s a moot point now. We’ve been summoned, not much we can do about it.” He cut into his strawberry-coated pancakes. “Eat your bacon. Something tells me we’re going to need our strength.”

Bunny pulled the Jeep to a stop outside the two-story Craftsman style home. A dark gray gable roof was set off by rich mahogany brown shingles and bright white trim work, with rich red fieldstone set around the base of the house. The front had that beautiful pillar and post design, with a covered porch that wrapped around to the left side of the house. An attached garage had been seamlessly integrated into the right side of the house. Huge glass double doors with an art deco design waited to greet visitors to the home. The house was warm, inviting and beautifully maintained. In the driveway sat a red Dodge Ram and a black Mustang. "Wow. Nice place."

Tabby nodded and opened her door. "Yeah. Nice."

He studied her face. She was pale and shaking. "It's okay, baby."

She took a deep breath and huffed it out. "The last time I got summoned by an Alpha, I was Outcast."

"Max has no cause to ask you to leave Halle. Besides, he's not *your* Alpha. Technically, he can't outcast you."

She shook her head. "Bears don't have Outcasting, do they?"

"Not really, no. We don't have the same kind of Pack or Pride structure." Not all shifters had traditional Alphas and Omegas and all that political crap. Most were simple family groups, like the Bears, Foxes and even the otherwise solitary Tigers. The loose-knit family groups would keep in touch via couriers in the old days and, in modern times, snail mail and e-mail. They held the vote for their proxies on the Senate that way, never having to meet unless they wanted to. Outcasting was something reserved for those who abided by the more stringent rules of the Packs and Prides, like the Wolves, Coyotes, Pumas and Lions, where one shifter's actions could endanger the lives of all.

"Then trust me, it's a really big deal." She shrugged her shoulders like she was shifting a heavy weight. "Let's go, I guess."

Bunny held out his hand, offering his mate his full support.

No matter what happened in that house, Tabby was his mate. That meant she could fall under either Pack law or Bear law. And since Bears had no Outcasting system, as far as he was concerned his mate had no problem.

One of the front doors opened. Emma Cannon stood there, a grin on her face and her hand on her hip. "I was wondering how long you two would stand out there. C'mon in. We won't bite, I promise."

Bunny moved forward, enjoying the warmth of Emma's greeting. He could already tell there would be few problems on that front. Emma was greeting them like old friends. "Thank you, Mrs. Cannon. I'm Alexander Bunsun."

Emma's lips curved up in a wicked smile. "I know who you are. You're the wereBunny who rode into town on a hog."

Bunny didn't know whether to laugh or not. "Um... Yeah. Maybe?"

A woman with wild curly hair down to her waist pulled Emma out of the doorway. "Don't worry, she has that effect on a lot of people." She ignored Emma's rolled eyes and pulled Bunny inside.

Bunny took a second to look around the great room of the Halle Alpha's house. The sage green walls, cherry floors and white trim created a warm feeling of comfort and home. The skylights in the vaulted ceiling let in a great deal of natural light. A large, reddish-brown leather sofa dominated the room. It rested on a bold area rug done in a geometric pattern of reds, blacks and greens. It faced a set of built-in cherry cabinets along one wall that doubled as the entertainment center with bookshelves on either side. The fireplace, on the opposite wall, matched the fieldstone on the outside of the home. He really liked the feel of the place. He'd have to see if he could find something similar in the area. From the way Tabby was staring, wide-eyed, he had the feeling she liked it too.

The curly haired woman held out her hand. "I'm Becky Holt."

Bunny returned her greeting. "Alexander Bunsun. Nice to meet you. This is my mate, Tabitha Garwood."

Tabby smiled weakly and clung to his hand with a grip he just knew was leaving bruises.

Becky Holt pointed to a tall, dark-haired man with muscular arms and an easy grin. "That's Simon, my mate. He's the Beta of our Pride."

"Pleased to meet you." He exchanged nods with the Beta, keeping hold of Tabby's hand. He could feel his mate trembling next to him.

Emma nodded toward a striking couple seated on her sofa. The man was dark-haired, with the same golden skintone Tabby had. The woman seated next to him was the palest woman Bunny had ever seen, with snow-white hair, pale blue eyes and pearly skin. Lying at their feet was a golden retriever in a guide dog harness. "That's our Marshall, Adrian Giordano, and his mate, Sheri." The couple nodded at them, but quickly returned to their conversation. Bunny wasn't fooled. Something about Giordano's body language told him that he and Tabby had the lion's share of the Marshall's attention. "Gabe and Sarah, our Omega, aren't here yet, but they should be shortly. There were grumbles about coffee and doughnuts."

"Doughnuts?" Becky shared a wicked, intimate grin with her mate. "I love doughnuts."

Simon chuckled. "Bet I know something that tastes sweeter."

"Oh, for the love of God, people." Emma flopped down on the couch. "Get a room."

"Works for me." Simon grabbed a hold of Becky's hand and began to drag her toward the stairs, ignoring her indignant squawking.

"Simon, knock it off. Emma, stop encouraging them." Max stepped out of his kitchen and shook his head at his Pride leaders, ignoring Emma's snickers and Becky's slap to Simon's arm. "You're making us look like idiots." He walked over to Bunny and Tabby and shook their hands. "Alex, Tabby, welcome to my home. Please feel free to join the insanity."

"Thanks, but everyone calls me Bunny."

The room stopped dead. He'd never seen anything like it. It was like he'd picked up life's remote and hit *Pause.*

"I'm sorry. Did you say people call you Bunny?" Simon, his dark eyes twinkling, leaned back against the fireplace mantel.

Bunny nodded. He loved some of the reactions he got when he told people his nickname, especially other shifters. They tended to range from horrified disbelief to unstoppable giggles.

"And you *let* them? Why not strap a cracker to your ass and call yourself lunch? Ow! Damn it, Becky." He rubbed the spot on his arm his curly-haired mate had just smacked.

"Ignore Garfield, he hasn't had his Cat Chow yet." Simon's eyes flashed down at his mate, gold sparks dancing in the dark brown.

Bunny bit back his laugh. "And you're making fun of *my* nickname?"

Max rubbed the side of his nose. "Why don't you two have a seat while we wait for Gabe and Sarah." He walked away, pointing languidly at Emma. "Not a word."

"Damn. And I had so many of them, too."

Max stopped and stared at Emma, one eyebrow rising.

Emma gave as good as she got, staring right back at her

mate. From the way their mouths were curving, Bunny didn't think there would be a fight, but the tension in the room seemed to ratchet up a notch. He wondered if the blond Alpha was about to drag his small mate up the stairs, Pride meeting be damned.

The doorbell rang, breaking the staring match between the two Alphas.

"I'll get it." The Marshall stood, moving with easy grace to the front door. "It's Gabe and Sarah. One of you get a cold towel, she spilled some coffee on her hands again."

Bunny frowned. "How did he know that?"

Emma waved Becky toward the kitchen and followed her through. "He's the Marshall."

And?

Sheri, Adrian's mate, must have seen his confusion. "The Marshall can sense the physical well-being of every member of the Pride." She frowned. "Your scent. It's so...wild. Not like the other Bear in town." She stared up at him, her pale blue gaze unfocused. Suddenly her eyes widened. "You're a—"

"Hey, Bunny." Gabe slapped him on the back, interrupting whatever it was Sheri had been about to say.

"Anderson. Learn anything about Chloe's attacker yet?"

Gabe shook his head. "I wish I had some news already, but there were no witnesses. Nobody on the street heard or saw a thing. The evidence we've collected is still at the labs in Pittsburgh, so we have to wait." He shrugged. "I wish I had more, but that's all I've got so far. How is Chloe, by the way?"

Bunny could see the way the small brunette watched Gabe. Her short hair was windblown, her hands reddened. His fingers twitched, the urge to heal the small hurt nearly derailing his train of thought. This must be Gabe's mate, the one who'd given

Gabe fits over Chloe. “Still unconscious. Any idea when her mate is supposed to arrive?”

“Jimmy’s coming back?” Emma swept back into the room, a wet towel in her hands. “Here, Sarah. Wrap this around that burn.” She clucked her tongue. “That looks nasty.”

“Let me.” He took hold of the poor burned hands and breathed deep, the relief at being able to heal the small hurt releasing some of his tension. He opened himself up to his Bear and the spiral of the healing path. He mended the burned flesh, encouraged the new growth of tissue and forced the skin to reabsorb the swelling. When he was done, no trace of the burn could be seen, and his legs were trembling with fatigue.

“Holy shit.” Adrian stared down at the woman’s hands, his eyes wide. “I *felt* that.” He lifted his face, his gaze narrowed on Bunny. “I’d forgotten Bears could do that.”

The woman smiled up at him sweetly. “Thank you.” She patted his arm. “That really stung.”

Gabe took one of her hands in his own, stroking the healed skin. “I owe you one, Bear.”

Bunny shrugged, feeling uncomfortable with the awed reactions of the Pumas. This sort of healing was as commonplace as hello among Bears. “It was nothing.”

Gabe’s jaw clenched. “You healed my mate. That means I owe you one.” His jaw relaxed and his brows shot up. “Unless you’d rather not have the man investigating the attack against your mate owe you?”

“Attack?” Emma frowned, taking a seat on the huge leather couch. “All I heard at the restaurant was talk of harassment.”

“Tabby was attacked outside her place of business a couple of days ago. A stink bomb was thrown through the window, and when she and the other girls ran out, she was hit on the back of the head hard enough for her to black out.”

Bunny glared at Tabby. He hadn't known she'd lost consciousness. He might not have been quite so calm if he had.

"Look, before we get too far, why don't we fill the others in on everything that's been going on? We tend to get a little blind to what's going on outside the Pride, so they might not know what all's been happening." Gabe took a seat in one of the side chairs and pulled his mate into his lap.

She settled in with a sigh, resting her head against his shoulder. "Good idea."

Bunny took a seat on the couch again, Tabby next to him. Adrian and Sheri took up the remaining seats, leaving Emma in the other wing chair, Max standing by her side. Simon and Becky settled on the floor across from the couch, their backs to the entertainment center. "Okay, here's what I know so far. Tabby was Outcast—" he ignored the gasp of his mate "—for something she didn't do. She roamed as a Wolf for about eight years before landing in Halle." He stared at Gabe, willing him to understand what he was about to say. "And if anyone owes anyone else, it's me who owes you and your grandmother for taking care of Tabby."

Gabe nodded, acknowledging what he'd said. Bunny got the feeling he didn't quite agree with him, but that was all right.

"Because of her status, this guy Gary feels he can do anything he wants to Tabby without repercussions."

Max winced. "Unfortunately, he's right. She's without the protection of her Pack, set apart from them for a crime, whether she committed it or not. Unless she proves she's worthy of joining another Pack or manages to get her old Alpha to take her back, she's considered a criminal and fair game."

Emma's lips curled up in a wicked grin. He'd seen that grin before, on a cartoon when he'd been a kid. It was the same grin the Grinch had when he came up with his idea to dress as

Santa and steal Christmas. The look sent shivers down Bunny's spine. And from the looks her mate was giving her, he guessed the Alpha had no clue what his little mate was thinking.

"Great." Bunny sighed and ran his hand over his bald head. The stubble there rasped against his palm. *Time to shave again.* "Anyway, he's egged the store, bothered all of the girls who, by the way, are all human other than Tabby, and called her multiple times. I got to see him last night and, frankly, if I hadn't been there, I'm not certain he would have stopped at harassing her. As it was, he tried to warn me off, telling me he had every right to bother my mate. In other words, he's stalking her."

"He's given humans a hard time?" Max whistled. "Who's his Alpha?"

Bunny blinked. "I have no clue."

Gabe shrugged. "I've asked him, but he refuses to answer. The only thing I've been able to learn is he comes from New Mexico. I'm still running down his birth records. The college has been less than enthusiastic about turning over records and, without a warrant, they're right. I can't get one without probable cause." Gabe ran his hand up and down Sarah's back. Whether it was to soothe her or himself, Bunny had no clue. "Besides, technically speaking, shifter law *is* on his side. The girls at Living Art are aware of what Tabby is and who the Pride members are, so they're considered kin."

Bunny could feel the helpless rage building up in him again. Did this mean that the little fucker could keep on taunting Tabby, possibly hurting her, and there was nothing he could do about it?

Fuck. That.

A soft hand landed on his arm. He looked up into the warm brown eyes of the Omega. "We'll fix this. I promise."

A calm peace he'd never felt off a yoga mat settled over him. He nodded, knowing she was right. Everything would be fine. Sarah smiled and sat back in her mate's lap, her hands curled up in her own. Gabe took hold of her wrists, his thumb stroking the insides. Something about the caress had Bunny taking notice. He stared at the sheriff and his mate, and wondered...

"Alex?"

"Hmm?" He turned back to find Tabby staring up at him. The fact that his name was pretty much the first word she'd uttered since walking in the front door soothed something deep inside him.

Tabby took a deep breath. "Tell them about Chloe."

He growled. "Some asshole beat my cousin Chloe damn near to death and left her in the road like trash. She would have died if it hadn't been for Julian Ducharme. She's still in a coma. Nothing we've done so far will wake her up."

Max's blue eyes flashed gold for a moment. "I heard. We're going to look into that." He exchanged a glance with Gabe and Adrian, who both nodded.

Sheri bit her lip. "Chloe's such a sweet little thing. Who would want do that to her?"

"We don't know, but so far the clues are few and far between."

"I'm betting on Gary and the Gutless Wonders," Tabby muttered.

"Gutless Wonders?" Max's tone was not amused. "How many Pack members does Gary have with him?"

Tabby winced. "He has two others who follow him. Oh, and he sent a kid out for a tattoo of his Wolf. I recognized it from when he changed once, just before he found out I was Outcast." And from her tone of voice that conversation had not been full of warm fuzzies. "He told the boy that if he got the tattoo he could join his *fraternity*." Tabby made little quotation marks with her fingers and made a face. "For all I know, he's changed people around campus, but since I don't exactly hang out there, I have no idea what he's really up to."

Max growled, the sound feral and feline. His sky blue eyes were pure gold. A light mist pooled around his feet, his power spilling out into the room. Bunny had only seen something like that once before, when a Lion had tried to make his father bow down before him.

It hadn't worked on William Bunsun, and it sure as hell wasn't going to work on William Bunsun's baby boy. His chin lifted in the face of the Alpha's anger.

"Why didn't I know about this?" Max stared around the room at his core hierarchy, his expression full of outrage. "He's changing humans on my territory and I didn't know about it?"

"Shit. How the hell were we supposed to know? How many other Prides do you know of that are based in a college town with other shifters in it?" Simon showed why he was this man's Beta. Other than the twitch of his shoulders and a brief wince, he stood tall. Even the Marshall was hunched over, fighting his Alpha's anger. The only other person in the room who wasn't bowed down was Emma. Even Tabby had her head lowered. "For the most part, they've come, respected our boundaries, kept to themselves, and gone home when they graduated."

"Except now we've got a wannabe Wolf Alpha roaming the streets, a Fox in the hospital, a group of Bears on the warpath, and God knows what else on the way." Emma sounded more thoughtful than upset. She rested her elbow against her knee and propped her chin in her hand. "Who the hell stood over my cradle and talked about living in interesting times?"

Max turned to his spouse, amused. The mist retreated, his

eyes turning back from gold to sky blue. "At least we don't have any more Senators running through town and co-opting our people."

"Do you think it was Gary who attacked Chloe?"

Bunny turned to find Sarah, Gabe's mate, staring up at him. "I have no idea, but I'm not sure why he would. Does he even know she exists?"

They all stared at Tabby, who shrank in on herself. "How the hell would I know? I stay as far away from him as I can."

Max pointed to Adrian. "Thoughts?"

The man frowned. "We need to set Puma guards on Chloe, make sure no one can get into her room without authorization."

Bunny bristled. "My family is there. Trust me, *no one* will get to Chloe."

Adrian nodded. "I'll need to discuss with them a rotation, so that they can get some rest. I have some people I trust to put with her, and I'm sure Gabe can come up with a few names as well." Gabe nodded. "I'm going to assume you're researching any possible human involvement, like a work rival or a romantic one?" Gabe nodded again, his eyes rolling. "Okay." Adrian turned back to Max. "Everything's being done on the Chloe side that we can do for now. Without Chloe being Puma, there isn't any way for me to monitor her physically other than keeping in touch with Jamie Howard."

"Do that." Max pointed at both men. "I want regular updates on her condition. Once she's awake, we can find out from her what she saw of her attackers. Maybe she'll be able to identify whether or not it was shifters who did this."

"And if it was?"

Max eyed Gabe. "We find out if it was Pumas, specifically *my* Pumas, who did this. If it wasn't, whoever it was is all yours.

Hell, if it was my Pumas, they're all yours after I Outcast them."

Gabe's answering grin was feral.

Whoever hurt Bunny's baby cousin was going to pay in a big, big way.

"We still need to deal with the Gary issue," Emma pointed out. "Whether or not he's involved in Chloe's attack we *know* he did something to Tabby."

Speaking of which... "Gabe, could I talk to you alone for a moment?" Tabby tried to ignore the questioning look on Alex's face. If he found out about Gary's little stunt in the woods last week, he'd blow his top. There was no way she'd risk letting him go off in a rage. He'd get himself killed.

"Sure." Gabe helped Sarah to her feet and stood, settling his mate back down in the chair they'd been occupying. He kissed her forehead and released her wrists. "Be right back."

Tabby pointed at Alex, who was about to rise and join them. "Sit. Stay. Good Bear." She followed Gabe out onto Max's back deck, ignoring the giggles coming from Emma.

Gabe stood in front of her and crossed his arms, his expression concerned. "Okay, Tabby. What did you want to tell me that you didn't want Bunny hearing?"

She described what had happened in the woods. Gary and his proto-Pack surrounding her, the look of lust on their faces. The way Gary had tried to punch out her windshield to get to her.

By the time she was done, Gabe's eyes had gone gold and he was cursing up a blue streak. "Why didn't you call me immediately?"

"I meant to, I really did. But I kept getting distracted."

He glared at her.

She winced. Damn it, he knew her so well, and they'd been friends for only six months. "Fine. I was worried that some people would blame me." She *was* Outcast, despite Bunny's unwavering support. There were those who would hear what Gary had done and shrug, thinking it nothing more than she deserved. Some would actively encourage Gary, hoping to drive her away. It was one of the many reasons she'd stayed Wolf for years rather than try to find a home in the shifter world. Real wolves didn't care that she'd been Outcast.

It had been lonelier than anything she'd ever been forced to endure. She prayed every night that she'd never have to face living like that again.

"Admit it. You were worried Max would kick you out of Halle."

She bit her lip. "Yeah. I was."

"*Tabby.*" Gabe ran his hands through his hair, obviously frustrated. "How many times do I have to tell you? You're *home*, okay? No one is going to take that away from you, especially not Max."

Max could take it away by simply turning his back on her. "You don't have the authority to say that, and you know it. You aren't the Alpha."

"No, but the Alpha listens to me, especially when it comes to Outcasts and rogues. I'm a Hunter, for crying out loud. Hell, his Marshall has vouched for you, his Omega thinks you're wonderful and wants a fucking tattoo now, thank you very much, and even his Curana is in there fighting for you! And Emma barely knows you! So let it go, Tabby." He pulled her into a hug. "Whether you believe it or not, you're home."

She shuddered, collapsing into the embrace. Gabe was solid warmth, his feline scent tickling her nostrils in a—

"Excuse me. Is this a private party or can anyone join?"

She lifted her head to find the back door open. Alex stood there, leaning against the doorjamb, his hands jammed into his pockets. His fangs had descended. He was eyeing Gabe's hands at Tabby's waist.

Gabe's hands lifted up and stepped away from her. "Mind out of the gutter, Bunny. Tabby's like a sister to me."

"Just like Chloe, huh?"

Gabe groaned. "When will people get over that? We never dated! God, as soon as she wakes up, I'm kicking her ass all over again."

Alex relaxed and chuckled, his fangs receding. "No kicking girl ass. That's just wrong."

"Please. Like Chloe wouldn't willingly kick my ass up and down the block if she thought I deserved it." Gabe shook his head. "It's hard to see her in that hospital bed."

"Tell me about it." He studied Gabe's face for a moment. "Are you going to fill me in on what my mate's hiding from me?"

Gabe shook his head. "Wish I could, but she has to be the one to tell you."

"Thanks a lot. Traitor." Tabby glared up at Gabe, ignoring the way Alex was watching her. All of his attention was suddenly focused on her, and not in a good way.

Gabe hesitated only for a moment, then shrugged and headed back inside. "Do me a favor, Tabby. Tell him. Trust him. He's your mate."

She nodded. It wasn't that she didn't trust Alex. She just didn't want Gary to get his hands on him. Gary would fuck him up without thinking twice about it.

Alex stepped out. Gabe shut the door behind him, giving the two of them their privacy. "Tabby?"

Better rip the Band-Aid off. "Gary attacked me one morning after a run. He and his goons cornered me out in the woods, up against my car. I'm pretty sure they were going to rape me."

Alex's whole body rippled. His fangs descended. His nails blackened, lengthening two inches. He freaking *grew* about six inches, the seams of his shirt popping, his jeans creaking against the strain. Considering he was pretty massive to begin with, it was impressive. "Where does Gary live?"

Tabby gulped. This was an Alex she didn't know. His voice had turned gravelly, deepened until he sounded like something out of a horror film. "I don't know."

"*Tell me.*"

"I don't know!" She did her best to stare him down, but her heart was racing a mile a minute. "And if I did, I wouldn't tell you."

"Tabby." His fingers twitched. She wondered if he was picturing Gary's neck between them.

"No." She tried to soothe him, resting one hand against his arm. "One Bear against a Wolf wins. One Bear against a Pack loses. I'm not worth your life, Alex."

He blinked, his hazel eyes turning dark brown. "*What?*" He roared, startling the birds from the trees. Tabby clapped her hands over her ears and wondered if they would start bleeding. "Would you care to repeat that?"

"I'm not worth dying over?" She gulped again, watching fury etch itself into Alex's features.

The door slammed open. "Okay, break it up." Sarah, the Pride Omega, stepped onto the deck. "Whatever's causing Mt. Vesuvius here to erupt has to stop now. You're going to scare the straights." Alex growled down at her. Sarah growled back. "Calm down, big guy. No one's going to touch your mate, okay? She's safe here." She patted Alex's arm. "Why don't you both go back inside? We have a few more things to discuss, and Max was thinking we might have you and Gabe run out to Frank's for some burgers. Doesn't that sound good? We could order some fruit for you, maybe a salad." Sarah tugged on Alex's arm, dragging him inside the house. The chatter continued all the way back into the great room. "We could get some pie. How about blueberry? Frank's pies are some of the best in town."

Alex's body began to retract, shrinking back down to his normal size. His muscles relaxed, his fangs receding. Whatever mojo the Puma Omega wielded was working, calming her big Bear down. She decided to help, adding her own hands to Alex's back, stroking him through his T-shirt. "Pie's good. Maybe we should get Ryan and Julian here too. Their mates are being harassed by Gary too." The grumbling under her palm was more irritated than pissed now, thank God.

"Good idea. Tabby, why don't you call them, get them over here? Ryan can let his family know that we plan on helping guard his sister while we're at it." Sarah's gaze never left Alex. Her hand continued to pet him until he'd completely calmed down. A fine sheen of sweat was covering the Omega by the time she had Alex down on the sofa, a confused look on his face. "Gabe? Could you get everyone's orders please?"

Tabby looked at Gabe. His jaw was clenched as he watched his mate tame another shifter into the palm of her hand. Tabby didn't know if he was jealous or concerned for her safety. "Sure. I can do that."

Sarah smiled at her mate. "Everything's fine, Gabe. Just take the orders and call it in. Bunny would never hurt me."

Alex shook his head. He looked like he was waking up from a trance. "No, of course I wouldn't." He looked over at Tabby. "Baby?"

Tabby rushed forward and threw herself onto Alex's lap. She curled into him, burying her face against his neck. His scent wrapped around her, warming her, comforting her as nothing else could. "It's okay, sugar. Everything will be okay."

He buried his face in her hair and breathed deep. "If he lays a hand on you, I *will* kill him. You need to understand that." He tipped her chin up. "You may not think you're worth dying over, but I know you're worth killing over."

Crap. His eyes hadn't returned to normal. They were full of savage anger, the eyes of a predator. That scary fury she'd seen on the deck was still there under the surface, barely contained by his force of will. "Alex, let it go. For me. Please?"

He took a deep breath. He closed his eyes and rotated his head. When he opened his eyes again, they were back to warm hazel. "For you."

She nodded. It wasn't over yet. Not by a long shot. She cuddled up against him and let him press his face to her neck. She knew what he was doing. He was breathing her in, filling his senses with her. If that was what it took to calm him down, she'd stay in his lap for the rest of his life.

"I need to know if you're a danger to my Pumas."

Bunny settled into Anderson's car with a wince. He'd really lost it out there on Max's deck. Just the thought of someone trying to *rape* his mate was enough to send him right back to that blistering rage. "Are any of them planning on assaulting Tabby?"

Gabe's brows rose. "Not that I'm aware of."

"Then no." He smiled sweetly, knowing that Tabby's chosen lifestyle was in jeopardy and he was the cause. If the Hunter believed he was a danger to his Pride, the two of them would be run out of town that same night.

Gabe studied him for a moment, his lips twitching. "Hands off the Wolf. Got it." He pulled out of the driveway and headed off to Frank's. "Where are you thinking of house hunting?"

Bunny shrugged. "Near here, I think. The houses are nice."

Gabe shot him a startled glance. "No offense, but can you afford it? Even with the housing market on a downturn, places near Max go for a pretty penny."

"I can afford it, especially if some of my family is here. We'll probably start up a branch of the family business here."

"And that business would be?"

"Bunsun Exteriors. Corporate specializes in commercial landscaping and hardscaping, but I want to start some residential options here. I'm a landscape architect."

"So your family is rich?"

Bunny made a face. "We're comfortable. Besides, it's my father's business, not mine. If a branch opens up down here, it will be run by my Uncle Steven." He was pretty sure Uncle Steven would fall in with what he wanted to do. Hell, he'd probably put Ryan in charge just so Bunny wouldn't be forced to do the paperwork. The last time they'd put an expense sheet in front of Bunny, he'd drawn big pink azalea bushes on it. Ryan was this generation's money man. "I wonder if I could get Eric down here or if he'll stay in Oregon?"

"Eric?"

"My brother. Dad left him behind to deal with the business while he's in town."

"Ah." Gabe pulled into the parking lot and turned off the ignition. "How many of you are there?"

"Family or Bears?"

Gabe frowned. "Huh?"

"Aunt Laura, Chloe's mom? She's a Fox. Her brother, Uncle

Ray, married Uncle Steven's sister, and they have three kids, one Fox and two Bears. So most of the family is half Fox, half Bear. Dad is the only one who mated a human, so Eric and I are both Bears. What makes it even more confusing? Uncle Steven and Aunt Stacy are Dad's cousins." He glowered at Gabe. "And no jokes about rednecks and first cousins."

Gabe's lips twitched. "I wouldn't dream of it." He got out of the car and headed to the diner, not bothering to wait for Bunny. From the set of his shoulders, Bunny figured he was still fighting a laugh.

He got out of the car, noting six bikes sitting off in a row. He frowned, something about those bikes looked familiar. Bunny followed the sheriff into the diner, a scent tickling his nose he hadn't encountered in a long time. He smelled Bears, ones he thought he recognized.

Gabe was standing just inside the door, his hands loose at his sides, his back straight and tight. "I'm going to ask you one more time. Back off and leave the girl alone."

Bunny blinked at the hard note in the Sheriff's voice. "Gabe? What's going on?" He looked over Gabe's shoulder to find six men, all above average height, surrounding a tiny woman. She held a tray in her visibly shaking hands. "Harry? Is that you?"

All six men flinched. "Alex Bu-Bunsun?"

Bunny smiled. "Well hell, Harry. How've you been?" He hadn't seen these guys in dogs' years. "Doing good since I last saw you?" That had been, what, ten years ago?

"Better. Better. Arm's all healed up, thanks. Gives me fits in the rain, though. Not so bad off as Barney. He still can't use his hand."

Bunny grimaced. He hated being reminded of Barney. He'd done everything he could to make up for what he'd almost done to the man, but Barney would have nothing to do with him. Bunny didn't blame him. He wouldn't want anything to do with the man who nearly killed him either. Last he heard, Barney was in Alaska, owned a bar, and was happily mated with two cubs. Rumor had it he'd moved there to put as much distance as he could between himself and Bunny, yet still remain in the United States.

Harry swallowed hard. "You, uh, just passing through?"

Harry's five gang members backed away from the waitress, wary eyes glued to Bunny. He shrugged. "Nah, I'm living here now. My, um, fiancée is here." The human waitress was looking at them strangely. No way could he use the word "mate" here.

Harry's eyes went wide. He managed to turn even paler. "F-fiancée? You're engaged. Congratulations." He feebly waved at the bikers behind him. They all took a polite seat at the counter, watching him with fear-filled eyes.

"Yeah, she's a tattoo artist." One of the six men moaned. Bunny thought it might have been Mikey. Despite his rough look, he'd always been a little more delicate than the others. You'd think a man with a flaming skull tattooed on the nape of his neck would be a little less wimpy. "Why, you thinking of getting one? She does good work." He'd seen that when he caught a look at Mrs. H's cross. She was a true artist, someone whose work he'd be proud to wear.

"Um, no." Harry shook his head so hard it should have snapped off his neck. "We're, uh, just passing through."

Lee, the smallest of the six men, gently tapped the waitress on the shoulder. "Can we please get that order to go ma'am?"

Bunny rolled his eyes. "C'mon guys. It was *years* ago."

"He took on all of us. *All* of us," Lee whispered. "He didn't even get a scratch."

Mikey whimpered. The wuss.

"You shouldn't have picked on Heather. She was only ten." And a Fox, which left her completely vulnerable to the seven teenage Bears who'd chosen to make her life miserable. He'd had no choice but to come to his cousin's aid. The decision to nearly kill the worst offender was something he had to live with every day. "I did ask you to stop." And he'd made each and every one of them apologize to Heather after he was done with them, even Barney.

It had taken two years for Heather's nightmares to stop. All of them had starred her cousin rather than her attackers. She still eyed him warily whenever the family got together.

Gabe was staring at him like he'd suddenly sprouted wings. "And Tabby's worried about you facing Gary?"

Bunny shrugged. He'd tried to tell her he could handle it, but she didn't want to believe him. She was too used to Julian. Black Bears would run from a fight they knew they couldn't win. Kermode, for all that they were some shade of cream or white in Bear form, were still a species of black bear.

Brown Bears, on the other hand, were a lot more aggressive. They'd stand until they dropped dead. And Bunny was still considered more aggressive than most. "She's used to Julian, but she'll learn." The men in front of him twitched. Bunny looked around, noting the curiosity of the rest of the diners. He smiled, hoping to reassure them. These people were all potential clients, after all. "So. It was nice seeing all of you again."

Food was plunked down in front of Harry, six large boxes and six smaller ones. The waitress pulled two bags out from under the counter. The relief in Harry's expression would have been amusing if it hadn't reminded Bunny of just *how* aggressive he could be. That look right there was one of the many reasons Bunny had learned how not to fight.

He didn't like it when people were afraid of him. Of all the people in this room, only Harry and his friends were truly aware of what Bunny was capable of, and they were *terrified.* He sighed. He rammed into this every time he saw someone who knew him from his wild teen years. He decided to try one last time. Maybe he could still show them he wasn't the same person he'd been when they knew him. "Where are you all headed?"

"Um. West." Harry picked up the bags and held out a credit card. "We're going west. Possibly California." The five other men nodded their agreement. "Maybe even Washington."

Bunny nodded. There'd be no convincing them he was a changed Bear. "I see. I wish you well on your journey."

Harry signed his receipt and stood. His fellow Bears fell in behind him. "We need to get going. Losing daylight and all that. Nice running into you, Bunsun."

"You too, Harry." He stepped aside, giving the men plenty of room to get out the door. "Have a good ride." He waved, not surprised when none of them waved back.

"What the hell, Bunny. What was that all about?"

He turned back to the sheriff. "Long story. I'll tell you on the way back." He knew his cheerful expression wasn't fooling the other man, but right now he couldn't be bothered to put much effort into it. "Let's get our order and get out of here."

"Yeah. Let's do that." Gabe went to the counter and asked for their food. Bunny stayed by the door and listened to the sound of motorcycles riding off into the distance.

Ryan arrived shortly before Alex and Gabe got back and introduced himself to the Pride leaders. He was just settling in near Simon when Gabe and Alex walked in the front door carrying their burgers. Gabe had the strangest look on his face, and Alex looked like someone had run over his dog. Tabby, concerned, sat forward. “Alex? Gabe? What’s wrong?”

Gabe shot Tabby a wild look before handing the food over to Emma and Becky.

Alex shared a long look with Ryan. “Ran into Harry and his buddies over at Frank’s Diner.”

Ryan groaned. “Shit. What were they doing here?”

“Heading west. Far, far west.”

“You think…?” Ryan let the rest of the sentence trail off.

“Nah. They’re still terrified. They wouldn’t risk it.”

“True.”

Tabby looked back and forth between them. There was something there that she didn’t understand. “What are you two talking about?”

Alex had the weirdest look on his face. He looked almost apologetic. But why?

“Harry and his friends harassed one of our cousins years ago. Bunny taught them not to do that anymore.”

“Taught them how?”

“He nearly ripped their leader’s arms off.”

Tabby blinked. *He did not just say what I thought he said.* “He what?”

Alex turned on his heel and walked right back out the door.

“Alex?” She got up and ran after him, ignoring Ryan’s voice calling after her. “Alex!”

He stopped. “I know you think you understand what’s going on.”

“In what universe?”

He turned. He looked harsh, drawn. “Fine. What do you think you know?”

“Other than the fact that you seem to be turning into an idiot? Not much.”

He took a deep breath, rotating his neck. “A long time ago, I had anger management issues.”

She waved her hand for him to keep going. The fact her mate seemed to have a temper hadn’t been lost on her.

“Some Bears went after my cousin, Heather, who’s a Fox like Chloe. She was only ten years old. They thought it would be fun to see if they could force her to shift.”

Tabby winced. That was bad, very bad. Most shifters couldn’t make the change until puberty started. “Why would they do that?”

“They were drunk, and...stupid.” He raised an eyebrow at her, his expression turning even harsher.

“Ew!” Tabby shuddered. “A ten-year-old?”

“They tried to force her into puberty. They thought it was a fucking joke. Of course the idiots didn’t realize that puberty isn’t something you can force. Heather was terrified.”

“I bet. What happened?”

“I found them.” He sat on the front step and leaned against the porch rail. He looked lost. “I almost killed them. All seven of them.”

“Seven?”

He nodded. “Seven.” He patted the step and she sat next to him. “I maimed one of them.”

She snarled. “Good.”

He stared at her, stunned. “Good?”

“They traumatized a *child*. I’d have maimed them too. Did

you go for the balls? Please tell me they aren't going to procreate."

His eyebrows shot up. "Um. No. I tried to rip the leader's arms off. Then I forced all of them to their knees and made them beg for forgiveness. When the first one said no, I snapped his arm like a twig. The rest fell into line after that."

"I bet." She grinned savagely and wriggled with excitement. "Did they whimper like little babies?"

His laugh sounded shocked. "Bloodthirsty little thing."

She cuddled up against him. "You protected your family, your Pack. There's nothing wrong with that. I'd have done exactly that if given the chance."

"Then you understand why I need to protect you."

She froze. Damn it, he *would* turn this around on her. "Pain in my ass."

He stuck his hand down the back of her jeans. "Yup. And you loved every minute of it." He pinched, making her squeal. "Now stop changing the subject."

"Okay, fine. You could probably take on Gary and his idiot friends without *too* much trouble."

"That's putting it mildly. Tabby, if Gary so much as gives you a papercut, he'll be eating his own ass."

"Can I watch?"

He snorted. "You just don't get it, do you?"

"Alex."

"Hmm?"

"I'm not afraid of you."

He sighed. "You will be."

"Right, Yoda. Sure I will." She kicked his shin when he pinched her again. "You'd sooner chew off your own paw than hurt me."

"True." He pushed until her head was resting against his shoulder. "After lunch I want some ink."

She cuddled close, loving the way he seemed to surround her. "Done."

"Food's getting cold." Emma stepped out onto the front porch. "And for the record? I'm not afraid of you either."

Alex stood slowly and pulled Tabby up alongside him. His hand nearly crushed hers. Her big Bear was nervous.

"Neither am I." Max took up position next to his mate. "I heard all about what you did. You protected your own. There's nothing to be ashamed of in that."

"Ditto." Adrian nodded respectfully to Alex. "Now come inside. Julian should be here any minute and rumor has it he loves cantaloupe."

Alex chuffed out a laugh. "You're all nuts."

"Nope. I trust my people, and they tell me you're worth it." Max waved them into his home. "Alex?"

Alex stopped. He looked startled at the sound of his name on Max's lips. "Yeah?"

"Welcome to Halle."

Tabby felt Alex tense beside her. "Thank you, Alpha."

Tabby nearly collapsed in relief. They weren't going to be turned away.

They were finally home.

Chapter Seven

"There's no change."

Tabby collapsed against the door, watching Alex visit his cousin. Chloe still hadn't moved.

He sat by Chloe's side and picked up her hand. He watched his cousin, his expression so full of sorrow Tabby's eyes filled with tears. The shades in the room were drawn, hiding them from the night. They'd stayed longer than planned at the Cannon's house, and visiting hours were almost over.

"Where is her supposed mate?"

"No clue. Last I heard, he wasn't in town yet. Gabe told me his plane got delayed." She watched him run his hand over his bald head. "The longer she's in a coma, the worse off she's going to be."

Chloe's mother stifled a sob. "She's going to be all right."

"I know she will, Aunt Laura."

A hand landed on Tabby's shoulder. She turned to find Julian standing behind her. His eyes showed the strain of being in the hospital, even though his lips smiled. "Hey, girlfriend. Long time no see."

She poked him in the side, knowing how ticklish he was. She'd left him twenty minutes ago sitting on the Cannon's couch, arguing with Emma about which reality TV show was better, *America's Next Top Model* or *American Idol.* She wasn't certain which one he'd been for, only that he and Emma seemed to be having a really good time. He'd refused to discuss Cyn, giving the Pumas that weird, secretive smile of his and changing the topic. Not even Max had been able to get him to talk about his would-be mate.

Julian jumped and shimmied away, batting at her hand. "I have an idea, but I need to talk it over with Chloe's family before I try."

Tabby stopped poking. Julian had his serious face on.

Alex stood. "What have you got?"

Julian tugged his braid. It was a nervous habit and told her just how much he really didn't want to be doing whatever it was he was about to propose. "I might know a way to wake her up, but if it works, it will change her profoundly."

"Do it." Chloe's father, Steven, didn't even blink.

"She'll still be Chloe, but might also be something more. Are you willing to risk that?"

Steven's mouth opened, but he stopped at a touch from his wife. "Changed how?"

Julian shook his head. "I don't know. What I do know is she and I will be connected in some very strange ways." He stepped into the room, lowering his voice. "What I'm discussing is not done lightly, and can only be done by the Kermode. Are you willing to risk having your daughter's life tied to mine?"

Alex frowned. "She has a mate."

"This won't be a mate bond. This will be something a great deal more...spiritual. I'm not sure I can adequately explain it." Julian looked frustrated. "There's so much that you can't see or feel. It's like trying to explain red to a blind man."

"It's hot." Tabby shrugged her shoulders when everyone

turned to her. “What?”

Julian rolled his eyes. “You watch way too much TV, Tabby. What movie was that from?”

“Does it matter? Is she going to wake up all Freddy Krueger?”

Julian snorted. “Hardly.”

“Is she going to become a Stepford Wife, all cheerful and homicidally creepy?”

“Nope.”

“Will she still be Chloe?”

“Of course!”

Tabby didn’t understand. “Then what’s the problem?”

Julian tilted his head. “She could become more in tune with the spirit world than other shifters. I’ve heard of ones who were awakened this way who could talk to the dead, or see into other people’s dreams.”

Tabby waited. “That’s it?”

Julian growled.

“No, she’s right. I’d rather have a psychic daughter than no daughter.” Steven held out his hand. “Please. Wake my girl.”

Julian smiled grimly. “I’ll do everything in my power.”

Tabby pulled out her phone. “Should I call Cyn and let her know what’s going on?”

The look Julian shot Tabby was lethal. “Do it and you’ll regret it.” His grin showed way too many teeth. “You’d look really cute with brown hair.”

“Don’t you dare.” Tabby glared at him. She hated her brown hair, always had. “I’d rather be b—” she glanced at Alex “—blonde.”

“Nice save.” Alex winked at her and the others chuckled,

easing the tension somewhat. “Julian, what do you need to wake Chloe up?”

“Privacy, and lots of it.” He headed for the door. “I’ll start tonight.”

“How will we know it worked?” Laura Williams stood, her gaze anxious as she watched Julian leave her daughter’s room.

“Trust me, you’ll know.” Julian left, leaving behind a group of very confused, very hopeful shifters.

“We need to get going too.” Alex hugged both his uncle and his aunt before taking hold of her arm. “We’ll stop by again tomorrow after we go house hunting. Let us know if you need anything.”

House hunting?

“Sure thing, Bunny.” His uncle pounded his back. “We’ll call you if anything changes before then.”

“With luck, her mate will be here when she wakes up.” His aunt gave him a peck on the cheek. Almost immediately, her eyes went back to her daughter. “Love you, Bunny.”

“Love you too, Aunt Laura. Uncle Steven.”

“Bye, Tabby.” Tabby flinched as Bunny’s uncle gave her a hug.

“Um. Bye.” She wasn’t used to this family stuff. She had no idea what had happened to her own family and, frankly, she really didn’t care. But watching Chloe’s parents watch over their child had her longing for something she’d never had. She wondered how she would she feel if it were *her* daughter lying on that bed?

Alex’s hand landed on her stomach, his fingers caressing her through her shirt. A sudden thought hit her.

Holy shit! They hadn’t used condoms at least once that she remembered. What if she *was* pregnant? She gulped, suddenly terrified. What the fuck had they been thinking? Her hand moved to rest over Alex's. She looked up at him and saw the way he was watching her, his gaze full of affection. She knew how he'd react if they were pregnant.

She blinked. If *they* were pregnant. She had a sudden vision of Alex sitting in a chair, their child resting in his arms. And the vision didn't scare her at all. He'd be an amazing father. Alex would never kick his child out of his home. He'd be more likely to kick the ass of anyone who tried to hurt his baby.

"Take care." Laura offered her a hug as well. "Bunny, your parents said they'd sit with Chloe for a little while tonight while Steven and I get some rest, so if you need them, call here."

"Will do. We'll see you tomorrow."

Alex took hold of her arm and led her out the door. "Ready to do my ink, baby?"

Tabby smiled. She might not know families, but she knew her art. "Sure thing." They headed for her Jeep. "Shop's closed, but I'm pretty sure Cyn won't mind me working on you after hours. Do you have any idea what Julian's planning on doing?"

Alex shook his head and drove for the shop. "Not a clue. Think we should tell Cyn anyway?"

"And risk that sneaky bastard figuring out a way to dye my hair brown again? No way."

They passed Frank's diner, drove through the nicer shopping district that contained Emma's shop, Wallflowers, and finally arrived at the little cluster of shops and convenience stores nearer the campus. Alex pulled around back and got out of the car. She settled back down when he waved to her, letting him check the area out with eyes and nose. He came around to the passenger side and helped her out, ignoring her grin. "You have someone watching the shop during the day, don't you?"

He shrugged, not even bothering to deny it. She bet he'd

had Gabe recruit some Pumas for the job. She hadn't scented any Bears and the scent of Puma was much more common than any other shifter.

Tabby dug her keys out of her purse and led the way to the back door. "So, do you have an idea of what you want?" Tabby clicked on the lights only in the back of Living Art. No sense advertising that someone was here when they weren't supposed to be.

"Other than the bear and wolf? No."

She led him into her workspace. "So, I get creative license, huh?" He just grinned at her and settled into the chair. "Cool. What kind of bear?"

"A grizzly."

She plopped down on her stool, stunned. "Grizzly?"

He nodded, watching her closely.

"You're a *grizzly*?" *Wow. That explains a lot.* He said he had anger management issues? Talk about an understatement. Grizzlies were considered the most aggressive of all the Bears. Some would say they were the most aggressive of all the shifters. She whistled. "Okay. Feel free to protect me from, y'know, anything you feel I need protection from." It wasn't like she'd be able to stop him. Grizzlies could, and would, face down entire Packs. Those confrontations usually ended in the Bear's favor, unless the Pack was particularly large or themselves extremely aggressive.

He chuckled. "Have any ideas what you'd like to do?"

She leaned back and studied him. "Where would you like the tattoo? And what size?" A glimmer of an idea was building inside her. Watching Alex with his family had made her long for things she'd thought she'd never have. She'd dreamed of a roof over her head, food on the table, cubs at her feet and a man by her side who'd love her forever when she ran as a Wolf. Now

Alex was offering her everything she'd ever wanted on a silver platter.

Yeah. She had an idea of what she'd ink onto him. Their hopes and dreams, permanently on his flesh.

He sat up and pulled off his shirt. He pointed to his chest. "Here, and whatever size you'd like."

She ran her hand over the smooth skin, felt his muscles ripple under her hand. Oh, he'd look so good with her ink right there, her signature for anyone to see. "I know what I'm going to do." She handed him a magazine. "Give me about twenty minutes, okay?"

He nodded. "Mind if I put on the radio?"

"Nah, go ahead. Just stay out of the front of the shop. We don't want anyone thinking we're open or wondering if we're being robbed." She grinned at him and headed back through the curtain. She smiled to herself. Cyn obviously hadn't found the ladder yet; the sign she'd tacked up was still there. She sat down at the desk and began drawing.

She drew the outline of her Wolf. The darker and lighter browns would blend together, the colors of her fur melding with his skin. The Wolf would stare out at the viewer with golden brown eyes. She was lying on her side, her expression serene. Behind the Wolf sat Alex's Bear, its massive head dwarfing her Wolf's. The Bear gazed down at the Wolf, his body hovering protectively over hers. Behind them a Wolf cub and a Bear cub frolicked in the mouth of a cave, a den for all of them.

Family. Home. Dreams etched into flesh.

Alex was going to love it.

She took the sketch to him and showed it to him. "What do you think?" He stared at it so long she started to get worried. "Well?"

"I want it in color." His voice was reverent, his finger tracing over first the Wolf cub, then the Bear cub.

Like she would ink it any other way. It was going to look magnificent in full color. "I just need you to do one more thing for me."

"Anything."

The ease with which he said that had her smiling like a love-struck groupie. "Take all your clothes off."

His lips curved up into a wicked smile. "Going to have your way with me?"

Now there's a thought. She shivered. The thought of riding him while he sat in her chair had her nipples hard in seconds. "Maybe, afterwards. But first I need to know what you look like."

One eyebrow rose. "I'd think by now you'd be intimately acquainted with how I look."

She giggled. "I want to see your Bear, you perv."

"Oh," he drawled. He looked up at the ceiling and sighed. "Okay. You asked for it."

She watched him undress, amazed anew at how lucky she'd been in the mate lottery. Alex truly was stunning when naked, all rippling muscle under smooth brown skin. Her fingers twitched. God, he had the best ass.

"Ready?"

She nodded. She was eager to see him, draw him. She wanted *them* on the tattoo, not two random animals.

Alex began to shift. Her eyes grew wide as his body grew, and *grew*. His head easily hit the height of the eight-foot ceiling and he bowed down, landing on his front paws. She figured he had to break the ten-foot mark when upright. As it was, his head was still above her own. "Um. Big."

His head dipped, brushing against her chest. She took the hint and rubbed his massive head. His eyes closed, his chest rumbling, the Bear equivalent of a purr.

"Damn, Alex." His eyes opened and he stared at her. It was hard to read his expression. "You're beautiful." His eyes closed on a sigh. She suspected it was relief.

She ran her hands all over him. She fingered the lethal five-inch claws, giggled at the huge hump of muscle on his back. He sat down, watching her move around him. When she reached his face again, his tongue reached out and ran up the side of her face.

"Blech." She wiped away the Bear drool and picked up her digital camera. She snapped off a shot of him sitting there. The tattoo would show him from the front. "Change back, smart-ass. I have a tattoo to do."

He shifted. "So?"

She frowned absently and used the USB cable to plug the camera into the photo printer. She pressed the button to print out the picture of her Bear. *So what? Ah, there we go.* The picture was almost done. She'd have to make sure no one else saw the image of her Bear sitting in the middle of the tattoo parlor. *Well, maybe I'll show Cyn and Glory.* They'd get a huge kick out of it. "Almost done. Let me make some adjustments to the sketch, make the transfer and we'll get started."

He settled back into her chair, still naked, and watched her while she cleaned off his chest. She shaved off any stray hairs, making sure there was nothing that would interfere with the clarity of the design. She transferred the image to his chest, smiling at the sight. It looked perfect. Tabby mixed her inks and snapped on her rubber gloves. "Ready?"

"C'mere." Alex pulled her down, kissing her so sweetly she damn near melted at his feet. "Mark me, Tabby. Make me yours."

She shivered. She kissed the center of the tattoo. She'd lined it up so that his Bear rested at his heart. "Mine."

He settled back down with a smile and closed his eyes. "Yours."

Tabby picked up her gun, dipped it in the ink, and began to draw.

She hadn't freaked. She'd seen his Bear and, instead of being terrified, she'd been fascinated.

He was such a goner. If he hadn't fallen for her before, he certainly was in love now. She'd reacted with joy, told him he was beautiful, played with his *claws*. No one ever played with his claws.

She'd touched him like he was a treasure. She'd made him hers more thoroughly than any mating mark could.

He'd almost had her move the image so that her Wolf rested over his heart, but changed his mind at the last minute. Bear had led him to his mate. She was healing his heart, and that heart would protect his Wolf with everything in him. Having her image there, below his Bear and his heart, forever protected and loved, was just right.

She was so close to him, her thigh brushed his leg. She hovered over him, her gaze intent on the art she was creating. The sting of the needle was nothing. He watched her etch their love, their life, into his skin and smiled. This was what he wanted, his Wolf, his family, and a home of their own. His cock hardened at the thought of Tabby round with his cubs.

"What are you thinking about?"

He wondered if she'd freak if he told her. "My new ink."

"Which part?"

"The cubs."

The needle didn't stutter. "You're okay with pups?"

"Cubs."

She looked up at him through her lashes. "Pubs?"

He tried not to laugh. "Cups?"

She wrinkled her nose. "I don't think so."

He moved his hand, let his fingers brush her thigh. "Children?"

The needle lifted. Her fingers shook. "Yeah. Children."

For a second, she sounded breathless. He nodded. "I'm okay with it."

"Good." She took a deep breath, her expression once more intent. The needle hit his flesh, the ink sinking into his skin. A deep peace settled over him. Funny. Usually he had to do an hour of yoga and mediation to achieve this level of just...being. He knew it had nothing to do with the tattoo and everything to do with the artist.

For hours, he lay there, watching his mate, his lover, mark their future, the figures taking shape under her skillful hands. Every now and then, he'd smile, visions of what they both needed dancing in his head. He could picture the house he wanted for them, the way he'd come home after a long day and find his mate, all green hair and big sparkling eyes, waiting for him. A warm, loving smile would be on those full pink lips. Maybe they'd both get more ink, maybe they wouldn't. And sometimes he'd be the one standing at the door, waiting for his love, their cubs safely tucked in bed.

It was after midnight by the time she was done. She sat up, set the gun down and stretched. He heard popping noises. She'd been bent over so long her back crackled. "Take a look."

He sat up and stared at himself in the big mirror over her

counter. He kept his hands away, knowing he couldn't touch, but damn if he didn't want to. Her Wolf's eyes practically jumped off his chest. "It's perfect."

He heard her snap off her gloves. "Let's get you covered so we can get out of here."

He turned, smiling when her gaze drifted down to his cock. "See something you want?"

She rolled her eyes but he could see the flush working its way into her cheeks. "You're going to have to be careful with your tattoo. You can't really work up too much of a sweat for at least a few hours. You need to give it time to heal." She frowned. "Wait. Can you heal it?"

He shook his head. "Nope. If I'm not careful, I could cause scarring. I have to let it heal naturally."

"Oh."

He reached down and stroked his erection, loving the way her eyes locked on his hand. "You know, we could always turn up the air conditioning."

"Lie down so I can bandage you, horn dog."

He chuckled and got back into the chair. His erection bobbed against his stomach. "Like this?" He raised his hands up until they clasped the headrest. He spread his thighs and waited to see what she'd do.

"I should have had you put your clothes back on first." She rubbed the ointment into the tattoo with gentle hands, bandaging him up carefully. "You know the drill. You've gotten ink before. No soaking the bandages, mild antibacterial soap for washing, use A&D ointment. No Neosporin or it'll scar."

He nodded. He knew what to do, and if he fouled up, his own little artist would kick his ass to remind him.

"Are you just going to leave me like this?" He waved at his

erection.

She folded her arms over her chest. "What will I get out of it?"

He grinned. "Orgasms. Lots of them."

She bit her lip, looking like a naughty little girl. "If Cyn finds out about this, I'm in so much trouble."

His hips jerked. "We'll clean the place up when we're done." He hadn't actually thought she'd go for it. He figured she'd argue, he'd get dressed and he'd take her back to the hotel room. Having sex in her chair? Talk about a fantasy come true!

Her smile was slow and languid, her eyes heavy with passion. She leaned down and took the head of his cock into her hot, wet mouth. "Oh, fuck." He reached for her head, eager to guide her rhythm just the way they both liked.

"Nuh-uh. Keep those hands up, mister, or this stops."

His hands latched onto the headrest. As far as he was concerned, they were chained there.

"Good boy." She patted his hip and swallowed him down, taking him to the root.

"Oh, shit." He fought to keep still. He didn't want to choke her, but *damn* that felt incredible. He'd never had anyone take him the way she did.

Her head began to bob, her tongue playing his cock like a fucking virtuoso. He lost himself in the sensation of his mate pleasuring him. God, he'd never felt anything quite so good. The cool air of the tattoo parlor blew over him, the pictures on the wall reminding him of the art she'd done on other people. He'd have to get her to take a picture of his new work, add it to the gallery on the wall of her station.

Oh. Oh *hell.* That tongue of hers was a lethal weapon. She lapped at the head of his cock, long, languid strokes, tasting the drops of precome that dripped from him. He clamped down on the headrest, desperate to grab hold of her head and force her to take him all in.

This time it was her space, her show, and he'd be damned if he didn't let her have that.

Tabby sucked him down again, watching his face through the fall of her bangs. He looked so gorgeous with his head thrown back. He was staring at the ceiling, his lips pursed. She wondered if he was doing something to hold himself back, prolong the pleasure. Counting ceiling tiles, maybe?

She wasn't sure if she wanted him to come now or if she wanted him to fuck her. Her hands ran along the insides of his thighs, came to rest at the juncture of his groin. Her fingertips grazed over her mating mark.

She did her best not to give away what she was about to do. He looked so ready to blow. And he was being such a good boy.

She lifted her head and, before he could react, bit down on the mating mark.

He roared and practically levitated off the tattoo chair. Startled, she pulled back.

Bear looked out of Alex's eyes. "Uh-oh." The last time she'd seen that look, he'd bent her over the bed and claimed her most thoroughly. Her pussy clenched in anticipation.

This was going to be fun.

She found herself off the floor and screeched. Alex had her on the counter so fast it was dizzying. Her head hit the mirror, her legs were spread wide and he was ripping at her jeans.

"No! No shredding!" He paused. She had maybe two seconds to come up with something to save her jeans. "You want everyone seeing me bare-assed?"

He growled, the sound low and threatening. She hadn't known it was possible to get even *more* turned on, but fuck that possessiveness of his was hot.

He undid her jeans and slid them down her legs. When he reached her boots he paused, the heat in his expression intensifying. "I love these boots."

Before she could ask what he meant, he was lifting her again. She found herself on her feet, her back to him, her hands clenching the edge of the countertop. Her panties were pulled down, exposing exactly how wet she was. He nipped her ass cheek with sharp teeth before licking a long line between her cheeks. "No lube, so this will have to wait."

She thought about the A&D ointment, but decided against it. She didn't know if it would work or not, and the way he was acting, she'd rather be lubed for the pounding she expected to get.

"God, I love your ass." His hands kneaded the globes. Little nibbling kisses peppered her cheeks. "So beautiful." He gave it one last lick before reaching under the edge of her shirt. "Your back is gorgeous too."

My back? She giggled. No one had ever called her back gorgeous.

He slapped one of her ass cheeks.

"Ow! What was that for?" She scowled at him over her shoulder.

"When I say you're gorgeous, you don't laugh."

He looked dead serious. "Why not?"

He leaned over her, caging her against the countertop, one arm on either side of her. "Because you are."

She shrugged. She knew she was cute on her good days,

but gorgeous?

"Are you calling me a liar?"

She blinked. He sounded almost pissed. "Um. No?"

"Good." He yanked her shirt off, his fingers going to her bra clasp before she could take a breath. "Your back is lean and strong, capable of carrying any burden. Just like you." He undid the clasp and stroked the bra away, his hands hot on her skin. "Your arms can wrap themselves around a Bear most find terrifying and love him until he can't breathe without filling himself with you."

She met his gaze in the mirror. His eyes dared her to lie to him, to tell him it wasn't love.

She nodded. She wouldn't lie to him. Not ever to him.

Some of the anger leached away, warming the dark brown eyes of his Bear. He rested his palm against her chest, nestling it between her breasts. "You've got the most loving heart I've ever been privileged to know. So don't tell me you aren't gorgeous. Everything about you is beautiful."

Damn. He was going to make her cry. "I'm not perfect." She'd screw up, she always did, and if he put her on a pedestal, she'd destroy them both when she fell off of it.

He smiled. "I never said you were. I said you were beautiful. I know the difference." He slid his cock between the folds of her pussy, getting the tip nice and damp. "You're stubborn, but you've had to be to survive. You've got a smart mouth. Sometimes I don't know whether to laugh or fill it full so you'll shut up."

"Hey!"

He laughed softly and began to slide into her, filling her up. His scent surrounded her, making her feel safe and loved. "And I've told you not to wear these boots to work. They scream 'Fuck me'."

"You did not, and they do not." He was all the way inside her now. She bit her lip and moaned at the fullness.

"I want to bend you over every time I see you in them."

She shot him a sultry look in the mirror. He brushed her hair way from her neck and nibbled, his gaze locked on hers. His tongue snaked out and stroked the mating mark.

"I thought I had everything necessary to make me happy. I had a good job, a family who loved me and accepted me. I could go out on my Harley and see the world, and they'd be waiting for me with open arms."

She raised a brow. She had a pretty good idea what he was leaving out. "And all the action you could handle?"

He shrugged. "What do you want me to say?" He thrust, jarring her forward. "Once I saw you, none of it mattered." He thrust again, driving his point home. "Without you, I have nothing."

She reached back and stroked his cheek, smiling when he kissed her palm. "Not true. You have everything I lost."

He began to finger her clit, driving her toward the edge. "Remember explaining red to a blind man? Explain what a mate means to someone who has never had one. Then explain to your mate why you cherish every breath she takes." He licked his mating mark again. "Now explain to your very stubborn mate that she *is* your necessity. Nothing else is worth shit without her."

"Alex." She sighed. She knew what he meant. He was her home, her heart. Her necessity. "I know. Believe me, I know."

He smiled. He understood what she was, and wasn't, saying. He bit down, throwing her over the edge into orgasm.

Her head flew back, her hands clenched the countertop.

She groaned, long and low, the orgasm rippling through her. If he hadn't clamped his hands on her hips at the last moment, she would have hit the floor.

He used that grip to begin truly pounding into her, his point finally made. He hammered her relentlessly, driving her through the orgasm and to the brink of another one.

Holy shit. The man was a machine. How did he keep doing this to her? She'd just had an orgasm so intense she thought her brain might explode, and here he was, pushing her toward another one that felt like it would shatter her world. He kept her pinned in place, his teeth sunk into her neck, his hands dug into her flesh. One of his hands lifted from her hips to tangle in her hair, keeping her head up. She could read what she could see of his face. He wanted her to watch what they did to each other, even if she could only see it from the stomach up.

She didn't need to see much more than that, she could feel it. And oh, how good it felt. She reached down and began to strum her clit, chasing after the orgasm his body promised her. He moaned against her neck, his face grimacing. His fangs sank even deeper into her. She felt the tug on her hair, the pleasure/pain at her throat and exploded around him. It robbed her of breath, her mouth opening on a silent scream, the sensation so intense she almost blacked out.

He lifted his head and groaned. "More."

Oh fuck no. More might kill her.

He licked the blood dripping from her mark. His power filled her, healing the puncture wounds instantly. "Hold on tight."

Hold on? "Whoa!" He lifted her again, keeping her seated on his cock. He managed to get them to her tattoo chair, draping her over it. His hands landed on the padded armrests, using them for leverage.

Gonna have to disinfect the cha-air... He began to fuck her hard, groaning behind her. Her flesh slid on the slick vinyl.

"Come for me."

Nuh-uh. No way. Too much more and she'd pass out for real.

"C'mon, baby. I know you've got it in you." Flesh slapped against flesh, the sound so erotic she could feel her body beginning to respond. "God, I love fucking you. So hot and wet, so tight. Gonna make me come, baby."

Good idea. Tabby hid her face in the chair clenched her muscles, squeezing his cock as hard as she could.

"Oh, *shit*!" Bunny slammed into her and came. His arms strained against the chair. She thought she could hear the sound of metal bending and hoped they weren't about to break anything.

He damn near sobbed as his orgasm drew to an end. "God. Love you, baby."

She smiled. "I know."

He kissed the spot between her shoulder blades. "And?"

"You're not so bad yourself."

"Tabby?"

She could hear the uncertainty in his voice. Even after everything they'd shared tonight, he still doubted? "Love you too."

He sighed. "Thank you. Stubborn woman."

She peeked through the small space where the armrest joined the rest of the chair. "We still need to clean up."

He moved his hips, his cock flexing inside her. "One more for the road?"

She turned her head as much as her position would allow

her and glared up at him.

He lifted off of her. “Fine. But your ass is mine when we get home.”

She couldn’t stop the stupid, silly grin that crossed her face.

Home. She loved the sound of that, even if home right now was a hotel room. And she loved the man who’d given it back to her.

The phone rang at four in the morning. Bunny opened one bleary eye and glared at the nightstand where he’d dropped his cell before collapsing into bed.

“Alex?”

“Shh.” He rubbed Tabby’s back with one hand and snagged his phone with the other. “Go back to sleep, baby.”

“’Kay.” She squirmed, settling back down.

He didn’t even check the caller ID before answering. “’Lo?”

“Alex? It’s Dad.”

“Mm-hmm.” *Wait. Wasn’t he supposed to be with Chloe tonight?* Heart pounding, Bunny sat up. “Chloe?”

“She’s awake, son.”

Yes! “Then it worked?”

“Yup. We owe Julian more than ever.” William chuckled. “Your uncle is considering adoption. Your aunt says it’s a done deal.”

Bunny chuckled. “I wonder how Julian will feel about that.”

“Speaking of which, we tried calling him to make sure he was all right and didn’t get an answer. You mind going to his place and checking on him?”

How the hell had they gotten Julian’s number? Bunny

shook his head. His family had ways of finding things out he still didn't get. "Yeah, no problem. And let Chloe know I'll be there first thing in the morning."

"Will do. Thanks, son."

"Night, dad." Bunny hung up and rubbed his eyes. He'd gotten maybe three hours of sleep, but getting up now would be worth it. Julian had just become a Bunsun-Williams, whether he knew it or not, and the family took care of its own. He got out of bed and reached for his jeans, wincing slightly at the pull of his tattoo.

"Alex?"

Damn. He hadn't meant to wake Tabby. "Go back to sleep, baby."

"Everything okay?"

"Chloe woke up."

Tabby sat halfway up, propping herself on her arms. "Really?"

He nodded and pulled on his pants. "I'm heading out for a little bit. If I'm not back in time for you to head to work, I'll see you at lunch, okay?"

"Will the hospital let you in at this time of night?"

He thought for all of a second about lying to her. "I'm not going to the hospital. The family wants me to check on Julian, make sure he's okay."

She sat up fully. "I'll go with you."

He shook his head. "You have work tomorrow. Besides, if something is wrong I'm a Bear. I can try to heal anything that might be wrong with him."

"He's my friend, I need to be there."

He put his hand on her shoulder and gently pushed her back down. "He's family, and I'll take care of it. If I'm out later than planned, I can always sleep. You have to turn people into living art, remember? You can't do that if you're exhausted."

She blew her bangs out of her eyes. "You'll call me if anything's wrong."

It wasn't a question, but a demand. He nodded. She'd want to know if Julian was all right. "I promise I'll call if I find anything more than Julian sleeping."

She bit her lip and nodded reluctantly. "Okay. Be careful. Whoever attacked Chloe is still out there."

He raised one brow at her.

"I don't care if you are a fucking grizzly. Even you can be taken down with the right hit to the head."

"Yes, Mama." He wondered if she knew that small-caliber bullets would literally bounce off his skull when he was in Bear form?

She shook her head and settled back down. "Please. Take care. For all we know, whoever attacked her is going after your family."

He paused. That thought hadn't occurred to him. He figured it had something to do with Chloe being alone, or being a Fox. Why would anyone go after her for being a Williams? "That makes no sense."

"Your family is well-off. It could have been a kidnapping plot gone wrong."

He shook his head. "No. She was beaten, remember? That speaks of anger." He sat on the edge of the bed.

"You think whoever beat her knew her?"

"Maybe." He rubbed his face. It was too damn early to think, but he had to. If Tabby was endangered because of what had happened with Chloe, he'd never forgive himself. "I'll find out if she remembers anything when I see her later." He pressed a soft kiss to Tabby's forehead. "You go back to sleep. I'm going to finish dressing and get out of here."

"Okay. Take care, sugar."

"Love you, baby."

She smiled sweetly. "Ditto."

He chuckled and stood, buttoning his jeans. "Brat."

"Your brat."

He grinned. He loved the warm feeling he got whenever he realized that, yes, she was his. "Damn straight."

He finished dressing as quietly as he could. He pocketed his keys and phone, threw on his jacket and boots and headed for the door. The fall air would be cold this time of morning. He listened for a moment, reassuring himself that Tabby had gone back to sleep before slipping out of the hotel room. He made his way to the parking lot and started his bike.

It didn't take long to get to Julian's apartment. He wasn't surprised when, at this hour, there was barely any traffic. He pulled into the parking lot and headed for Julian's door.

He reached the door and pulled out his cell phone. He was starting to wake up, thanks to the brisk air. He dialed Julian's number and listened to it ring.

No answer. Shit. He rang the doorbell.

Then he rang it again.

He knocked. Then he pounded. "Shit." Something was wrong.

He called Gabe. The man answered on the second ring, sounding wide awake. He didn't bother with a greeting. "Julian isn't answering his door or his phone. He used his abilities to wake Chloe up, and now I think he's in trouble."

Gabe didn't even hesitate. "I'm on my way."

"I'm breaking in. Don't arrest me."

"You have reason to believe he's in distress. Break away."

Bunny hung up the phone, reared back, and kicked Julian's door in. He found the Bear passed out on the floor.

His hair was completely white.

Bunny ran his hands over his bald head. What the fuck did this mean? Julian's hair should have gone back to black by now. "Shit." He picked Julian up and put him on the sofa. He summoned Bear and settled into the healing spiral. Down he went, deep into Julian's body, looking for any signs of trauma. A side effect would be the partial healing of his own tattoo, but that couldn't be helped. He could only hope that it didn't scar and ruin his mate's beautiful work.

Nothing. Julian was completely healthy and thoroughly unconscious.

He pulled himself back up the healing path, wondering what the hell he should do now. *Wait.* He peered closer at Julian's head and huffed out a relieved breath. Black strands were slowly appearing among the white. The Spirit Bear would be fine.

He sat back and waited for Gabe to arrive.

"Hell. What did you do, rip the door of the hinges?"

Speak of the devil. Bunny grimaced. "Dude in distress, remember? I kicked it in."

Gabe whistled. "I didn't think Bears were *that* strong."

"Black Bears aren't," Bunny muttered. Were Julian's lashes fluttering?

"Right. Grizzly. I keep forgetting that." Gabe propped the broken door in the opening and made his way to the sofa. "How is he?"

"Waking up, I think."

"Why is his hair white?"

"He's Kermode, remember? Their hair does this when they're healing."

"Or spirit-walking," Julian groaned. His eyes opened and Bunny gasped. The man's normally deep brown eyes were a steely gray. "Chloe's awake."

"Yeah. I got the call. The family asked me to come check on you when you didn't answer your phone."

Julian grimaced. "Told them I needed lots of privacy."

"In this family? You'll be lucky if you get to take a piss alone from now on."

Julian frowned. "I'm not family."

Gabe began to laugh. "That's what you think. I just came from the hospital. Trust me, you've been informally adopted. By a bunch of grizzlies, no less."

Julian's eyes went wide. "*Grizzlies?*" He stared at Bunny, his expression a mixture of shock and wicked amusement. "Does Gary know you're a grizzly?"

Bunny smirked. "Not yet."

"Besides, the ones you really need to worry about are the Foxes," Gabe added. "They're sneaky. You'll never see them coming."

Now it was Bunny's turn to laugh. Foxes were notoriously good at hiding their scent. Gabe was right. Julian wouldn't know what hit him if *that* half of the family decided to show up on his doorstep. Uncle Ray, Aunt Laura, Chloe, Tiffany and Heather could be formidable when they banded together. God help him if those four decided Julian needed nursing.

Julian shivered. "Why is it so cold in here?" He looked over at his door and frowned. "What the hell happened to my door?"

Bunny rolled his eyes. Gabe really needed to stop laughing.

"So she's awake?"

"Yup."

"Julian woke her?"

Tabby sighed. Cyn had been up her ass all morning. "Yup."

"And Bunny said he's fine?"

She eyed her boss. "Julian's fine, just very tired." And what an understatement that was. Alex told her that whatever Julian had done to help his cousin had taken a lot out of her friend. He'd stayed awake long enough to "come back completely" (whatever the hell *that* meant) before sleeping again. Alex figured he'd sleep for at least twenty-four hours.

"She. I meant *she*. Chloe's fine, right?"

Tabby hid her face and groaned. "Chloe's awake but she's not fine. She doesn't remember who attacked her."

"Crap." Cyn leaned against the countertop. "What does she remember?"

"She says she thinks she got a phone call from a friend. She was walking to meet the person when bam. Lights out. She woke up in the hospital last night, wondering what the hell happened."

"Shit. So it could have been Gary?"

Tabby shook her head. "I don't think so. Gary hasn't made a move toward anyone but me. He'd have no reason to go after her."

"Does he need one?" Tabby lifted her head, ready to argue the point. Cyn held up her hand, stopping her. "Hear me out. He's an asshat. He doesn't *need* a reason to go after someone he sees as weaker."

"How would Chloe be weaker?"

"She's unprotected, right? Not part of a Pack?"

Tabby snorted. "No Fox is part of a Pack. They live in family groups, remember?"

"No, because, duh, I'm not a member of the furry set. Remember?"

"What happened, couldn't find someone to give you a bite?"

Cyn glowered. "Julian got to them before I did. I went to talk to Chloe's aunt like you told me to. She turned me down."

"Oh." Tabby hid her face again. It wouldn't do to laugh in Cyn's face.

"She told me her *adopted son* would take care of it when the time was right."

Tabby's shoulders shook. She hoped her arms were muffling her laughter.

"What the hell? She told me it wasn't her place to change me and that the *honor* belonged to my *mate*."

"He'd probably prefer it that way, actually."

Cyn growled.

"Seriously." Tabby lifted her head again and let Cyn see the evil grin on her face. "If it's anything like a mating bite then you'll *want* him to do it." She waggled her eyebrows at her friend and waited for the explosion.

"In his dreams!" Cyn stomped toward the back of the shop. "Don't think I won't find a way around this. Fucking asshole. Thinks he can stop *me*, does he?" She eyed Tabby speculatively. "So. Does your offer still stand?"

Tabby groaned. "Julian said if you become Wolf or Puma, your life will be in danger. I *can't*."

Cyn growled.

"Believe me, if I could, I would in a heartbeat. But I'm not willing to risk your life. If Julian's right, you could die, Cyn." Tabby shook her head. Julian was in for an interesting time of it. Cyn had taken it into her head that Julian was holding out on her for no good reason.

"Fine," Cyn ground out between her teeth. "I'll be in the back doing paperwork." She stormed off, and Tabby knew it wouldn't be long before Cyn took matters into her own hands.

Truthfully, Tabby didn't know why Julian was waiting to mark Cyn. Cyn was his mate. He had to have known it for some time. So why was he insisting that they needed to wait? Tabby had wanted to mark Alex the moment she saw him. She couldn't imagine leaving either one of them hanging, especially now that she'd gotten a taste of him.

The bell over the front door jingled. Tabby got off her stool and turned to greet the new customer. Hopefully the customer would take Cyn's mind off becoming a shifter, at least until she could get Julian to explain things to Cyn personally.

"Hello, Outcast."

"Gary." She stepped away from the countertop, her back hitting the wall. Gary was flanked by his two idiot bits of muscle. *Fuck.* He had a baseball bat in his hands.

"C'mon out, Tabby. You know what we want. Give it to us and no one will get hurt." He grinned, his fangs showing. "Especially that pussy mate of yours."

She shuddered. No way was she letting Gary get his hands on her.

"Tabby?" *Aw hell.* Before Tabby could stop her, Glory stepped out from behind the curtain. "Um. Gary. What can we do for you?"

She'd said it just a little too loudly. Gary scowled at her before gesturing to one of his minions. "Get Cyn. I bet she's in the back."

Tabby scooted out from behind the counter. "Leave them alone, Gary."

He smiled, his expression cold. "Now why would I want to do that?"

The two goons laughed. One of them pushed past Glory and headed into the back.

"Get your hands off me!"

Tabby stiffened at the dull sound of a fist landing on flesh. She didn't know if it was Cyn or the goon who'd landed a blow. She hoped it was Cyn. If Cyn got hurt, she had no idea what Julian would do.

Cyn was shoved through the open curtain. Gary's friend took his place next to Gary. Tabby risked looking back. Hell, Cyn had a big red mark on her cheek. Julian was going to flip out.

Glass shattered. Glory shrieked. Tabby turned back to Gary to find him standing over the broken remains of their glass counter, the baseball bat stuck through the metal shell. "Pay attention, bitch!"

Tabby held up her hands. She moved in front of Cyn and Glory, protecting them from the three Wolves menacing them. "You really don't want to do this."

Gary smirked. "You're Outcast. I can do whatever the fuck I want to you." He tilted his head. "We don't want to hurt the little humans too much, though." His grin turned mean. "We don't want to cause trouble."

"I hate to tell you this, son, but you're already in trouble." Gabe stepped into the shop followed by a tall, golden-haired man in a suit. Max Cannon glowered at the three wolves, his gaze raking across the women's faces, assessing the damage.

Oh, thank God, the cavalry is here.

Gabe's hand rested on the gun at his hip. He was in full uniform. "Put the bat down. Now."

Gary glared at Tabby. "I'm Wolf. I have the right to lay claim to the Outcast."

Max chuckled, but there was nothing of amusement in the sound. "In your dreams." He straightened. "You're on my territory, asshole, threatening one of mine. Back off." An invisible wave of power flowed from the man. The strength of the Alpha who stood in the doorway was subtle, but strong, a lot stronger than Tabby's old Alpha. "You don't really want to piss me off, do you?"

Gary's packmates cringed and backed away from the women. Gary merely sneered. "You can't claim the bitch as one of yours. She's a Wolf and an Outcast."

Max Cannon merely lifted one golden brow. "Oh? Why not?"

Gary turned to face the Puma Alpha. "It's against Protocol!"

Max grinned. "In case you hadn't noticed, I'm not a Wolf." He pointed to Tabby, Glory, and Cyn, his gesture encompassing all three of them. "And these ladies are under *my* protection."

Tabby shivered. Something shifted deep within her soul, her Wolf reacting with a mix of confusion and happiness. She'd never felt anything like it before.

Max took a step forward, menace dripping off of him, an Alpha defending his territory. "Do you want to go a few rounds and see which one of us wins?" His eyes had turned from pure crystalline blue to molten gold. Puma eyes. His hands flexed, his claws coming out. "I guarantee you don't."

Gary shook his head, his expression full of disbelief. "You can't do that."

Max cocked his head, his golden eyes narrowed "She's

proven herself to me and, more importantly, to my Second. Who, by the way, happens to be a Hunter."

Gary paled.

Gabe's deep blue eyes had also turned gold. He winked at Tabby over Max's shoulder. "Welcome to the Pride."

She gaped at Max, who nodded, his gaze never leaving the stunned, furious Wolf in front of him. She hadn't even realized what had been missing until Max accepted her. She was part of something again, even if it wasn't a Pack. The deep burden of loneliness that had dogged her steps for years was finally gone. "Thank you."

"You *can't*. You're not a Wolf. You don't have the right to take her in."

Max grinned. His fangs were showing. "You've already pointed out she's Outcast. That means she'd have to prove herself in order to join a Pack. In case you missed it, I just happen to be an Alpha. She's proven herself to me, and now I've chosen to take her in. That makes her mine." In the blink of an eye, Max moved, wrapping his hand around Gary's throat. Tabby could see the little dents in Gary's skin where Max's claws pressed hard enough to leave a mark, but not hard enough to draw blood. "Are we clear?"

Gary gulped. "Yes."

"Yes, what?"

"Yes, *Alpha*," Gary whimpered.

"Good. Now. If I find out you're harassing my Pridemate again, I will kick your ass so hard you'll be eating through your sphincter. Do you understand me?" Max shook him lightly.

"Yes, Alpha Cannon," Gary gritted out through clenched teeth. He'd just acknowledged Max's right to protect Tabby and he didn't look very happy about it.

"And you're paying for the damages to this shop and Cyn's face. Understand, pup?" Mist swirled around Max's feet, almost invisible, but incredibly powerful. Tabby trembled. Her shoulders bowed and her head dropped, Max's power pulling her to her knees. Behind her, Glory and Cyn both groaned, obviously feeling the same effects.

Gary's eyes changed, turning deep brown. Wolf's eyes. He stayed on his feet; he had no choice. Max's claws were still digging into his neck. "Yes, Alpha Cannon."

Max let go slowly, drawing his claws across the outside of Gary's neck. "Now, get out of here before I have Gabe arrest you. Or worse." He tilted his head, his gaze never leaving Gary's face. "What happens to Hunted shifters, Gabe?"

"I'm not Outcast!" Gary's face turned beet red.

"No, but you're bordering on rogue, boy." Gabe took a stance to Max's left, placing himself between the girls and the Wolves. "And rogues are my specialty."

"Go back to school, little boy. If you grow up to be a *real* Alpha, you'll understand what I'm doing here. Until then? Stay out of town. You're not welcome here anymore."

"You might want to consider going to another school. Maybe one closer to home?" Gabe frowned. "Who *is* your Alpha, anyway?"

Gary gulped. "We're leaving." He scrambled out the door, dragging his friends with him.

Gabe shook his head, glaring at the trio rushing down the street. "What the *hell* is going on?"

"I have no idea, but I plan on finding out." They exchanged a look before Max turned to the girls. "You three okay?"

"One of them hit Cyn." Tabby lifted her head and took her first real breath since Gary had entered Living Art. Max had reined in his power. She could stand again. She rose, grimacing at the sounds of broken glass underfoot.

Glory groaned, staring at the shattered glass counter. “Hell. We can’t open for business like this. Somebody will get hurt.”

“How did you know that you could make me Pride?” Tabby was still stunned. She was part of something again. She hadn’t even realized how tense she’d been until Max accepted her into his Pride. She felt so loose, so relieved, she was dizzy with it.

Max shrugged. “I didn’t. I just know Rick’s Luna is a Puma, and she’s now part of his Pack. I was hoping you wouldn’t need a Puma mate for it to work.”

Tabby paled. “What would have happened if it hadn’t worked?”

Max grinned. “You’d still be under my protection until Rick arrives.”

Arrives? “Um. The Poconos Alpha is coming?” Tabby backed away, bumping into Cyn and Glory.

“Ow. Shit. I can’t believe that asshole punched me.”

Tabby turned, thoughts of the scary Wolf Alpha driven from her mind. “Oh crap. Cyn, you okay?”

“Let me see.” Max walked around her to help Cyn and Glory to their feet. His fingers lightly stroked the red, swollen flesh. “You’ve got one hell of a bruise.”

“Ow.” Cyn winced, pulling away from Max’s fingers. “That mutt is going to pay for this.”

“Let us deal with it.” Gabe picked up a piece of art, placing it on a stool near the shattered counter.

“Change me so I can deal with it myself! I’m sick and tired of the Fuzzy Club traipsing in and out of my place and wrecking my life!”

Max chuckled. “I heard that a certain Bear had it in mind

to take care of that himself."

Cyn screamed. Everyone stared at her, shocked. "Does *everyone* know about this but me?"

Max backed up, his eyes wide. "Maybe we should just go now."

Gabe backed up right along with his Alpha. "Good idea." The two men fled, heading in the opposite direction from Gary.

"Cowards!" Cyn shouted after them.

Glory giggled. "You just scared off one of the most powerful men in town."

Cyn wrinkled her nose. "He may be an Alpha, and he may be powerful, but deep down inside? He's still a *man.*" She kicked a piece of glass across the floor. "Put a pissed-off woman in front of him and he runs like the yellow-bellied coward he is."

Tabby's jaw dropped. "You *have* met Max's wife, right?"

Glory was laughing so hard Tabby wasn't certain she was breathing.

Cyn rolled her eyes. "C'mon, let's get this cleaned up before The Three Bears show up. God knows which of us will have to play Goldilocks if they do."

"Want me to have Julian look at that bruise?"

The glare Cyn shot at her should have turned her into a pile of ash.

Watching her two friends get mated was going to be so much fun!

She took the broom Cyn handed her and sighed.

Yeah. Fun.

Chapter Eight

"Well?"

"Nope. Nothing."

Bunny sighed. Ryan was even more frustrated than he was. He'd dragged his cousin out of the hospital for lunch, hoping to get the man to relax. Hell, he'd even let Ryan have all the cantaloupe this time.

If Ryan clenched that fork any tighter, he'd bend it right in half.

Yup. This is working out well. His cell phone rang. "Tabby?" He winced. He'd meant to pick her up for lunch, but he'd gotten sidetracked. "I'm sorry, baby. I forgot. I took Ryan to lunch."

"That's not why I called." She paused. "Well, okay, that's *one* reason."

Bunny frowned. She sounded shaken. "What happened?"

"Couple of things. Don't freak out."

Okay, those three words had him on his feet, reaching for his jacket. "Tabby. Tell me."

"Gary came to the shop. There's some damage but no one was seriously hurt."

Bunny growled. He gestured to Ryan. "Gary was at the shop."

Ryan was on his feet in two seconds flat. He dropped some

twenties next to their half-eaten food and they raced for the door.

"You all right?"

"Yeah. Max and Gabe showed up and rescued us."

Bunny slowed down. If the Puma Alpha and Second had been there, he doubted Gary got much more than threats out. "Anyone hurt?"

"One of Gary's minions landed a blow on Cyn, but she'll be all right."

"You called Julian yet?"

"I've been ordered not to."

But she hadn't been ordered not to tell Bunny. "Good girl."

"Thanks. I'm not supposed to tell Ryan either."

He laughed. "Too late. We're headed your way." He put his hand over the receiver. "They're fine. Gabe and Max rode to the rescue."

Ryan straddled his bike and reached for his helmet. "Good. But I'm still heading over there."

"I know. Let me call Julian. Cyn's the only one who got hurt, but the girls are pretty shaken up."

Ryan nodded and strapped on his helmet.

"We're on our way, baby. Need us to pick anything up for you?"

"Lunch would be good."

He winced at the amusement in her voice. "Sorry."

"It's okay." She sighed dramatically. "You forgot me. I understand."

He could feel himself blushing. Damn it. How did she keep doing that to him? "Pizza good?"

"Works for us. Oh, and make sure there's at least one meat

lovers, extra bacon, okay?"

"Done. We'll be there as soon as we can."

"Love you."

"Love you too." He waved Ryan off before dialing Julian's number.

"'Lo?"

He didn't bother with any preliminaries. Julian sounded really out of it. "Gary attacked Cyn. She's okay, but we're heading over to Living Art to check on her."

No response.

"Julian?"

"When you finally face him, make sure you give him a swipe from me."

"So you think he'll go after them again?"

Julian sighed. "Let's just say I don't see any other possibilities."

"Are you heading to the shop?"

"Does a bear shit in the woods?"

Bunny laughed shortly. "Meet you there." He clicked shut his phone, called Lou's Pizza and ordered three larges. He straddled his Harley and started off, wondering what else had Tabby upset. More than Gary's visit was bothering her. She'd sounded...excited. And he bet that Max and Gabe were the source of that excitement. Maybe Gabe had something on Gary, or would be able to get a warrant now that the man had vandalized the shop and harassed Cyn. He sort of understood why the sheriff hadn't arrested him on the spot. Putting a shifter into a human jail was always problematic. Still, knowing Gary and his friends were locked up, even overnight, would go a long way toward easing his mind.

Hell, at this point he bet all of them could use a break. He'd help the girls get the shop cleaned up and locked up for the day. Then he was going to take Tabby house hunting.

He arrived at Living Art with the pizzas, a plan already forming. All thoughts flew right out of his head when he saw the shattered glass countertop with the baseball bat stuck in it. “Son of a bitch.”

“That’s what I said.” Ryan’s jaw was clenched so hard Bunny was surprised his teeth hadn’t snapped off.

“We’re fine.”

Ryan glared down at Glory. “He attacked you.”

She shrugged. She was doing her damndest to look nonchalant but Bunny could see the way she was shaking. “He attacked Cyn and Tabby. I was along for the ride.”

Ryan took a deep breath. Then he took another one. Bunny could see his Bear shifting under his skin, dying to get out, hunt down the man who’d dared threaten his mate, and tear him to pieces. “I’m going to fucking kill him.”

“Get in line.” Julian stepped into the chaos. Silver still peppered his hair, and his dark eyes sparkled with gray lights. “Where’s Cyn?”

Glory inched away from Ryan and earned herself a low growl. “She said she was going out for a bite.”

The three men froze. “She wouldn’t.” Bunny stared at the curtained-off area, wondering if she’d really be that stupid.

“She would.” Julian walked around him, his gait still unsteady. “Where’s Tabby?”

“She left. She said she had to make sure Cyn didn’t do anything stupid.” Glory frowned, staring at the three groaning men. “What?”

“Did you think she was going out for lunch?”

“Well, yeah.” She blinked up at Ryan. “Wasn’t she?”

"Shit. You think she went to Aunt Laura?"

Ryan shrugged. "She did before. Mom told her no, that it was up to Julian to do the honors."

Julian groaned. "Crap." He ran his fingers through his hair. "This keeps getting better and better."

"We'll find her, Julian."

"And then I'm going to tie her fine ass down and mark her." Julian stomped out of the store.

"I thought you said it wasn't time?" Bunny shouted after him.

"Yeah, well, the timetable just got screwed all to hell and back."

Bunny chuckled. Tabby would try to keep Cyn from doing anything stupid, but still. Maybe Glory knew something about what was going on. "Do you know where the two of them went?"

"I think Cyn said something about talking to Emma."

The two Bears exchanged another glance. "You think Emma would do it?" Ryan shifted next to Glory, boxing her in. She glowered up at him.

"I don't know her well enough to say." They'd only met the petite Curana the other day, but her power was undeniable. Bunny didn't think Emma would do something she'd been specifically asked not to, but with an Alpha female, you could never tell.

"Maybe you'd better follow him, then."

"Yeah. Ryan, stay here, help Glory clean up. I'll get Cyn and Tabby back here in one piece." He held up his finger, stopping Glory's automatic protest. "Do this, please. It will ease Tabby's mind to know that someone is watching over you."

She snapped her mouth closed. Her sigh sounded so put-upon, he almost laughed. "Fine. The furball can stay."

"Gee, thanks." Ryan rolled his eyes. "Take care of them. I'll call Mom and Dad and let them know what's going on."

Bunny waved and headed out, leaving the cooling pizzas on a stool. He hoped Glory was hungry. He had the feeling he wouldn't be back before they'd turned stone-cold.

"C'mon, Cyn. You know Julian is going to turn you. Can't you just wait?"

Cyn turned on her. They were only half a block from Wallflowers, the curio shop Emma co-owned with her Beta, Becky. It was the closest she'd been able to park. "Do you know why I'm not sitting around waiting for him?"

Tabby bit her lip. No, she didn't, but now that Cyn was talking, she wasn't going to interrupt her and risk her shutting up. Cyn rarely talked about why she did things, she just did them.

"My mom always waited for my dad. Always. To the point where she didn't fucking *sneeze* without his say-so. She let him make all the decisions, run her life for her. And after he died, she was fucking *lost*. She could barely function without him there."

"Cyn. How do you think I'd feel if I lost Alex?"

Cyn blinked. "That's different."

"Maybe. I'd be able to function if I survived. I know I can take care of myself. I've proven that."

"What do you mean, if you survived it?"

Tabby winced. "Most mates don't survive the death of their partner."

Cyn's jaw dropped. "Seriously? Your lives are tied together?"

"Duh. That's what mates are, Cyn. We're two halves of a whole. If half your body died, if half your heart stopped beating, what would happen to you?"

Cyn's jaw snapped shut. She looked freaked out. "Huh. Maybe this whole mating thing isn't such a hot idea."

"And maybe this is exactly why Julian chose to wait. You need to be certain it's what you want before you tie your life force to him."

Cyn stepped closer, lowering her voice. "You wanted this? You wanted your life tied to someone else's?"

Tabby nodded. "It's the most incredible feeling I've ever had. I'd gladly do it all over again if it meant I get to keep Alex." She put her hand on Cyn's arm. "He's my home, Cyn."

"Whoa." Cyn's shocked expression faded. She knew exactly how much home meant to Tabby. "So if he left Halle?"

"I'd be on the back of his bike, *after* I got a very good reason for the move out of him." Tabby grinned. "Mate doesn't mean doormat, Cyn."

She nodded slowly. "I'll have to think about this." She took a step back and turned on her heel. "But I'm still talking to Emma."

Tabby groaned. "C'mon, Cyn. Alex was bringing pizza, damn it!" Her stomach rumbled. She was *starving.*

Cyn laughed and opened the door to Wallflowers.

"Good afternoon, ladies. How can I help you?" Becky Holt rose from the Victorian, cream-colored sofa with a smile. This was the first time Tabby had been in Wallflowers and she looked around with interest.

Wallflowers was a business that catered to people who enjoyed hand-crafted, artisan-made pieces. The eccentric store carried hand-carved cuckoo clocks, paintings, old-fashioned mirrors, masks, plaques...anything that could be used to decorate a wall. An antique rug covered the distressed hardwood floors. A small Victorian sofa covered in soft cream brocade graced the center of the floor. A Queen Anne coffee table in rich cherry wood sat before it, bearing a silver tea service. Two matching chairs in that same cream fabric faced the sofa, creating an inviting little conversation group. Against one wall was a gas fireplace with an ornately carved mantelpiece, where black-and-white and sepia photos were displayed in silver frames. A cherry and glass counter, as Victorian as they could make it and still have it be functional, graced one wall, with an antique cash register.

Emma and Becky had created an atmosphere of a bygone era, and the shop was warm and inviting. A fire crackled merrily in the fireplace on this cool September afternoon, the light glinting off lovely cherry-wood wainscoting. Rich rose floral wallpaper warmed the walls above it. It was very feminine, and both women obviously loved it. Tabby could see herself spending time here, enveloped in the welcome Emma and Becky exuded to everyone who entered.

"I'm here to talk to Emma. Is she here?" Cyn cocked her hip and flipped her dark hair behind her. To anyone who didn't know her, she looked singularly unimpressed, but Tabby had seen the way her dark eyes gleamed at the sight of that beautiful cherry-wood counter.

Becky's smile wavered as she stared at Cyn's battered face. Her eyes narrowed. "What happened?"

"Nothing. I just want to talk to her about a bite. I'm Cyn Reyes. I own Living Art Tattoos."

The two women stared at one another for a moment before Becky sighed. "Is this about the problems with Gary or the fact that you're mated to one of the Bears?" She turned to Tabby when Cyn's jaw dropped. "What's his name?"

"Julian," Tabby supplied. She ignored Cyn's glare, smiling at the Beta. *Her* Beta, now that Max had accepted her into the Pride.

"Huh. Simon mentioned something about that." Becky tapped her teeth with her nail. "And I think Emma said something about leaving that up to your mate."

Cyn shifted and her lips tightened. That Latina temper was getting the better of her again.

Becky laughed. "Hey, if it were up to me, you'd have the right to choose. I didn't get that right and neither did Emma."

"So you didn't want to be changed or mated?" Cyn pounced on the Beta's words with childish glee.

Becky laughed. "Oh, hell yes, I wanted it. I just wanted to choose *when*."

Tabby laughed. "See? I told you it's not that bad."

Becky's slow smile was wicked. "Nope. Not bad *at all*. And having your mate change you makes it even more special. Emma and I were both human when Max and Simon marked us. They'd been changed by the old Alpha, Jonathon Friedelinde, and from what Simon said, he wishes it had been a little bit different."

"Why?"

Cyn had a good question. Tabby hadn't met a made shifter before. Her old Alpha wouldn't allow it, except between mates.

"The mating bite masks the pain of the shifting bite. The only other human I know of who was changed by a non-mate is Sheri Giordano, and she had been beaten nearly to death. She still bears the scars of the fight she had with a rogue Wolf." Becky's hand drifted up to her neck. Tabby knew she had a set of scars there from her own run-in with a rogue. "It can be done, and has been done, but I for one would rather have pleasure than pain. I don't like pain. It hurts me."

"Becks? Who are you talking to?" Emma walked in from the back room, her brown eyes twinkling merrily until she caught sight of Cyn's face. "Cyn! Tabby! How are you? Oh, your poor face!"

Tabby bowed her head in respect to her Curana. "Emma."

Emma's eyes widened. "It's true. Max accepted you into the Pride." She laughed, the sound loud and merry. "Rick is going to shit a brick."

"*Emma!*" Becky rolled her eyes. "Ugh. Ignore her. Listen, Cyn? I'm going to get you some ice for that cheek, okay? Have a seat, I'll be right back."

Cyn sat. "Thanks."

"Rick should be here in a day or two." Emma smiled gently at Tabby. "Did you think I was going to leave you an Outcast?"

Tabby shuddered. She did *not* want to meet the Poconos Alpha or his Luna!

Becky returned with the ice pack and handed it to Cyn. "Put that on your face. Do you need some ibuprofen?"

Cyn shook her head no, her eyes darting around the shop.

Tabby leaned closer to Becky and whispered, "How the heck do I get out of meeting Rick Lowell?"

Emma snorted and handed a glass and two pills to Cyn. "Take that, no arguments. You need to go to the hospital?" Cyn shook her head again and swallowed the pills, looking stunned. "And you!" She pointed to Tabby. "Rick isn't that bad. And Belle is going to *love* you."

Tabby was horrified. "That's what I'm afraid of. Would she prefer my ass with A-1 or Heinz 57?"

"Wuss," Emma coughed into her fist. She laughed when

Tabby blew her a raspberry. “I mean it. Rick really isn’t as bad as he’s made out to be. He just *looks* scary.”

“I’m a Pride member though, right? He can’t make me go away?”

Emma’s expression softened. “No, Tabby. No one can make you go away now except you.”

“Okay. Wow.” Tabby blinked away the tears that sprung up out of nowhere. God, she was turning into such an idiot. “Thank you.”

“The worst Rick could do is decide he wants nothing to do with you, and knowing him, that won’t happen. Be honest with him, about everything. He’ll treat you fairly, I swear.”

Tabby bowed her head again. “Yes, Curana.”

“Cyn?”

Tabby flinched. Julian had found them.

“What?”

Cyn’s belligerent tone wasn’t a surprise to Tabby, but from the shocked looks on Emma and Becky’s faces, it was to them.

His eyes flashed at the sight of her bruised face. “Do you want to talk about this?”

“What’s to discuss? You made a decision about my life without bothering to… What’s wrong with your hair?”

Tabby turned. Fully half of Julian’s hair was still white. Gray lights danced in his eyes. Whatever he’d done to help Chloe, he wasn’t fully back from it. He looked exhausted, otherworldly. “The healing was more difficult than I anticipated. She was farther into the dreamscape than I’d originally thought.”

Huh? “What the hell does that mean?”

Julian smiled at her. “Don’t worry about it.” He turned his attention back to Cyn. “Let me heal that. Please?”

Tabby grabbed hold of Cyn's arm. "Please let him, Cyn."

"All right." She handed the ice pack to Becky and moved toward Julian.

The man was shaking, whether with exhaustion or rage, Tabby couldn't quite tell. His eyes were still deep, dark brown, but those silver flecks were throwing her off.

His fingers drifted across Cyn's face. The white in his hair deepened, the bruise disappearing under his hand. The swelling went down, the black and blue turning a healthy pink.

When he was done, he was shaking like a leaf.

"Wow," Emma breathed. Tabby was pretty sure it was the first time the woman had ever been shocked speechless.

"I know you don't trust me. I was hoping to give us both some time, get to know one another before I changed you. Is that such a bad thing?"

Cyn shrugged, looking uncomfortable. "You also said it wasn't time yet. Can you please explain that to me?"

His eyes closed wearily. "I...know things. It's part of who and what I am, but what I see is incomplete. All I know is that if I change you before it's the right time, there will be serious repercussions."

"What kind of repercussions?"

He opened his eyes. Something in his expression sent a shiver down Tabby's spine, and suddenly she knew why Julian had been holding off on marking Cyn. "Neither of you will survive."

Julian nodded. "It's coming soon. I can't see what's going to happen, but I know that a decision must be made that will change everything." He held out his hand to Cyn. "Please. Trust me."

Cyn studied Julian. Tabby couldn't read her expression. It

was closed off, introspective. She figured Cyn must be weighing her own past against what she saw of her friends' future. "Give me one thing. One piece of information I don't know. Everything I've learned about you, about *us*, I've had to hear from other people. Give me something of yours."

Julian lowered his hand. "I'm not sure I'll survive what's coming next."

Cyn took a deep breath and nodded. "That's the reason you haven't *marked* me?" She made little quotations with her fingers.

"One of them, yes."

She took her eyes off of him. Her foot started to tap. "You were trying to save my life." She glared at him. "We're going to have a nice, long chat about what you should and should not hide from me. Understand?"

He nodded. Whether or not he agreed with it, Tabby had no clue.

"All right. You do what you have to and I'll do the same."

"If you become Puma or Wolf, you'll lose your life."

He sounded so certain, Tabby couldn't doubt him. "Cyn, you should wait."

She nodded. "I'm not an idiot." She turned back to Julian. "Give me reasons why you want things from me. I'm a lot more likely to listen to that than some bullshit about not being ready. Got it?"

He nodded again.

"I will deal with you later." He opened his mouth to speak, but Cyn held up her hand, stopping him. Tabby could tell she was still furious, that Latina temper still riled. "I have to go clean my shop. Tabby, do me a favor. Make sure he gets home. He looks half-dead."

"We can drop you off first."

Cyn smiled. "I could use the walk." She headed for the door, making sure to avoid touching Julian on her way out. "Bye, Emma. Bye, Becky."

The women echoed her goodbye and watched her through the plate glass window. Julian kept his back to the door, his expression blank. Tabby knew he was hurt by Cyn's rejection.

"Well. That was fun. Not." Emma shook her head, her hands on her hips. "Someone needs to give her a time-out. Maybe a nap."

Tabby started to laugh. Julian rolled his eyes. "I'll take care of her, don't worry."

"Whether she likes it or not?"

Tabby jumped to her friend's defense. "She doesn't think she needs taking care of. She's got reasons for why she's acting the way she is. I know some of them, but not all of them. Emma, remember what you told me about Rick, that I should be honest with him and tell him everything? Julian, that's what you need to do with Cyn. She sort of had a mushroom childhood."

"A what?"

"She was plunked down in the dark and fed a lot of bullshit."

"Oh. Yeah, that would do it." Emma waved. "Listen, I have inventory to sort out. I'll talk to all of you later. And Tabby? Be available when Rick gets here, okay?" Before Tabby could protest, Emma was back through the curtain, effectively cutting her off.

"Nice exit." Tabby turned back to Julian. He was smiling. More of his hair was its natural black. Very little could keep Julian down for long, not even rejection from his mate. Tabby bet he was already figuring out ways to get around Cyn's temper.

"She's good at those." Becky settled back down on the couch. "Crisis over?"

"For now," Julian said. He gave Tabby a long look. "We need to talk."

"Ugh. More talking? I'm all talked out. How about hunting?"

Julian's expression blanked. "Hunting?"

"No lunch. The pizza's probably long cold by now and Alex already ate without me."

"He wouldn't want you out there by yourself."

She grinned. "I won't be. You'll be with me." She reached up and patted his cheek. "Couldn't you go for a nice warm rabbit right about now?"

"Fine, but you're letting him know where we are."

"Can do. C'mon, let's go. I'm dying for a good run."

"Amen." Julian shuddered all over. "I'd love to get into my fur."

"Then it's a done deal." She knew just the place to take him, too. Far enough away from the college that Gary couldn't give her grief without disobeying the local Alpha, yet close enough that she wouldn't have to drive into the next town over just to avoid the college. She waved bye to Becky and dragged Julian out of the store. "C'mon, the car's this way."

Julian's smile turned grim. "Of course it is."

She stopped. "Uh-oh. Why do I have the feeling this is one of those I-know-something-you-don't-know moments?"

Julian stopped. "You're taking me into the woods northeast of Halle, the ones farthest from the college. We'll change, run, and Gary will be there. We'll fight. I'm pretty sure you'll survive."

Tabby blinked. "How the *fuck* does Gary know we're going running? We just decided that!"

"He doesn't. He's deliberately ignoring Max's direct order to stay on the college campus. Why, I have no idea, but there it is."

Shit. "Okay, maybe Burger King for lunch." Or maybe they could go in a completely different direction, like right behind the campus?

He shook his head and grabbed her arm. "If we don't do this now, people will die."

Well, shit. "Where's Alex?"

Julian shook his head. "I don't know. I don't know anything after..."

Oh. Oh shit.

After he's dead.

She pulled out her cell phone and handed it to Julian. "Start dialing."

He looked startled, but only for a moment. He began to punch in numbers, his face tight. "Bunny? Meet Tabby and me in the woods northeast of Halle. We're going hunting." He winced and pulled the phone from his ear. Tabby could hear Alex roaring on the other end. "Listen to me! It's *important.*" The commanding tone was back in Julian's voice. On the other end of the line, Alex stopped roaring. "I had a vision. You need to meet us there. Got it?"

"Got it," she heard Alex rumble. She unlocked the doors of the Jeep and settled in, buckling her seat belt. Julian joined her and she started the engine. "Keep her safe, Julian."

"I'll do my best."

She took off with a squeal of tires, heading for the outskirts of Halle.

"Do better."

She felt a grim smile flirting around her mouth. Her big, overprotective Bear was having a fit that he wasn't the one there to protect her.

"We'll be in those woods in about twenty minutes. Get there as fast as you can." Julian hung up the phone and placed it on her console.

She blinked. "That's it? Alex is our only reinforcement?"

Julian smiled, one of those enigmatic expressions she was beginning to realize meant he knew more than he was willing to share. "Everyone else will come when needed. I know that much."

"Okay." She wasn't certain a few well-placed phone calls wouldn't be better, but she had to trust that Julian knew what he was doing.

"Ryan, we gotta go."

"No." Ryan's eyes hadn't left Glory once. They'd remained a deep chocolate brown the entire time. "You go. I need to stay and protect my mate."

"I don't need protection!" Glory gritted through clenched teeth.

Bunny agreed. "She's right. Julian had a vision. He and Tabby are headed into the woods, and I think they're going after Gary. They need us. Glory doesn't."

Glory's eyes narrowed. "And you are *not* leaving me behind while my friend is in danger."

"You want to come?"

She opened her mouth to answer and saw the smirk on Ryan's face. "I want to *go* with you. Asshole."

He threw his head back and laughed. "You aren't going anywhere."

"Says who?"

"Says me. Gary might have more friends we don't know about. I'm not leaving you unprotected."

Glory's pixie face turned grim. "Your cousin's mate is in danger. You could solve your problem by putting me on the back of your bike and taking me with you, thus protecting *both* of us. You'll know where I am even while you fight." She suddenly glared up at him. "And if you think you can keep me locked up in here while Tabby's in trouble, you're sorely mistaken. I *will* figure out a way out of here and when I do I will make your life a living hell." She reached up and yanked on his shirt, bringing the much larger man down to her. Bunny knew Ryan allowed it, if he'd wanted she'd have a better chance of lifting herself off the floor that way than dragging him down. "Do we understand one another?"

Ryan pretended to think about it. "Define living hell."

She snarled at him. "Have you ever had Icy Hot smeared inside your jock strap?"

His expression blanked. "Um. Yes. That would be a version of hell."

They didn't have time for this. "We have to go now, people."

Ryan sighed. "You stay where I put you, Glory." When she went to argue, he covered her mouth with his hand, a hand that took up almost half her face. "I mean it. You aren't in any way ready to get into a shifter battle. I can't fight and protect you at the same time. Got it?"

She nodded.

"Get the keys to the shop and start locking up."

She ran into the back room.

"You always meant to take her." Bunny was sure of it. His stubborn cousin had given in way too easily.

Ryan shrugged. "I need her to start trusting me. If giving her this helps, then fine. But understand, she's my first priority. Any sign she's in trouble or distress and I'm done."

Bunny nodded. He understood. He felt the same way about Tabby.

"Let's go." Glory somehow managed to both stomp and drift out of the room. It was amazing. Bunny figured it had something to do with the wispy, gypsy-like clothes she favored.

"You heard the woman. Let's go." Ryan followed Glory out the door, Bunny leading the way.

He hoped the Pumas understood how badly he wanted to end this thing with Gary. If the Wolf laid one paw on Tabby, he was going to wind up a rug.

Tabby got out of the Jeep and began undressing. You couldn't change in clothes; you'd get tangled up in them. Rumor had it that Emma's first change had happened that way, although the details were sketchy and she tended to yowl whenever her mate brought it up. She folded her clothes neatly and laid them on the passenger seat.

"Here."

She turned to take Julian's clothing and faced him naked for the first time.

Dayum. The boy was *fine*. She eyed him up and down, wolf-whistling at him. Smooth skin glided over defined muscle. Well-defined pecs without a trace of hair drifted down to a washboard stomach and a cock that, even with her limited experience (and his limited interest), still managed to look impressive. His legs were long and lean. Hell, even the man's feet were sexy. Julian had the build of a runner, strong and sleek. Alex was built more like a body builder or wrestler. She could very easily see Cyn totally losing it when she finally got Julian naked.

He waggled his eyebrows, a cheeky grin crossing his face. "You're not bad yourself."

She eyed him appreciatively. "Cyn is in a hell of a lot of trouble."

Some of the amusement left his face. "Yeah. If I get out of this."

She could sense his nerves and his determination. Whatever was going to go down was inevitable now. She would do everything she could to see that Julian came out of this alive. "Let's change."

He nodded, and began to shift.

Watching another person shift shape was incredible. There was no blinding flash of light and bam, you had a bear. Nor was there the sound of crunching, grinding bones and sizzling agony seen in horror films. It was more like watching water flow through the person, moving them, bending them, blending them with their animal in a liquid haze of a dream until the man was gone and only Bear remained. She knew if she'd touched him during his shift all she would have felt was warmth, the comforting presence of man and beast flowing through her fingers. Anyone looking on from the outside would assume the feeling would be wet or slimy, but it wasn't. It was airy and tingled in her palms. It was sensual and innocent in a way a non-shifter could never understand.

When Julian was done shifting, she got her first good look

at a Kermode Bear. He was almost pure white, with a smattering of light gold fur at his shoulders and along his back. He had a thick, stubby tail and a long snout with a black nose. He had the general shape of a black bear with his rounded ears and sleek body, unlike Alex's more blunted face, heavy ruff and humped, muscled back. He was easily a few feet shorter than Alex's Bear. Make his fur black instead of white and he'd look right at home in these woods.

Julian grumbled at her. He wanted her to call her Wolf. With a smile, she allowed the change, pulling her Wolf to the front, more than ready to run on four paws. She lifted her nose to the breeze, catching the faint scent of rabbit, mouse, and the occasional deer.

No sign of Gary or his friends. Not yet, anyway.

The big white Bear sat back and began rolling on the ground, a strange sound coming from him. If she didn't know better, she'd swear he was laughing at her. She yipped at him, dancing around him, eager to get him moving.

Julian got up and shook his head, swiping his tongue along her ear. He made that strange sound one more time before settling his weight on all fours, waiting for her to lead the way.

With a flick of her muzzle she pointed toward the north. Julian nodded his great white head and followed her. She kept the pace easy for him, unsure how much energy he would need in the coming battle.

And, from the prickling of her ears, the battle was almost upon them, with or without Gary's scent.

He saw her Jeep, but not her. Damn it. She should have waited for him before heading off on her own. God knew what kind of trouble she'd get into before he found her. Fuck the fact that Julian was with her, *he* needed to be the one protecting her.

Bunny tried his best to still his growing anxiety. He didn't know if she'd run into Gary yet or not, but from here on out they were moving silently, leaving the bikes behind. The sound of their Harleys would alert Gary to their presence, and they definitely didn't want to do that. If they were lucky, they'd catch up to Gary before he did any damage. If they could get him to the Alpha and prove he'd disobeyed a direct command from the local authorities, he'd be banished from Halle, possibly even disciplined by his own Pack Alpha. Bunny could only hope so.

He parked the bike next to Tabby's SUV and stopped the engine. "Ready?"

Ryan pulled off his helmet and dismounted. "Just a minute." He held out his hand for Glory's helmet. Her pale blue hair tumbled down to her waist. From the dazed expression on her face he'd say she'd never ridden a motorcycle before. Either that or she'd always remained on tarmac. The drive through the woods had been rough. "You okay?"

"I think my tailbone is broken." She got off with a wince, shaking out her filmy skirts. "Well, damn. You broke my ass."

Ryan stopped her. "You stay where I put you, right?"

She glared at Ryan and slammed the helmet into his stomach. He coughed out a surprised breath. "Let's go, Teddy."

Before they could start off, another motorcycle pulled up next to them. Bunny grinned. He recognized the bike. "Hey, Dad."

Ryan waved. "Hey, Uncle Will."

"Boys." His father got off the bike, his hazel eyes somber, his dark hair ruffled by the breeze. "I understand you might need some...help?" He frowned at Glory for a moment before a big grin crossed his face. Bunny bet it was the powder blue curls.

"Julian called you?"

William shrugged, his attention diverted from Ryan's mate. "Not sure you could call it that, exactly. Let's just say I was sleeping and I had a dream that I should head over this way. So here I am."

"Bear is looking out for us," Ryan said solemnly. Bunny nodded, agreeing. Only Bear himself could have sent his father that vision.

"Anyone want to fill me in?"

"Gary is somewhere in these woods. So are Tabby and Julian."

William growled, the sound low and fierce. "He's going after my daughter-in-law?"

"They're not married."

All three Bears turned and stared at Glory.

She crossed her arms defiantly over her chest. "They're not."

"She's right. We're mated. That's much more permanent than marriage." Though, if Tabby wanted to go through a ceremony, he'd be proud to stand up in church and recite his vows. In fact, the more he thought about it, the more he considered insisting on it. It would be one more way to make it known she belonged to him.

Ryan rolled his eyes. "C'mon, Glory. Let's go." He took hold of her arm, ignoring her attempt to pull away from him. Bunny was pretty sure the attempt was automatic at this point. "They went that way."

"Mm-hmm." He looked into the Jeep and saw two piles of clothes. "And they shifted." His eyes darkened. He did *not* like the thought of his Tabby seeing any male but him naked. He didn't care that in the Packs and Prides nudity meant nothing during a shift. It meant something to *him*, dammit. His father never allowed his mother to run around naked, that was for sure.

Of course, she laughed at his growls and did what she damn well pleased, but his father didn't exactly *allow* it.

"Follow me." Ryan led the way, Glory stomping in her delicate looking boots right by his side.

Bunny hid a smile. Something told him she'd give his cousin hell, but in the end she'd be just what he needed.

Tabby growled. The son of a bitch had stayed downwind. He was still in human form, but he was naked and ready to shift at any moment.

"Wow, what a coincidence. Here I am, out for a leisurely run, and who do I run into but the fucking Outcast and her baby polar Bear."

Tabby rolled her eyes. Julian was going to kick his ass just for the polar Bear comment.

She couldn't attack, not yet. Not until he made a threatening move. She wouldn't do anything to jeopardize her new place in the Pride, and kicking Gary's ass without cause would definitely make problems for her.

The two idiots Gary took everywhere laughed. Hell, after six months in Halle, she *still* didn't know their names. They'd moved to flank Gary, protecting their precious wannabe Alpha. Tabby snorted. *Right. He's an Alpha. And I'm a Teletubby.*

Gary looked over her shoulder at Julian. "I have no quarrel with you, Bear. Back away and you won't get hurt."

Julian's answer was the deep, throbbing roar of a black

bear, echoing through the woods to be heard miles away.

Gary smiled. "So be it. I've always wondered what it would be like to fight a Bear."

Gary and his buddies began to shift.

Bunny's head lifted at the sound of the other Bear's roar. "They're farther than I thought."

"They must have shifted." William began tugging off his clothes. "You two go on ahead; I'll guard my soon-to-be niece."

"Not in this lifetime." Glory stomped past William, stopping just short of Ryan.

Ryan just sighed and began to pull off his clothing. Bunny was already tugging off his own clothes, terrified that Gary had managed to catch Tabby before he could get to her. It didn't matter that Julian was with her. Black Bears rarely won a fight with a Wolf Pack. They would run, knowing the Pack could take them down. Maybe he thought because the Pack was so small that he'd be able to defend Tabby?

"Why are you getting naked?" Glory's wide eyes brought him back to what they were doing.

"We can't shift in clothes. If we do, we'll get tangled, which makes us vulnerable to attack." Ryan was completely naked. He stretched, muscles flexing, joints popping. Bunny rolled his eyes. Ryan was showing off for his mate.

From the poleaxed look on her face, he'd succeeded. Her gaze couldn't decide which part of his body to settle on. Ryan tipped her chin up and planted a kiss on her open mouth. "Stay with Uncle Will. He'll keep you safe."

Her jaw snapped shut. "I can take care of myself."

Ryan pointed behind him. "He can take care of you better."

Once again her jaw dropped. Where Bunny's father had been now sat a grizzly Bear calmly scratching its ear. "Oh." She nodded at the huge Bear. Bunny's father was the only one in the family who rivaled him in size. "Okay. I'll, um." She sat down hard, bouncing a little. "Sit. Stay. Got it." She reached under her without moving her eyes off Will Bunsun and removed a rock, tossing it aside absently.

That's going to leave a mark. From the look on Ryan's face he'd enjoy healing it, too.

Bunny rubbed his chest and sighed. He was forced to heal the tattoo the rest of the way and hope for the best, otherwise it would heal when he shifted. God knew what would happen to the glorious picture if he did that.

He did *not* want to meet his mate if her Wolf looked like a Shar-Pei.

Bunny nodded at Ryan and began to shift. He could see the shock still on Glory's face as the two men both turned into grizzlies.

The shock turned to disgust when a long Bear tongue swiped up her cheek just before the two Bears charged into the woods.

"*Ew!* Bear spit!"

Tabby was shocked when she hit the ground. Julian had batted her aside with one swipe of his paw before looming over her prone body. He snarled at the Wolves facing them, daring them to go after him.

They did, nipping at his flanks, trying to draw him away from her. He refused to go more than a few yards away, darting back to her when it looked like one of them might be ready to pounce. And every time she tried to stand, he pushed her back down with one paw, easily holding her in place. He was acting like a mama protecting her cubs. She growled up at him, demanding he let her go so she could fight. He couldn't take on even this small a Pack by himself.

Julian looked down at her and shook his head. He wasn't going to let her go.

Tabby bided her time, watching the Wolves harass Julian. Julian moved, going after one of the Wolves.

Now.

She shot to her feet and raced after Gary. She had one shot to save Julian and she wasn't going to waste it.

She heard Julian's pained cry behind her. She paused in her charge, glancing back. Julian was on the ground, his neck bloodied, two wolves dodging in and out, trying to get another bite in and finish the kill. But Julian continued to snap at them, his wounds healing before their eyes.

Too slowly. Tabby knew they were healing too slowly. He was still drained from saving Chloe. If he took a wound that was too deep, his visions would come true.

She tried to jump toward him, determined to protect him, when strong jaws clamped on her hind leg and dragged her back. She threw back her head and howled in pain, desperately hoping Alex would hear. If he didn't come soon, she was going to lose Julian.

The pained howl of a Wolf had him sprinting through the trees. The top speed for a natural grizzly had once been clocked at thirty miles an hour. Bunny did his damndest to top that.

Bunny was furious. It wasn't long before he could hear the yips and cries of the fight. He put on an extra burst of speed, knowing seconds could mean the difference between life and death.

Ten more steps would see him where he needed to be. Nine...eight...seven...

Tabby yelped, the sound full of anguish. And Bunny, terrified, ran faster.

Julian was barely breathing, his fur matted with blood, the color a dark golden green to her Wolf's eyes, almost blending with the soft gold of his shoulders. She could smell the coppery scent of his blood, her own and the Wolves around them. At least they'd managed to get off a few shots of their own before going down.

She snapped at Gary, trying to get him off of her. She struggled, but couldn't break free, not without snapping her leg. She gave up and let him drag her back, knowing what he would attempt to do next.

He would try to mount her. And when he did, she would try to kill him.

Bunny skidded to a stop, taking in the scene through furious eyes. Bright red blood matted Julian's fur, his throat almost shredded. He could already tell the Bear was unconscious, unable to assist Tabby in her fight.

Tabby was under Gary, the would-be Alpha Wolf attempting to mount her. Her dark brown and tan fur was matted with blood and dirt, the small tuft of green at the very top barely visible. She whimpered in pain when she tried to put weight on her back paw. The leg gave way beneath her, the shock nearly giving Gary the chance to enter her. She snapped and snarled, trying to toss Gary off, but he had a hold of her neck now and was hunching his hips forward, trying to fuck the smaller Wolf.

Gary was trying to rape Tabby.

Bunny roared and relaxed his iron control over his rage.

And it felt *good.*

Tabby started at the terrifying roar. She knew who that was and renewed her struggles.

Alex was here.

Her hind leg was killing her, her neck was sore, and she couldn't get the son of a bitch off her to save her life. She looked up as far as she could with Gary's teeth buried against her throat. There were two grizzlies. One went after the Wolves trying to finish off Julian. The other, larger one raced straight for Gary.

Gary let go of her and tried to back away, but he was too late. The grizzly swiped with his massive paw, sending the Wolf flying through the air. Tabby whimpered, her neck bleeding from where Gary had tried to embed his teeth.

Gary landed against a tree with a yelp of pain and a sickening thud, his sides heaving. Alex stood over her battered, bleeding body and growled. The expression in his eyes was full of pure rage. His muscles were tense with the need to kill, pure predator as he stared at his downed prey.

Sometimes it was easy to forget that Bears were omnivores. She didn't think she'd ever forget that again.

She struggled to her feet, wincing, unable to put her full weight on her back paw. It wasn't broken, but it felt badly sprained. She nuzzled Alex's leg as he settled back on all fours. He was massive, much larger than the other grizzly. She stretched up and licked the underside of his jaw, barely able to reach him with the tip of her tongue.

Alex's eyes never left Gary, but the insane growls lessened with her display of affection. Now, pure rage was filtered by determination, turning what might have been a massacre into an execution. She had no doubts that Alex would win.

She did have to wonder how many pieces Gary would be in when Alex was done.

Bunny stared at the Wolf struggling to his feet. Off to his left, he could hear Ryan quickly dispatching the lesser Wolves. Now it was up to him to deal with Gary.

He started forward, snarling when he felt Tabby trying to keep pace. He needed her to stand back, let him deal with her attacker, but he couldn't tell her that in this form. He didn't dare take his eyes off the Wolf. Gary would take any advantage he gave him, and Bunny had no intention of bleeding for the asshole.

But Gary would bleed for him. Oh, would he bleed.

Gary rose to fight him, using those darting tactics Packs used to bring down large prey, but the shifter was off balance. Bunny, thanks to Bear's gift, knew Gary had banged his head pretty hard and was probably fighting off a concussion. That, added to the ribs he'd cracked when he hit the tree, were making him slower and much clumsier than he'd been when he'd faced Tabby and Julian.

Poor puppy. Bunny grinned, showing his fangs. He reached out one long arm and knocked Gary sideways. He wasn't ready to finish the kill yet. He wanted Gary to suffer first.

Tabby yipped. He darted a quick glance at her, startled when she limped her way toward Julian. The other Bear did not look good. He wasn't healing as quickly as he should. Those legendary Spirit Bear powers seemed to have deserted him.

Shit. Whatever Julian had done to help Chloe must have weakened him more than Bunny had first thought. He needed help, and he'd need it soon.

Sharp, cold pain sliced across his side. He whirled back to face his opponent. He'd taken his eyes off Gary for too long and the Wolf had gotten him for it. He roared and knocked the Wolf back, his claws raking along Gary's side. The Wolf howled. Blood dripped from wounds inflicted by five-inch claws. As Wolf, he wouldn't heal, not without help, or without shifting. And shifting right now would merely give Bunny the opening he needed to finish him.

He narrowed his eyes and gathered himself. It was time for the real battle to begin.

Sharp claws, flashing teeth, flying fur, and the smell of blood assaulted her senses. The battle was joined for real. Each shifter tried his best to savage the other, Gary fighting for his life, Alex fighting for his mate and the life of her friend. The two Wolves who had come with Gary were down, defeated by Ryan in such a short amount of time that Tabby was surprised at how long it was taking Alex to finish the battle. The two Wolves who'd shadowed Gary's every move had even changed, lying there naked and pathetic, covered in dirt and blood and tears. They were babbling, begging the huge grizzly for mercy.

Ryan chuffed at them and turned his attention to Julian. She knew the healing powers of the Bears and hoped he'd be able to help him. Because she could hear Julian's heartbeat, and it was slowing down.

Julian was dying.

Bunny stopped Gary from darting under him. He couldn't afford to expose his soft belly to the Wolf. He got a good bite on the Wolf's tail, earning a pained yip from Gary before he pulled free. They circled one another, each watching for another opening, another chance for claws and fangs to do some serious damage. Without the rest of his Pack, there was no way Gary could win, not against someone like Bunny.

Bunny saw his opening and charged the Wolf, raking his claws down Gary's left haunch, opening his hip down to the bone. The Wolf went down, unable to put weight on the leg.

Bunny pulled himself around quickly, his snarl daring the Wolf to get back up.

Gary didn't. Panting, the man changed, turning human. He clutched his hip, moaning in agony. If Bunny let him live, he'd need a hospital.

Bunny was debating that. He was leaning more toward not.

Tabby limped back to him, and the pain she felt sealed Gary's fate.

Chapter Nine

Tabby tried to stop Alex from killing Gary. Too many questions would be asked if a man was found naked, mauled by a grizzly bear. But even limping as quickly as she could, she wasn't fast enough. So she was surprised when a golden body separated Bunny from his prey. She stiffened, knowing who was blocking Alex. Emma could have gotten hurt if Alex hadn't pulled his blow at the last minute, recognizing the scent of the Curana.

"Really, you don't want to do that." Max Cannon stepped out from the trees, gloriously naked. She ignored Alex's glare and got a good eyeful before politely turning her back on her Alpha's nudity. Simply put, the man was built like a fucking golden god. How could she *not* look?

From Alex's low growl, she'd be paying for that bit of gratuitous eye candy later. Right now, they had more important things to deal with.

"For one thing, I have some questions for Gary Sanders of Phoenix, Arizona." Gary whimpered.

Arizona? I thought he was from New Mexico.

"Like, who his Alpha is, and why he thought it was okay to disobey me on Pride lands?" That invisible mist poured out of the Alpha, demanding compliance from all around him.

"Jesus Christ on a pogo stick. You're *huge*!" Tabby's eyes

rolled and landed on the naked form of Emma Cannon. She stood, staring wide-eyed at Alex, her head barely reaching his chest. "What the hell do they feed you guys in...where are you from? Do elephants look at you and say, 'Goddamn, you're *big*'?"

There was a gusty sigh. "Emma. Could you focus on the bad guy here?"

"Sorry." But she didn't look sorry as she quickly shifted to Puma.

Tabby ignored her Curana and bowed down, baring her belly for her Alpha. Out of respect for Alex, she kept one eye closed.

The other eye was for the man candy. The Alpha was seriously *hot*. And, as the saying went, she was mated, not dead.

A female Puma bounced over to her and tilted her head, snarling when she saw Tabby's eye open and trained on the Alpha. Tabby knew who it was immediately and closed her other eye. Apparently the Curana was *not* amused, and she was much larger than Tabby.

Gary was still panting, but Tabby didn't dare open her eyes to look. "This isn't Pride land."

"Oh? Are you sure?"

The only response was the renewed whimpers of Gary's minions.

"Thought not. Bunny, why don't you change back? I'd rather not have to explain a bear mauling in Halle, especially a grizzly mauling. If you and your family are staying, we need to keep your presence as quiet as possible. We don't need Fish and Wildlife sniffing around, wondering how to move your fuzzy ass back west."

She heard a rustling sound. “Tabby?”

She opened her eyes to find her naked mate bending over her. She damn near growled when she saw her Curana sizing him up. Tabby changed back, then laughed when the big cat was plucked up by Max and carted back toward the other Pumas.

A soft moan had her looking back at the great white Bear. “Julian!” She scrambled to her feet, ignoring her own wounds. She’d heal with time. Julian might not.

Ryan was over him, eyes closed. The concentration on his human face was hard to miss. He was doing his best to heal the other Bear. Wounds began slowly closing, but without the graceful flow she’d seen Julian use. “Alex?”

“On it.” Alex joined his cousin over Julian’s prone body. He closed his eyes and drifted away from her, down what he’d called the spiral of the healing path. She had no clue what he meant by that, but if it saved Julian, she was all for it.

“Tabby.”

She turned around and faced her Alpha. She made sure to keep her gaze glued to the small scar on the side of his nose. She had no idea why that seemed to amuse him, but it did. “Yes, Alpha?”

“What punishment should Gary suffer for his attack on you?”

“And attempted rape,” Alex growled behind her.

The amusement fled Max’s face. “Attempted *rape*?” He glared down at Gary. “You tried to rape another man’s mate?”

“Stop.” Gabe Anderson stepped forward, the Pride Marshall behind him. Both men looked grim. “This man is hereby declared rogue. Therefore, he’s *mine.*” He grinned, the look vicious. “I wondered how it would feel to go on a Hunt. Now I know."

Gary cringed for the first time. "What?"

"You not only disobeyed the local Alpha, you attempted something that is considered anathema to all shifters. You tried to rape another man's mate. That makes you rogue." Gabriel Anderson suddenly seemed ten times more dangerous than he'd ever been. He lifted Gary by his neck, ignoring the choking sounds the Wolf made and the astonished gasps of his Pridemates. "Had you succeeded and run, I would have Hunted you down. Maybe I would have turned you over to the Senate for justice." He dragged Gary's face closer, his fangs displayed, his eyes flashing gold. "Maybe." He dropped Gary to the ground. "Now you'll be taken in. You'll be taken before a Tribunal. And I'll see to it that you pay for what you've tried to do today." He leaned down. Gary shuddered, his face pinched and gray. "And if you try to escape me, I'll let Bunny have you." He whispered in Gary's ear for a long time. Tabby couldn't quite make out what was said, but she got the impression that Gabe was filling Gary in on Alex's reputation and how he'd gotten it. "Do we understand one another?"

Gary looked ready to piss himself as he darted a horrified glance toward Alex. "Yes sir." He no longer looked like a wannabe Alpha. He looked like the young punk he really was, and he was terrified.

"Good." Gabe clapped his hands together loudly, startling not only Tabby, but everyone else as well. "You two morons, get up. You'll be spending a few days in jail while I arrange for your Tribunal."

The Wolves got to their feet, shuffling pathetically. Tabby had no sympathy. They'd nearly killed Julian and her, and for what? Sport? Because they could? "Why?"

The Wolves stopped. Gary turned to her. There was fear in

his eyes. "Why what?"

"Why did you do this? Why have you harassed me? What did I ever do to you?"

He blinked. One of the wolves behind him opened his mouth, but shut it at a sharp gesture from Gary. The Wolf's eyes darted to Gabe, and if she didn't know better she'd swear there was something he was dying to tell the Hunter. "We're Wolves. You're weak, alone. Abandoned by your Pack for being unworthy. What were we supposed to do, ignore you?"

Max shook his head, looking disgusted. "We aren't animals that turn into humans. We're just the opposite, humans blessed with the ability to share our lives with our animals. And Tabby's Pack might have been stupid enough to let her go, but she's part of my Pride now. That means she's no longer fair game for idiots like you who think they're in a bad werewolf movie." He waved his hand. "Get them out of here before I change my mind and let Bunny eat them."

The two morons *did* wet themselves in fear. Tabby felt better already.

Max was staring at Julian, his expression concerned. "Get Julian to Jamie. He'll make sure the Bear is taken care of."

"He'll live." Ryan sat back on his ass, his face full of weary triumph. "I got most of the bleeding stopped, but if he doesn't wake up soon, he's going to have scarring."

"Jamie can help with that. Can he be moved?"

Ryan eyed the Puma Alpha. "Care to lend a paw? Because I'm not hauling a three-hundred-pound Bear through the woods all by myself."

"We'll all carry him." Bunny gestured to Adrian and Simon. "Grab his ass, I'll get his head."

The two men exchanged a glance. Adrian shrugged. "I don't

know about you, but I really don't swing that way."

Simon snickered.

"Oh, move, you big dorks." Emma Cannon, now human again, bounced around her mate. She wrapped both hands around Julian's ass and heaved. And *heaved.*

Julian didn't even jiggle.

Emma glared at the Pumas, her hand under the Bear's ass, her own stuck up in the air. Every single pair of male eyes went immediately to the treetops overhead, save one. Those sky blue eyes admired his mate's naked ass as she strained to lift a five-hundred-pound Bear by the butt. Yet she still managed to sound like a queen when she demanded, "A little help here, please!"

The Pumas moved en masse to obey their Little General. "It's like watching Super Grover," Ryan muttered.

And despite everything that had happened, Tabby found herself laughing as she hauled an unconscious Bear back to her car. "Guys? What do we do with him once we've got him there? Tie him to the hood?" *Ow. Stupid stick.* She hopped on one foot and almost dropped the butt cheek she was currently hoisting.

The white Bear opened one eye and winked at her. He was going to be all right. She chose not to say anything, but let her Pride carry him. After what he'd done both for her and for Chloe, Julian deserved a little pampering.

"Hey! He winked at me!"

Simon laughed. "You may not swing that way, Adrian, but apparently *he* does."

"Did you know you have a green Mohawk when you're

Wolf?"

His Tabby blinked up at him. "Huh?"

Bunny laughed, wiping wet green hair from her eyes. "Yup." He ruffled the top of her head, rinsing out the shampoo. "Right about here. Lime green, just like your hair."

She snorted. "I do not."

"Do too."

She tickled his side, earning an undignified giggle. "Do not."

He slapped her hands away carefully. "Do too."

"I've seen myself in ponds, Baloo. Trust me, there's no green there."

"Oh, yes there is, baby." He reached for the washcloth and soaped it up, being careful to be very gentle with her bruised flesh. Inside, he was still snarling and snapping. There was blood on her skin, *her* blood. If he knew where Gabe had taken Gary, the Wolf might not live to see the Tribunal. But he didn't know where Halle's jail was. Tabby had refused to say, and then the little cheater had gotten naked. One look at the bruises and marks on her body and he'd whisked her into the shower, eager to ease her hurts. The only way to soothe his Bear was to wash away the evidence of her ordeal from her sweet skin, using his powers to heal as much of the damage as he could without falling over. "I'll make a deal with you."

"Hmm." She leaned into the strokes of the washcloth, her eyes closed, her throat exposed. It was fucking incredible the way she trusted him to take care of her. To never, ever hurt her. "Okay. What deal?"

"You shift and I'll take a picture. If I'm right, I get the sexual favor of my choice." He stroked the washcloth between her legs, grinning when she gasped. "If I'm wrong, you get a sexual favor, anything you want." He blinked and added, "That doesn't include a third party."

She chuckled. "Fine." She stroked his hardening cock, slanting him a sultry look from under those long lashes of hers. "I already know what I want. Do you?"

Bunny shuddered. Oh yeah. He knew what he wanted.

"I'll dry you off before you change." She tilted her head, looking confused. "I don't want the room smelling like wet dog."

She tickled him again. Damn it, how had she figured out he was ticklish? It wasn't fair. Despite everything that had happened that day they were both laughing when they tumbled out of the shower. He towel-dried her hair as best he could. It wasn't like he had a hair dryer. *Speaking of which...* "Would you do me a favor?"

"Sure." She folded the damp towel and put it back on the rack.

"Shave me later?"

Her eyebrows rose. Her gaze drifted to his head, her lips twitching. "Trust me that much?"

He stroked her cheek, the bruise fading a bit as he unleashed some of his healing power. He was tired after healing the worst of Julian's and Tabby's wounds, but not too tired for what he wanted to do to his mate. "With everything."

She smiled. "Dig out the camera. I've got *plans* for your ass." She sashayed out of the room, damp hair clinging to her face, her rounded ass calling to him.

Damn. His mate was so sexy. He ran for his luggage and pulled out the digital camera. "Ready?"

She shrugged and shifted. He snapped the shot and grinned. He already knew he'd won. "Take a look."

She shifted back and looked. "Well. Damn." There, in full

color, was a wolf with a green tuft right over her eyes. "How come I never noticed that and you did?"

"Wolves are partially color-blind, right?"

"Yeah, we have trouble with greens, they tend to look gray to us."

"Bears have full-color vision no matter what form we're in."

She rolled her eyes. "That was not a fair bet then."

He smirked down at her. "Hey, I told you and you didn't believe me. That makes it more than fair." He narrowed his eyes, his smirk turning to something more feral. "On your knees, baby."

She pouted up at him through her lashes before gracefully sinking to her knees. She knew what he wanted, too. She took his cock in her hot little hand and sucked the head in. Her tongue swirled around the opening, lapping up the precome that had begun to seep from the tip. God, she looked so good with his cock in her mouth, those full, ripe lips wrapped around him, straining to hold him. She sank down, burying her nose in his curls and he damn near lost it right then and there. He didn't think he'd ever get tired of the way she took him down to the root. He'd never had a lover who sucked him the way she did. She pulled back, dragging her tongue along his length.

"Oh shit." He was going to blow in an embarrassingly short time if she didn't take it easy on him. "Stop!"

She stopped, halfway down his cock, her nostrils flaring.

"On the bed. I want a taste too."

She let him go, only to stand and turn him. He let her, curious to see what she was going to do. She pushed and tugged at him until he was on his back in the middle of the bed, her legs straddling his face, her mouth once more descending on his cock.

Perfect. He had that luscious ass of hers right above him, that delicious pussy riding his mouth. This right here was what he was talking about. He began to eat his mate, licking her in steady swipes, clit to hole, over and over again.

Her mouth paused, her groan sending shockwaves through him. He used one hand to hold her hips steady. The other went to the back of her head. He planted his feet on the bed and began thrusting, fucking her mouth, his fist clenching in her hair. Dominating her, just the way his little Wolf liked it. And from the way her tongue went to work and she groaned around him, he knew he was right. With her, he could let go, be a little rough, and she'd lap it up and demand more.

God, she was everything he'd ever needed.

Tabby loved it when Alex held her like this, letting her know just how much he desired her. She wrapped her hand around his cock, just in case he thrust a little *too* hard, and he growled his approval. She took what he was giving her with abandon, wriggling her hips, desperate to get his mouth right where she wanted it.

Oh yeah. Right there. He sucked her clit into his mouth and hummed and that was all she needed. She came, howling around his cock, her tongue working furiously to bring him off.

But he wasn't done with her. Not yet. That hand in her hair tightened, bringing a fresh spurt of pleasure with the stinging pain. He pulled her off him, rolled her beneath him, and attacked her pussy with his mouth, nibbling, licking, sucking until she was screaming under him, begging him to fuck her. It didn't even occur to her until he moved that he'd kept his cock from her mouth. He rolled around and impaled her in one long stroke, fucking her like a madman. She wrapped her legs around his waist and clung to him, her nails raking his biceps, leaving long scratches on his back. His hazel eyes darkened and he snarled down at her. He took her hands in his and held them over her head, ignoring her growl of protest. He bent his head and nipped her breast, licking all around her nipple until she was ready to bite him in frustration.

When he marked her there, right above her nipple, she came so hard she almost passed out.

"Yes, yes, *Tabby,*" he ground out through clenched teeth. He pulsed inside her, his eyes screwed shut in ecstasy, a deep, shuddering groan escaping from between his lips.

Alex opened his eyes and bent down to her, taking her mouth in a sweet, soft kiss. His hand was still wrapped around her wrist. "I love you."

She flexed her hips, earning a groan in response. "I love you too." She grinned. "Now, can I have my arms back?"

"I don't know." He flexed his own hips, making her gasp. He was still hard. "I don't think I'm done with them yet."

She licked her lips and dragged one foot from his back down to his ankle, stroking him with it. "Well, if you're still using them, I suppose I could let you keep them a while longer."

His grip tightened, but not so much that he caused her a moment's pain. Just enough to tell her she wasn't getting out of this bed any time soon. "*Let* me?"

She kept the grin off her face, doing her best to look sultry. She wasn't done with him, either.

"Emma?" She didn't know why the Curana had demanded Tabby come to Wallflowers, but the summons had managed to get her out of the last of the cleanup at Living Art. Glory had grumbled, but Cyn had waved her out the door with orders to return with lunch. That had shut Glory up. Alex waited outside, refusing to leave her alone even long enough to walk to Wallflowers. Whoever had injured his cousin was still out there, and Alex wasn't taking any chances with her safety.

Inside the store were two people chatting with Emma, but she couldn't quite get a good look at them. All she saw was a flash of red hair and the tinkling sound of feminine laughter.

"Tabby?" Emma Cannon glided up to her, hands extended. "I have someone I'd like you to meet."

She caught a strong, feral scent and damn near passed out. *Oh. Oh dear. I'm screwed.* Behind Emma stood a Wolf and a Puma. The Wolf had waist-length red hair, a nasty scar on one cheek, and eyes the color of a frosty day. He wasn't the handsomest man she'd ever seen, but there was something about him that demanded your attention and kept it. The Puma was a blonde woman with bright green eyes and an easy smile on her face. She was almost too pretty to be real. She leaned heavily on a cane, her free hand wrapped around the redhead's biceps. Whether that was to hold herself steady or just because she felt the need to touch that massive arm, Tabby didn't know.

"Rick and Belle Lowell, I'd like you to meet Tabitha Garwood, my newest Pride member."

Rick's eyebrows rose at the words *Pride member.*

"Tabby, these are the Poconos Alphas."

Yup. I'm screwed. She nodded respectfully. "Mr. and Mrs. Lowell."

"I've just been telling them about what happened out in the woods."

Rick's power slammed into the room. "Tell me *everything.*"

Tabby shuddered and did. She told him her date of birth, how her mother's obstetrician had declared her a girl, how her mother had knitted her first cap. She told him about her first scraped knee, her first fistfight, her first kiss. Then she told him how she'd been made Outcast, abandoned by Pack and kin. She told them how she had lived like a Wolf for years, found her way to Halle and met Mrs. Anderson. She described Gabe, Julian, Alex, Ryan, Cyn, Glory, and Brit, the girl who couldn't handle a drunken Wolf. She told him about Gary's stalking and how the Pumas had saved her and claimed her as their own.

She almost told them about all the sex she and Alex had been having. She decided at the last minute they probably weren't interested, since by that point, both Rick and Belle's eyes had begun to glaze over.

By the time she was done, Emma's mouth was hanging open. "Note to self. Never ask Tabby to tell me everything."

"Can I have a drink of water?" Tabby croaked. Her mouth was parched, but at least that heavy weight of the Alpha's power was gone.

Rick had a bemused look on his face. "Are you done?"

"God I hope so." Belle limped toward the sofa, ignoring the way Rick nearly jumped to her side. "I don't know if I can handle another round of *This Is Your Life.*" She settled in with a sigh, rubbing her hip with a wince.

"Who was your old Alpha?"

She stared at Rick. *Hell, at least he won't head to Georgia and try to eat him.* "Dennis Boyd, sir."

"Out of?"

"Marietta, Georgia."

"Address."

She supplied it with a wince. She figured he'd check up on her story and decide for himself whether or not she could stay.

"Calm down, Fido. You're scaring the crap out of her."

Tabby blinked and turned toward the Luna. "Ma'am?"

Belle glared at her. "Don't ma'am me. Makes me sound like my mother." Belle's glare turned into an evil grin that had Tabby backing up a step. "Tell her, Rick."

"We've already checked out your story, Tabitha." She turned back to look at the Wolf Alpha. His expression had softened significantly, making him much more approachable. He might even be likeable. "Dennis Boyd is no longer the Marietta Pack Alpha. His son has taken over for him. He's been Alpha for about two years now, and he's been trying to find you. He wants to make amends for what was done to you."

"He wants you to go home. Even your parents want to see you again. They know now what the Alpha did was wrong." Belle patted the cushion next to her. Tabby fell into the seat, stunned by what she was hearing. "You have options. One, you can do what Micah wants and return to Marietta. No doubt everyone will want to fawn all over you and show you the *boo-hoo, oh-how-sorry-we-ares*. Two, you can stay here in Halle and tell them to go fuck themselves, thank you very much. Which, frankly, is the option I would personally go for." Belle gave her the most vacuous grin she'd ever seen, morphing from powerful Luna to bimbo Barbie in the span of seconds. The sharp intelligence behind those green eyes belied the look, leaving Tabby feeling bewildered and not a little off balance. "Make sure you use an air horn to drive the point home. They hate that."

"Belle."

The Luna grinned up at her mate, the empty-headed look completely gone. The Wolf Alpha sighed, but the sound was full of fondness for his blonde mate. "Three, you can come to the Poconos with us. I've already spoken to the Pack and explained your circumstances. They're willing to waive Protocol in light of what's been done to you and what you've done since then."

She gasped. Go to the Poconos? Leave Halle?

Join a new Pack? One that might actually *want* her?

"I mean, what self-respecting Wolf would want to live with all these...cats?"

She growled until she saw the wicked grin on the Alpha's face.

"Them's fightin' words, Fido." The Luna was laughing with him. "Besides, from the sound of that growl, I think she's made a decision."

"No one said she can't be both Pack and Pride." Rick lifted Belle's hand and kissed her knuckles. "You've proven that."

Belle tilted her head. "True. Emma?"

"Hmm?" The Curana calmly poured tea from the silver tea service, her brown eyes dancing with glee.

"Care to share her?"

Share? *Me?* Tabby's head was spinning. She hadn't done anything to prove herself to the Pack. Why would they want her?

"I haven't done anything to earn my way into your Pack."

"You helped defeat a rogue Wolf. That's all we need to know." Belle patted her knee.

Rick nodded. "You could have done anything during those years you were alone. You could have caused a lot of damage, done a lot of mischief. Instead, you chose to make your way as a Wolf, living off the land. Not once did you cause trouble. And when you did rejoin the human race, you started working toward your GED, got your driver's license, a job, and an apartment. That does not scream threat to me or to my Pack."

"But..." Only one thing was really clear in her mind. "I don't want to leave Halle." Halle was *home.*

"No one says you have to." Rick's eyes narrowed in thought.

"You could be our ambassador to Halle."

Emma snorted and handed over a cup of tea to Belle. "Ambassador? Rick, we see each other once a month."

"So? I like the thought of having an ambassador." Rick winked at Tabby.

She was pretty sure she looked like a landed fish, gaping and gasping like crazy. "How about I'm just the resident Wolf?"

"Works for me." Rick clapped his hands.

And just like that another mantle settled over her, one of acceptance. It was similar in feel to the Pride, but was somehow wilder, more earthy. More integrated.

"I'll satisfy Protocol and set up your formal introduction to the Pack later. For now, welcome to the Pack."

The mental voice of her Pack Alpha was strong and sure. Tabby buried her face in her hands and cried.

She'd gone from unwanted and unneeded to fought over and loved. The only thing that made her happier was Alex was there to share it with her.

"When do we get to meet the grizzlies?" Belle practically bounced in her seat. "I've always wanted to meet Bears."

Tabby laughed through her tears as Alex's hand stroked through her hair. "Wait until you get a load of Julian." The Luna was going to *love* her friend. She had the feeling they were two of a kind.

"How are you feeling?"

Tabby watched Julian shuffle around his tiny bedroom. He still wasn't fully recovered from the fight with Gary, or his healing of Chloe. She followed him in, pausing in the doorway. "I've been better." He settled on the edge of the bed with a wince.

From the amount of white in his hair, she should have known not to ask. Luckily, he was now working for Jamie Howard in his private practice. The man had taken one look at the nearly white hair and pale gray eyes, and put him on bed rest for the next two weeks. For once Julian hadn't argued. That let her know more than anything how poorly he was feeling. "We're going to take care of you."

"It's the least we can do." Alex strode into the room carrying a mug of Julian's favorite tea. Two days had passed since the incident in the woods and he still hadn't left her side for more than a few minutes. It was cute, in an overprotective, caveman sort of way, but she knew it was going to get old real fast. "Besides, you're family. Remember?"

Julian flopped back against the pillows with a weary groan. "Your aunts and mother are driving me insane."

"Aunts?" Alex put the mug next to Julian on the nightstand and stood back. "Aunt Stacey is here?"

Tabby settled on the bed next to Julian. From the amused look on Alex's face, he knew this was something the two had done more than once. Alex had nothing to worry about, and apparently he knew it. She'd fallen asleep in Julian's bed once, and he'd never touched her. He'd moved into the living room and slept on the couch, leaving her the queen-size bed. Of course, he'd forced her to cook breakfast by claiming a sore back. He'd been so pathetic, she'd agreed and made him pancakes.

Damn that boy could put it away. She'd wound up making three batches. She'd gotten two whole pancakes out of them. She felt lucky she still had all her fingers.

At least she'd gotten her fair share of the bacon. Sometimes it paid to cook.

Julian nodded and flung his arm over his eyes. "I swear, if I get one more bowl of chicken soup, I'm going to scream."

"Chicken soup?"

Julian lifted his arm long enough to glare at her. "For *breakfast*." The arm flopped back down when she began to giggle.

"I'll go get you pastries, maybe a burger from Frank's." She patted his knee, trying to soothe the poor, wounded baby.

"If Aunt Stacey is here then the cousins are all here, too."

"Cousins?" Julian moaned.

"Heather, Keith, and Tiffany." Alex clucked his teeth in mock sympathy. "You're gonna get so sick of chicken."

"Shit." Julian struggled out of bed. "I just remembered I have to go to Alaska for about sixty years."

"Cyn wouldn't like that."

Julian frowned. "Where is Cyn, by the way?"

"The shop's finally open again. We're getting wooden counters installed with glass on top and only part of the way down the sides. The carpenter's been there for the last two days." She didn't say anything, but she thought the carpenter had a thing for Cyn. Julian could deal with that when he was feeling better.

"And Chloe?" Julian turned to Alex. "I know she's feeling a little better but she seems…fuzzy."

Alex blinked. "She's having some trouble keeping things straight. The doc says it should wear off over time."

"Is she having problems with one of her hands?" Julian clenched his left one into a fist.

"Yeah. Shit. How tightly are you two tied together?"

"I know how she feels, and I think I can talk to her." He

frowned. “She’s not a very sympathetic person, is she?”

Alex shrugged. “She can be. It depends. Why do you ask?”

“I mentioned chicken soup and she started giggling.”

Alex just smiled, but the expression was weary. Not all was right in his cousin’s world, and the strain was showing in the whole family. “Jim finally got here. He’s been to see her twice so far.”

“I know.” Julian grimaced. “He told her again that she’s too young for him. Just what she needed to hear when she’s got a long recovery ahead of her.”

“Fuck.” Alex ran his hand over his shaved head. Tabby had taken care of the stubble for him that morning. “No wonder she seemed a little depressed this morning.”

“She’ll figure something out. And if she doesn’t, well.” Tabby allowed her fangs to show. “That’s what family is for.”

The evil grin the three of them shared did not bode well for Chloe’s reluctant mate.

“There’s something you two need to tell Max for me.”

“What?” Alex finally took the one chair Julian had.

“Something is still wrong. It’s tied into what happened with Gary, and he’s only the beginning. I think there will be trouble with the Poconos Pack as well.”

“Trouble from them, or they’re going to have similar problems?” Tabby rolled over and settled her head on her hand.

“They’re tied to the Halle Pumas. The problems of one will become the problems of the other.” Julian frowned and looked confused. “I think.”

“Shit, I hate that cryptic crap.” Alex rubbed his eyes. “What the hell does that mean, you think?”

Julian opened his mouth to reply when Alex’s phone rang.

"Hold that thought." He flipped open his phone. "Bunny here."

Tabby watched the play of emotion crossing Alex's face. She could tell it was Gabe on the phone, but couldn't quite hear what he was saying. When he hung up, he looked dazed. "Well, I think I know one of the answers. Gary was definitely working for someone out in the Midwest. Turns out he and his friends were hired to come here. Their records were doctored so they'd be listed in the university computers as new transfers."

"What were they doing here?"

Tabby pulled on Julian's arm when he tried to sit up, but he ignored her. "More importantly, did Gary say who sent them?"

Alex shook his head. "He's refusing to tell them anything more. All Gabe knows is that they were here to observe, but they wouldn't say why. Gabe's hoping that the Tribunal will get more out of them." If anyone was capable of finding out the truth, it would be the men and women who made up the Tribunal.

"Whoever it is must have a lot of money and connections if they can pull off getting them into the college system." Julian looked ready to start pacing. Tabby would sit on him if he tried.

"Wait." Tabby sat up. "Does Gabe know yet if Gary was the one who attacked Chloe?"

Alex's eyes went wide and he whipped his phone out. "I don't know. Let me call him back and ask." He dialed the phone again, asking the question they all needed answered. "He says he'll call back once he knows. They're going to run the DNA, but we might not have the results for weeks."

Julian settled back down. "Now what?"

"Now I order in pizza for lunch before I take my mate house hunting."

House hunting? Alex hadn't mentioned anything about house hunting. She was supposed to be at work by four, so they had some time if they hurried.

"You, sir, are a God. And please get me the Hawaiian, I'm in the mood for pineapple."

"Done." Alex headed into kitchen and bellowed, "Menus?"

"Third drawer on the left!" Julian grinned up at Tabby. "Are we having fun yet?"

"Hey, there's not a chicken in sight."

"Then I'd say yes." They heard Alex order the pizzas. One meat lover's, double bacon, one Hawaiian, and one spinach, tomato and garlic. "Well. Glad it's not *my* mate eating the garlic."

Tabby made a face and lay back down. "Cyn would rather eat Gary."

Julian growled.

"Not like that, you perv! Geez. She's been muttering about finding him and kicking his ass until he whines like a little baby."

"I'll leave that to Bunny. Speaking of which, why was any part of Gary's ass alive to be hauled off to jail? I'm surprised Bunny didn't just kill the fucker and be done with it."

"We needed answers that only Gary had. Besides, he'd shifted. We would have had a body to hide and that's just not as easy as it sounds."

Julian tilted his head. He looked like he was listening to something only he could hear. "It wouldn't be the first time."

Tabby felt a chill. "Dude. I personally have never hidden a body. I swear."

"Not you. And not Bunny, either. Bunny prefers to maim rather than kill." Tabby grimaced. She was still getting used to the fact that the Alex she knew was the same man other grizzlies backed away from in fear. “No, the Pumas have done it before. Not sure how, or who, though.”

“Well, Mr. I’m-A-Hunter said we needed him alive, so Alex let him live.”

“Is it true the guy who tried to rip out my throat pissed himself?”

“Yup.”

A serene smile crossed Julian’s lips. “Cool.”

“Okay, pizzas are ordered.” Alex flopped into the middle of the bed, wriggling until he was between Tabby and Julian. He turned onto his back, causing the bed to dip and sway. Tabby held on for dear life. “What were we talking about?”

“You not turning Gary into a grizzly bear Happy Meal.”

“Oh. Nah. I’d never wash the taste out.” He turned to Tabby with a grin. Only she could see how the smile didn’t quite reach his eyes. “Would you really want to kiss me if I had Gary breath?”

“Ugh.” She exaggerated her shudder and made a face. “Thanks for that thought. Now I’m not hungry anymore.”

The tension in Alex eased. “More for me, then.” He took her hand in his. “Not sorry I didn’t tear him apart then?”

“Nope. Let him face justice. From what I heard, Gabe says they’re going to make him wish he’d died on your claws.” She curled her fingers around his, contentment flowing through her. He was there beside her, and right then that was all she needed. “Any idea when we’ll hear from Gabe?”

“Depends on how long it takes for him to crack Gary. It could be minutes to days.”

“Fuck.”

“There’s another way.”

Tabby blinked at the thoughtful tone of Julian's voice. "What now?"

"I could enter Chloe's dreamscape again, see if I can find something. It's possible she remembers her attacker somewhere deep in her subconscious."

"Hell to the no." Bunny nearly shoved Julian off the bed. "Do it and I'll not only call the aunts, I'll call in the cousins. *All* the cousins."

"Shit. No need to be mean." Julian shoved back. Alex barely moved. "Fine. Maybe I can call in someone else who can help."

"Another Kermode?"

"No, Tabby. I'll dial one-eight-hundred-I-Need-A-Psychic."

Tabby rolled her eyes and climbed out of bed. "We can let him out of bed now. He's just fine."

Alex snorted a laugh just as the doorbell rang. "I'll get it. God, it's like I have a brother-in-law now. A pain in the ass, sarcastic, know-it-all brother-in-law."

"Is there any other kind?" Julian yelled after him. He put his arms under his head. "I like this town." He started to snicker. "Hey, Bunny? If I've been adopted by your aunt and I've already adopted Tabby as my sister, does that mean your mating is illegal? Because first cousins really shouldn't marry you know."

This time it was Tabby who almost pushed him off the bed.

Alex stared at the door to Living Art. He could see two of the women laughing and talking through the plate glass window. Cyn especially looked relaxed as she tried to coax Glory into doing God knew what. There was no sign of Tabby.

Inside, he was chilled to the bone. "So what you're saying is

Gary isn't the one who went after Chloe."

"Nope." The sound of Gabe's sigh was tinny through the earpiece. "He knew who Chloe was, though. She was one of the people he was sent to Halle to keep an eye on. And get this. Hunters in other parts of the country have found three bodies with similar MOs. All of them were half-breeds."

"Half-breeds?" Now there was a term he hadn't heard since the last time someone had called one of his cousins that. But hey, Harry said Barney's arm had healed.

Mostly.

"Like Chloe. She's half Fox, half Bear."

"No shit." He took a deep breath, mentally reciting a mantra to calm down. "Have they gone after children?"

Silence. *Fuck.* "Good question. If they have, they've managed to make it look like accidents."

"Why?" Alex wanted to punch something badly. It had been six weeks since Chloe's attack. The annual Halle Halloween masquerade was in two days, and they were going. He and Tabby were closing on a house just three blocks from Simon and Becky Holt's place the day after. She'd taken one look at the For Sale sign on the little red brick house and squealed in glee. How could he not buy it for her?

And this morning Tabby had told him she thought she was pregnant. Julian had met them for breakfast, taken one look at Tabby and ordered her a large glass of milk and a doctor's appointment. She hadn't been amused, but she'd drunk the milk and made the appointment with the doctor Julian recommended. She'd been saving the pregnancy for a surprise, not knowing Alex would more than likely have noticed within a day or two anyway. There was nothing about her body he didn't keep an eye on. The thought of his cub growing under her heart made his nearly skip a beat. The fear that someone was going after half-breeds, endangering his child and his mate, made him see red.

"No clue, but I'm going to find out, starting with the anonymous phone call to 9-1-1. Someone saw something that night and called it in or Chloe would have been dead before the ambulance got there. I'm going to find out who and what they know if I have to shake this whole damn town loose to do it." And as a Hunter, Gabe was more than capable of doing just that.

"My family is moving into the area. We're at your disposal." Once his father knew the family was in danger, they'd be more than at the Hunter's disposal. They'd be his fucking shadows. "Is Chloe still in danger?"

"I'd say so. She survived and, as time goes on, she might remember more about her attackers."

"Then we're *definitely* moving to Halle. *All* of us." His father had been formalizing plans to open a Pennsylvania branch of Bunsun Exteriors. This would give him the perfect excuse to get the family here and keep them together, all under circumstances no one would call suspicious.

"Shit. Let me know when so I can prepare Max and Emma, okay?"

Alex grinned. "Hey, this is what family does, right? We take care of our own."

Gabe groaned. He'd made the comment more than once that he considered Chloe a little sister. His Aunt Laura had decided that was enough to declare him de facto family.

"I think you should know Tabby's pregnant." And if anyone went after her or his cubs, he'd do what he needed to do. If he'd learned nothing else since coming to Halle, Tabby was the only real necessity in his life. He'd do anything to keep her safe. Even let the beast he struggled so hard to contain go.

Gabe blew out a breath. "Got it." And he knew the Hunter did. Gabe understood what it was to protect and serve those he loved. "Keep an eye on your mate. Do what you have to."

"And what will you be doing?" He watched Julian enter the tattoo parlor and wondered what the Kermode was up to. Cyn was still giving him a hard time, but she wasn't nearly as bad as she had been. He hoped his friend would be able to claim his mate soon. The Bear deserved some happiness.

"What I have to." The phone clicked, disconnecting him from Gabe.

"Goodbye to you too." Bunny pocketed the cell and crossed the street, following Julian into Living Art. "Tabby?"

Her green hair appeared before she did. A big smile graced those full, pouty lips. "Hey, sugar."

Cyn poked her finger into Julian's chest with a growl. "Goddamn it, Julian! For the last time, I am *not* going to tattoo "Property of Cyn" on your ass!"

Tabby began to laugh, and just like that his day was looking a whole lot brighter. He would protect this, what he'd found here, with every fiber of his being. God have mercy on anyone who tried to take this away from him. Because this?

This was *home.*

About the Author

Dana Marie Bell wrote her first short story when she was thirteen years old. She attended the High School for Creative and Performing Arts for creative writing, where freedom of expression was the order of the day. When her parents moved out of the city and placed her in a Catholic high school for her senior year, she tried desperately to get away, but the nuns held fast, and she graduated with honors despite herself.

Dana has lived primarily in the Northeast (Pennsylvania, New Jersey and Delaware, to be precise), with a brief stint on the US Virgin Island of St. Croix. She lives with her soul mate and husband Dusty, their two maniacal children, an evil, ice-cream stealing cat and a bull terrier that thinks it's a Pekinese.

You can learn more about Dana at: www.danamariebell.com

Love has a trick up its sleeve.

Foxes' Den

© 2010 Teresa Noelle Roberts

Duals and Donovans: The Different, Book 2

Some guys just don't take rejection well. Sure, Akane's affair with an uptight sorcerer's boy toy backfired, but two hundred years locked in a mortal body is cruel and unusual punishment for a Trickster avatar. To free her fox form, she needs sex magic with a male of her own kind. Except none exist.

Adorable Trickster-touched fox dual Taggart Ross-Donovan is the closest she's found. Even better, he's married to Paul Donovan, whose red magic sizzles the air around him. One night with them will generate the extraordinary power needed to set her free.

The last thing Tag and Paul expect to find under a sorcerer's curse is a kitsune, a beautiful one who gets under their skin without even trying. Tag is more than ready to take the risk she needs. Paul has reservations, but it's nothing Tag can't overcome with a little sensual persuasion.

No one goes into the ritual with more hope than Akane...or more fear. Failure will leave her forever entrapped. Worse, she's falling for two mortals. And there's only one thing that can kill a kitsune—unrequited love.

Warning: Contains sly fox men (with tails), foxy fox women (with multiple tails), sexy witches chasing tail, Trickster magic, cranky sorcerers, and enough gay, het and MMF sex to torch your Kindle.

Available now in ebook from Samhain Publishing.